ESAU AND JACOB

ESAU AND JACOB

by

Joaquim Maria *MACHADO DE ASSIS*

Translated, with an Introduction, by

Helen Caldwell

University of California Press

Berkeley and Los Angeles

1965

University of California Press
Berkeley and Los Angeles, California

© 1965 by The Regents of the University of California

Published with the assistance of a grant from the
Rockefeller Foundation
Library of Congress Catalog Card No.: 65-19249
Designed by Ann W. Hawkins
Manufactured in the United States of America

Translator's Introduction

Now, when comedy hereabouts appears to be dead, or in a profound coma, it is a mistake, perhaps, to bring forth this work of mirth from another age, another language, another hemisphere. At least, the unwary reader should be put on his guard. In these pages he will find no red-blooded realism, no naked women, no heavy breathing, no rapid pace, no raw meat for slavering jaws, not even any strange sexual perversions. Indeed, anything in the way of sex in this book will come under the heading, "comedy."

Published in 1904, *Esaú e Jacob* has the Rio de Janeiro of 1869–1894 as its setting. There are horse-drawn carriages, tipping of hats, and other manners from that faraway time and place. The fictional personages mingle in, and shadow forth, the events that led to the formation of the Republic of Brazil; the revolution itself is shown in the light of their various reactions to its various stages. One of these creatures of Assis' brain even has an audience with the historical Marshal Floriano Peixoto: it is a droll confrontation. But these comic characters and events are transformed in the light of their own greater significance, and the stronger colors of allegory, theme, and symbol fill our eyes. For, with this, his eighth and penultimate novel, Machado de Assis' narrative power reached its apex. This is the most tightly integrated of all his novels—a work that is wise, delicate, loving, gently funny, but intellectually conceived. To fathom it one must penetrate above, beneath, and deep within its story. It is not only a portrait of Brazil, it is the way of men in society in general. And the method of narration is so subtle, so strangely modern that it still fascinates and baffles.

Yet, the guideposts are there; the important thing is not to rush past them with a careless glance. The title, for example, is a key to the book's meaning—*if* we interpret it in connection with the epigraph that appears on the first page of Ayres' narrative. Title and epigraph will lead us to an understanding of the first chapter, the first to the second, and so on. But, if the reader hurries past the epigraph, say, or assumes that the title *Esau and Jacob* refers to some Old Testament story, then he is in for endless obfuscation and bewilderment.

In his foreword, Machado de Assis informs us that the name that Ayres, the fictitious author of the novel, gave it was *Last* (*Ultimo*), and he implies that he does not understand why Ayres gave it that title. Yet, Machado de Assis himself sold the novel to H. Garnier, his publisher, under the title *Ultimo;* and it is still, today, on the manuscript of the work, which is in the Brazilian Academy of Letters in Rio de Janeiro. Indeed, Machado de Assis did not change the title to *Esaú e Jacob* until after galley proofs.

It would seem that Machado de Assis decided *Esau and Jacob* was a better title. Why? Did the first title bear any relation to the final one? Was the title *Last* really given to the narrative by the fictitious Ayres?

Let us consider the final title, *Esau and Jacob* in the light of the epigraph. The epigraph is a line of Dante. And Dante, in his *Paradiso,* used Esau and Jacob, and in particular Esau's red hair, to symbolize God's practice of conferring diverse natures on men, even on sons of the same father and mother—twins—so that not only do brothers not necessarily resemble each other, children often do not resemble their parents. But the epigraph is a line from the *Inferno* (Canto V, line 7), though it too has reference to predestination—to souls predestined not to fulfill their destiny.

In Chapter XII, this line from the *Inferno* is applied to guests at the home of the banker Santos for being "insipid" bores. Chapter XIII, however, seems to indicate that it refers to a whole society. This is borne out by another quotation. In Chapter XXXII, which narrates the old diplomat's retirement to his native land, we are told that he withdrew from the society of men, taking as his device, "I fled afar off, and dwelt in solitude." The quotation is from the Vulgate, Ps. 54:8. The rest of the psalm relates how the singer came back and found Philistines in the city, and "saw the city all full of wickedness," and in the marketplace "nothing but usury and fraud." The psalm and the quotation from the *Inferno* seem to refer to the same persons. There is the further detail that the line from the *Inferno* is from the passage where Minos is consigning sinners to the various circles of Hell by the proper number of turns he gives his tail. In allusion to this, the banker Santos' tongue (Chapter LXXXIV) "made seven turns in his mouth"—which would land him in the seventh circle with the usurers, where he properly belonged.

When the character Ayres used the line of Dante, he was referring to a segment of the society he found in Rio de Janeiro in the 1870's; Ayres, the narrator, applied the verse to the whole narrative and everyone in it. He would perhaps have excluded all the women, because he liked the ladies, and in particular Santos' wife, Natividade, with whom he was in love. Machado de Assis, however, might well have intended to include everyone among these *souls*. But, when he turned over the narration of this novel to the ex-diplomat Ayres, he let him have his way. Although the narrative is in the third person, Ayres (like Julius Caesar) introduced himself as one of the actors. As narrator, Ayres remains rigidly in character: he is always the old diplomat; he is never Machado de Assis. As actor, he bears out the character of the narrator. And, in a sense, the story is his. True, his characters are free agents and autonomous: he only records their acts, words, and thoughts; he even defers to the reader in matters of interpretation; but, with each succeeding chapter, the character of Ayres grows clearer, takes on added life and meaning.

In Chapter XIII, Ayres partially explains his literary method. In alluding to the line of Dante that the actor Ayres wrote in his notebook, he says:

Well, there is the epigraph of the book, if I should wish to give it one, and no other occurred to me. It is not only a way of rounding out the characters and their ideas, but it is also a pair of spectacles with which the reader may penetrate whatever seems not quite clear or wholly obscure.

Furthermore, there is an advantage in having the characters of my story collaborate in it, aiding the author in accordance with a law of solidarity, a kind of exchange of services between the chess-player and his men.

If you accept the comparison, you will recognize the king and the queen, the bishop and the knight, and that the knight cannot become a castle, nor the castle a pawn. There is of course the difference of color, white and black, but this does not affect the power of each piece to move, and finally one side or the other wins the game, and so goes the world. Perhaps it would have been a good idea to insert, from time to time (as in chess books), the favorable positions or the difficult ones. With no chessboard, that procedure is a great aid for following the moves, but then it may be that you have enough vision to reproduce the various situations from memory. Yes, I think so. Away with diagrams! Everything will go along as if you were actually witnessing a game between two players or, to be more precise, between God and the devil.

That is, the good and the evil in their natures make the action; the characters write the story. At the same time, the collaboration between the two Ayreses is neat and effective. The banker Santos, for example, did not stand high in Ayres' opinion—I am speaking of the narrator: there are insinuations from the start, and Santos is permitted, again and again, to display his more unlovely and asinine traits, but it is Ayres the actor who is assigned the job of giving Santos the *coup de grâce*. (After all, he *was* in love with Santos' wife.)

"Your cigars are superb." [Ayres says to Santos.]
"These are new ones. You like them?"
"Superb."
Santos rejoiced in this praise: he considered it a judgment aimed straight at his person, his merits, his name, the position he held in society, his house, his estate, his Bank, his waistcoats. That is perhaps too much: it will serve as an emphatic way of explaining the strength of the bond between him and his cigars. . . .
These were the suspicions that roamed about through Ayres' brain, as he gazed mildly at his host. Ayres could not close his eyes to the aversion this man inspired in him. Not that he wished him any harm exactly. He might even have wished him well, if there had been a wall between them. It was his person, his feelings, his remarks, his gestures, his laugh, the whole soul of the fellow that offended him.

As already mentioned, narrator Ayres presses historic personages into his service, and, worst of all, he puts the reader to work. He leaves blank spaces in his narrative for the reader to fill in. "The attentive, truly ruminative reader," he tells us in Chapter LV, "has four stomachs in his brain, and through these he passes and repasses the actions and events, until he deduces the truth which was, or seemed to be, hidden."

From the title *Esau and Jacob*, the epigraph, and Ayres' psalm, we may fairly surmise that this society which forms the subject matter of the novel is not the child of the previous generation, and that it is predestined by its nature not to fulfill its destiny.

What *was* its destiny? Speaking historically, one answer would be "to found the Republic."

Armed with our spectacles and four stomachs, let us now look at Chapter I: its title seems propitious, "Things fated to be."

A society woman, Natividade, accompanied by her sister, climbs the steep, rocky hill, Morro do Castello, to consult a fortuneteller about her twin baby sons. The seeress predicts that a great destiny is in store for them: they will be great! In what way? asks the mother. That, says the fortuneteller, rests with the future. And she adds the, apparently, gratuitous information that the twins fought in the womb and will continue to do so in the world.

Who are these babies, who is this mother? The hill mentioned in the initial sentence is a clue to their identity. The Morro do Castello is here a monument of Brazil's past, a symbol of the history of Brazil's capital. As Gastão Cruls writes in his *Aparência do Rio de Janeiro,* there was no real city until the first Portuguese settlement removed to this rock. It was from there that the Portuguese drove the French from the bay in 1581. It was on this hill that Father Manuel da Nobrega founded the great Jesuit college in the sixteenth century. Anchieta taught there, and preached in the Jesuit church that bore the date 1567 on its lintel. It is clear that this lady, Natividade, has an intimate relation to the Morro, to the old Brazil, if she is not Brazil herself.

In 1871, when Natividade went there, all this early civilization was long since gone, church and college had been abandoned by the Jesuits. A fortuneteller reigned there in 1871, Ayres tells us. The situation is summed up by the "penance" of the ladies' feet and by the title of Chapter II—playful allusions to Dante's Mt. Purgatory (which was also located in the Southern Hemisphere).

With Dante's mountain of repentance, the ascent became easier the higher one went; with the Rio hill it was "better coming down than going up." This was a society that consulted fortunetellers, though the more sophisticated, like the eminent banker Santos, might go in for spiritualism. The Church and its culture had become a shabby thing, good enough for poor people and the dead, a cheap charity for the wealthy, who also used its crucifixes as personal lucky charms. The "Nobrega" of Ayres' tale is a begging lay-brother who steals from the collection bowl. This is an irresponsible, superficial society—in passions, morals, mentality, and religion, a society slightly contemptuous of things Brazilian, whether it be language, thought, art, manufactures.

The fortuneteller from the wilds, the *cabocla*—what is she? She probably represents the three racial strains of Brazil's substructure. In her are combined gentleness, innocent beauty, rhythmic grace, and the mystic ignorance of Indian, Negro, and Portuguese folklore and superstition. But she is the voice of destiny: "destiny" to Machado de Assis was synonymous with "nature." One feels she is something more basic than Rio's society at the end of the century. There seems to be an affinity between her and this mother. Natividade, we learn later, did not resemble her father; she was not the daughter of the Second Empire. She had a sky-blue soul like her grandfather's: she believed she was beloved of fortune. Although she consulted a fortuneteller about her babies' future, she had never once doubted that her sons were destined to have a great future. Brazil, land of the future! When did one last see that phrase? No longer ago than this morning's paper.

This lady *is* Brazil. She is married to a banker; she is faithful to her banker; she cannot be seduced by an intellectual, even though he is a man of good sense, and the banker is not. These babies are her sons, identical twins born in the year of the Republican Manifesto. They have a great destiny before them—a destiny they are, paradoxically, destined never to attain completely, because they are also destined never to agree, never to actually disagree. Their quarreling has no grand significance as in Genesis, where two nations struggled in Rebekah's womb. There is no Biblical Jacob in this story. The fighting of the twins, Paulo, the liberal, and Pedro, the conservative, has no political significance. Politics is only an excuse that serves a basic need. They are identical twins; Natividade recognized them as "two pieces of herself." Where the wish of their mother was concerned, they were like a man talking to himself. They represent the mutual attraction and repulsion that exists between individual human beings.

Now, we can see why Machado de Assis changed the title to fit the greater meaning. *Last* would refer specifically to the age, perhaps echoing a verse from Matthew, a gospel that Ayres quotes more than once: "And the last state of that man is worse than the first. Even so shall it be also unto this wicked generation." In other words, *Last* would restrict the author to a time, a place, and a subject —Rio society in the last quarter of the nineteenth century. The title *Esau and Jacob* embraces the whole destiny of a people. By carrying forward the message of the epigraph, it explains how the Republic was born of this society to which it bore no resemblance—just as the youthful heroine, Flora, did not resemble *her* parents. As Ayres remarked of her with allusion to Dante, "Children do not always reproduce their parents." Flora was the opposite of hers. *They* were working politicians of the old school, identical except in will power. Her father was a party man, conservative, weak-willed, not conspicuously honest or dishonest—just so-so. Her mother had tremendous drive and ambition. Like Lady Macbeth, she counseled her husband, in effect, "Look like the time . . . but be the serpent under it." She was not inciting to murder, however; she was merely trying to get him to change his party.

There was nothing of practical politics about Flora. There was nothing practical about her. She was given to dreams and visions. She herself was "Orpheus the sweet singer," a will-o'-the-wisp, a "fragile vase," "flower of a single morning," fit subject "for a tender elegy." There were many suitors for her hand—among them a capitalist, a bureaucrat, and young men from the provinces. But she would have none of them. She had eyes only for Natividade's sons, Pedro and Paulo, the one a conservative, the other a liberal, identical twins. And she was not content to choose one: she wanted them both. To her they were not two, but one.

Flora did not share her parents' dismay over the fall of the Monarchy. To get away from their pain, she took refuge with her piano. "For her, music had the advantage of not being present, past, or future: it was a thing outside time and space, pure idea." But, in her sonata there was "a kind of harmony with the present hour." Flora *was* the present, as the twins were the past and the future. She saw no difference between this past and future; *they* both wanted to possess this present. Love, in Machado de Assis' vocabulary, is the present, the moment; lasting love is a series of presents, of moments, and this is what life is. Early in the story, the personage, Ayres, tried to escape the present when he took as his device the verse of the psalm, "I fled afar off and dwelt in solitude." He fled into the past: into the streets of his boyhood, into old letters and memories. Like the two men who dyed their beards, he too tried to hold Time captive; but "God granted Time a writ of *habeas corpus.*" Ayres changed his device, fled back to the present, to love: a true Dantean, he prolonged himself by living in society.

There is a general concern, among the personages of this novel, with holding Time captive. Some try to accomplish it by making themselves new, others by clinging to the old. And many symbols multiply the images of the various aspects of Brazil, its monarchy, and its republic, for these are in, and of, time: Custodio's signboard with the legend, "The Imperial Pastry Shop," and its new paint, Perpetua's inkwell, the letter from the Marquês de Pombal to the Dutch minister, the five stars of the Southern Cross, the caboclo's song, the portraits of Robespierre and Louis XVI which were replaced by the portraits of the banker and his wife, the cushions and ribbons in the twins' bedroom, the unfinished house, the wall and the rose, Petropolis, Santos' cigars, the toilet water on Nobrega's face, and so on.

Wisdom, Machado de Assis used to say, came out of a well. The old Ayres, whose favorite authors were Homer, Dante, Horace, Erasmus, Father Bernardes, and other European classics, actually rejuvenated himself by returning to certain mineral springs in Europe. (He distrusted Brazilian spring water.) And the flower in his buttonhole is redolent of youth, innocence, young love, life. For, this old intellectual is also one of Brazil's *souls*. Soul, *alma,* is the keyword of this novel. The psyches of the various personages are all plumbed, as individuals, and as parts of a greater soul—the soul of Brazil.

For all the abstract terms in which the novel is couched, for all its deeper meaning, it is none the less a true and vivid account of a certain period of Brazilian history. Integrated into this work of symbolic fiction, we find not only the reactions of typical Brazilians from various walks of life to the historical events, but, also, in brief flashes of poetic description, such actualities as the imperial government's ball for the Chilean officers, the soldiers' march down the Rua do Ouvidor, the first ball of the Republic, the wild financial prosperity and speculation. Even Marshal Floriano Peixoto, in characteristic attitude, is made to add to the drollery of this book. For, Machado de Assis lived through these events: as a bureaucrat, he saw them at close hand; as a journalist, he commented on them in the press.

And this novel is no less true because Machado de Assis chose to make it a comedy, a story "without tears," chose to weave into it threads that tie in knots such various and sundry aspects of civilization as politics, religion, diplomacy, young love, old wisdom, and—perhaps most nicely of all—the naturalistic school of writing. As Ayres' "beloved Horace" put it, *ridentem dicere verum / quid vetat?* Like the other four of Assis' last five novels, this one satirizes the Brazilian scene and the world, Brazilian society and human nature—through characters that have a permanent life of their own. And it stands securely, a unique work of art among Machado de Assis' creations and among other works of universal genius.

Table of Contents

ESAU AND JACOB

Preface

When Counselor Ayres passed away, there were found in his desk seven manuscript notebooks with sturdy cardboard covers. Each of the first six had its number in Roman numerals I, II, III, IV, V, VI, written in red ink. The seventh bore the title *Last.*

The reason for this special designation was not understood then, nor later. Of course, it was the last of the seven notebooks, and it was the thickest, but it was not a part of the *Memorial,* the diary of thoughts and recollections that the Counselor had been writing for many years, and which formed the contents of the first six notebooks. It did not have the same arrangement by dates, with indication of the hour and minute, as the others. It was a narrative; and, although Ayres himself figured in it, along with his name and his title of Counselor, and with hints of several of his love affairs, still, it was a narrative unrelated to the material of the six other notebooks. And why *Last?*

The hypothesis that it was the late diplomat's wish that this notebook be published after the others does not seem likely, unless he wanted to force people to read the other six, in which he wrote about himself, before reading this, the seventh and last—a story written with a single, inner thought running through its manifold pages. If so, it was the fellow's vanity speaking; but vanity was not one of his vices. If it had been, was it worth the trouble to satisfy it in this way? He did not play a prominent role in the world: he went through the steps of the diplomatic career and was pensioned off. In the leisure moments of his

career he wrote his *Memorial,* which, if the dull and obscure pages were cut, would scarcely while away the time
(and perhaps will) of the Petropolis boat trip.

This is the reason for publishing only the narrative. As
for the title, several came to mind that would epitomize
the subject matter. *Ab Ovo,* for example, in spite of its
being Latin. The one that won out, however, consisted of
these two names that Ayres himself once cited:

ESAU AND JACOB

I   *Things Fated to Be!*

It was the first time they had ever gone to the Morro do
Castello. They began to climb from the Rua do Carmo
side. There are many people in Rio de Janeiro who have
never gone there, many no doubt have died, many more
will be born and die without ever once setting foot on that
rock. Not everyone can say they know a whole city. An
old Englishman who had wandered widely over other
lands confided to me many years ago in London that all
he really knew of London was his club, and it was all he
needed to know—of the metropolis and of the world.

Natividade and Perpetua knew other neighborhoods
besides Botafogo, but the castle rock, Morro do Castello,
for all the talk there had been about it and about the
cabocla that reigned there in 1871, was as strange to them,
as remote, as the Englishman's club. The steepness, the
unevenness of the cobblestones mortified the poor ladies'
feet. Still, they continued to climb, as if it were a penance,
slowly, eyes on the ground, with lowered veil. The morning was filled with a certain bustle: women, men, children, going up, coming down, washerwomen and
soldiers, a clerk, a shopkeeper, a priest, all looked at them
in amazement. Though they were simply dressed, still,
there is a certain ladylike air that cannot be concealed,
and it was not common there on high. Even the slowness
of their gait, compared with the briskness of the other
people, made one suspect that this was the first time they
had come.

A Negress said to a sergeant, "Wait and see if they
don't go to the cabocla's!" And both stopped at a distance,

overpowered by that invincible desire to pry into the lives of others, which is often all a man wants here below.

As a matter of fact, the two ladies were covertly looking for the number of the cabocla's house. Finally they found it. Like the other houses, it, too, climbed the hillside, and was approached by a little stairway, narrow, shadowy, suited to an adventure. They had intended to slip in quickly, but their way was blocked by a couple of men coming out, and they shrank back against the wall of the house.

One of the men asked them in a familiar manner if they were going to consult the fortuneteller. "You're wasting your time," he added furiously, "you'll only hear a lot of nonsense."

"It's a big lie," the other man said with a laugh. "The cabocla knows very well what *he's* up to."

They hesitated a moment. Then they decided that the first man's remark was a sure sign of the clairvoyance and candor of the fortuneteller: not all could have the same happy lot. But the lot of Natividade's babies might be wretched, and then . . . While they paused in thought, a postman came by, and this made them go up the steps more quickly, to escape further curious glances. They had faith, but they also had a fear of public opinion, like a devout man who blesses himself in secret.

An old caboclo, the father of the fortuneteller, showed them into the parlor. It was a simple room: bare walls, nothing to suggest mystery or inspire fear, no symbolic gear, neither stuffed creature nor skeleton, or picture of monstrosities. A copy of the Dogma of the Immaculate Conception, stuck up on the wall, might suggest a mystery, even in its grimy, frayed condition—but it did not inspire fear. There was a little guitar lying on a chair.

"My daughter is coming," said the old man. "What are your names, ladies?"

6

Natividade gave only her Christian name Maria, as a veil still thicker than the one she wore over her face, and received a card—the appointment was for but one— with the number 1,012. There is no need to be astonished at the figure, the patronage was heavy and went back for many months. Neither is it necessary to comment on the custom, which is ancient! most ancient. Reread Aeschylus, my friend, reread *The Eumenides*, there you will find the Pythia calling those who came to consult the oracle: "If there are Hellenes present, come, approach in the customary way, *in the order appointed by lot . . .*" By lot in the old days, by numbers now; the main thing is that truth conform to priority and that no one lose his turn for an audience. Natividade put away the ticket, and the two women went to the window.

To tell the truth, they were a little fearful. Perpetua less so than Natividade. The adventure seemed bold, and possibly dangerous. I won't describe their looks and gestures. You can imagine, they were uneasy and restless. Neither said a word. Natividade later confessed she had a lump in her throat. Happily, the cabocla did not keep them waiting. At the end of three or four minutes, her father led her in by the hand, raising the curtain at the back of the room.

"Enter, Barbara."

Barbara entered, while her father picked up the guitar and went out to the stone landing through a door to the left. She was a light little thing, her skirt bordered with lace, a tiny slipper on her foot. You could not deny she had an airy, elegant figure. Her hair caught up on the top of her head with a bit of crumpled ribbon made a natural zucchetto, whose tassle was supplied by a sprig of white rue. Here we have a touch of the priestess. The mystery was in her eyes. They were opaque. Yet not completely so, nor so much so that they were not sometimes clear and

7

sharp, and then they were also intense—so intense, so sharp that they entered deep inside a person, rummaged in his heart, and returned, ready to do it all over again. I do not exaggerate when I say that the two women felt a kind of fascination. Barbara questioned them. Natividade told why she had come, and handed her her sons' pictures and locks of their hair, since, she said, she had been told this would be all that was necessary.

"It is," Barbara assured her. "The babies are your sons?"

"Yes."

"The face of one is the face of the other."

"They are twins. They were born a little over a year ago."

"You may sit down, ladies."

Natividade said to her sister in a low voice that the cabocla was "friendly." Not in such a low voice, however, that the cabocla could not hear. Perhaps Natividade feared the prophecy, and wanted to make sure of a favorable destiny for her sons. The cabocla went and sat down at a round table in the center of the room, and facing the two women. She placed the locks of hair and the pictures before her. By turns she looked at these and at the mother, asked the latter several questions, then remained staring at the pictures and the locks of hair, her lips parted, her brows drawn together. It pains me to say that she lit a cigarette, but I must say it, because it is the truth, and the smoke accords with the rites. Outside, her father drew his fingers across the guitar, and softly sang a ballad of the tropic Northern wilderness:

> Naiad with skirts of white,
> Over the stream with a leap . . .

While the smoke from the cigarette curled upward, the face of the fortuneteller changed expression, radiant, somber, now questioning, now full of answers. As she leaned over the pictures, she clasped the locks of hair in either hand, and held them to her face, staring at them, smelling them, listening to them. And none of this seemed strange or ridiculous, as it does in the telling. Natividade did not take her eyes off her, as if determined to read her thoughts. And it was not without amazement that she heard her ask if the boys had fought before they were born.

"Fought?"

"Yes, fought, Senhora."

"Before they were born?"

"Yes, Senhora. I asked if they had not fought in their mother's womb. Don't you remember?"

Natividade, who had not had an easy pregnancy, answered that she had, to be sure, felt strange motions repeated, and pains, and sleeplessness . . . But then what did it mean? Why would they fight? The cabocla did not answer. A few minutes later she got up and walked around the table, slowly, like a person walking in her sleep, her eyes open and fixed. Then she returned to the mother and the pictures, looking at one and the other. She began to move restlessly, and breathe hard. All of her, face and arms, shoulders, legs, all of her was on the verge of wresting the *word* from Fate. At last, she grew quiet, sat down exhausted, then leaped up and came toward the two women, so radiant, her eyes so alive, so full of fire, that Natividade hung on them and could not keep from grasping her hands and asking her in an anxious tone, "Well? Tell me, I can hear everything."

Barbara, brimming with soul and with laughter, took a long breath. The first word seemed to fill her mouth, but withdrew again to her heart, without reaching the prophetess' lips or the ears of others. Natividade pressed for the response: she could tell her everything, without leaving out anything . . .

"Things fated to be!" the cabocla finally murmured.

9

"Bad things?"

"Oh! no! no! Fine things! things fated to be!"

"But that's not enough. Tell me the rest. This lady is my sister, and in my confidence, but if need be, she'll leave us, and I alone remain. Tell me in my ear . . . Will they be fortunate?"

"Yes."

"Will they be great men?"

"They will be great, oh! very great! God will give them many blessings. They will go up, up, up . . . They fought in their mother's womb . . . well? They will fight outside in the world. Your sons will be glorious. That is all I can tell you. As for the kind of glory, it rests with the future: things fated to be!"

From the inner court, the voice of the old caboclo went on with the song of the wilderness:

> Climb up my coconut tree,
> Throw down the côcos to me.

And the daughter, having no more to say, or not knowing how to say it, began to move her hips in the suggestive rhythms of the song that the old man kept repeating:—

> Naiad with skirts of white,
> Over the stream with a leap,
> Climb up my coconut tree,
> Throw down the côcos to me.
>   Côco break, Sinhá,
>   There'n the cocá',
>   Land on your head,
>   Split all the way!
> I'll have many a laugh,
> There'll be plenty of play,
> Cocô, naiá', lelê!

Better Coming Down
Than Going Up

All oracles are double-tongued, but they are understood.
Natividade understood the cabocla, in spite of the fact
that she did not hear her say another word. To learn that
the things fated to be would be fine, and her sons great
and glorious, was enough to make her happy, and to
make her take a fifty *milreis* note out of her purse. It was
five times the regular price, and was the equivalent, or
more than the equivalent, of Croesus' rich offerings to the
Pythia. She took back the pictures and the locks of hair,
and she and her sister left, while the cabocla retired to the
back of the house to wait for other customers. There were
already some standing at the door, with their numbered
tickets, as the two ladies, averting their faces, went rapidly
down the steps.

Perpetua shared her sister's joy. She shared the cobblestones, too, the wall facing the sea, the shirts hung up in
the windows, the banana peels under foot. Even the shoes
of a begging lay-brother, a "Brother of Souls," who was
turning the corner of the Rua da Misericordia into the
Rua de São José, seemed to laugh with joy, when actually
they were groaning with weariness. Natividade was so
beside herself with joy that when she heard him beg,
"Masses for souls!" she drew a brand new two-milreis
note out of her purse and put it in his bowl. Her sister

called her attention to the mistake, but it was not a mistake, it was for the souls in purgatory.

And they walked on with buoyant step toward the coupé that was waiting for them in the space between São José church and the Chamber of Deputies. They had not permitted the carriage to take them to the foot of the *morro* for fear the coachman and footman might suspect their purpose. The whole city was talking about the cabocla of the Castello. She was on everyone's lips, they ascribed infinite powers to her, a succession of miracles, winning numbers, found articles, marriages. If the two ladies should be found out, they were lost, although many respectable people had gone there. At sight of them giving alms to the Brother of Souls, the footman climbed up on his cushion and the coachman touched the reins to the horses; the carriage came for them, and they set off toward Botafogo.

III   *Alms of Happiness*

"God bless you, devout lady!" cried the Brother of Souls, as he saw the banknote fall on top of two nickel *tostões* and some old copper *vintens*. "God grant you all the happiness of heaven and earth, and may the souls in purgatory beg Holy Mary to recommend your ladyship to her blessed Son!"

When luck laughs, all nature laughs too, and the heart laughs like everything else. This was the Brother of Souls' explanation for the two milreis, though he put it in other, less speculative, words. The suspicion that the note might be counterfeit did not really get a firm footing in his brain: it was a momentary hallucination. He saw that the ladies were happy, and, as he had the habit of thinking aloud, he said with a wink while they were getting into the carriage, "Those two have seen a little green bird, that's sure."

Not to mince words, he supposed the two ladies were returning from some amorous escapade, and deduced this from three facts, which I must place here in order, so as not to leave this man under the suspicion of being a gratuitous destroyer of reputations. The first was their joyousness; the second, the size of the donation; the third, the carriage waiting on a corner as if they had wished to conceal the place of assignation from the coachman. But don't go concluding that he had once been a coachman and driven young ladies about, before he went in for serving the souls in purgatory. Do not imagine, either, that he had formerly been a rich adulterer, and open-handed each time he said goodbye to his mistresses. *Ni cet excès d'honneur, ni cette indignité.* He was a poor devil with no other calling than his devotion. Besides, he would not have had time, he was scarcely twenty-seven years old.

He bowed to the ladies when the carriage passed. And then he looked long at the banknote—so fresh, so valuable, a banknote that the *souls* would never see leave his hands. He went along the Rua de São José. He no longer had any heart for begging, the banknote had turned to gold, and the idea of its being counterfeit again entered his brain. The idea was now more insistent, and held its ground for several seconds. If it should prove counterfeit . . . "Masses for the *souls!*" he moaned at the door of a greengrocer's, and they gave him a copper, a dismal, grimy vintem, alongside the banknote that was so fresh it seemed just off the press. Then he came to a rich house, went into the entrance court, climbed the stairs, and begged. They gave him two vintens—twice the other coin, in value and in verdigris.

And the banknote, still clean, two milreis that seemed like twenty! No, it was not counterfeit. In the entrance court, he took it in his hand, looked hard at it, it was genuine. Suddenly he heard someone open the grilled gate at the top of the stairs, and hasty footsteps; he, still more hastily, crumpled the note and put it in his trousers pocket. There remained only the vintens with their dismal verdigris—the widow's mite. He went into the street, to the first workshop, the first store, the first house entrance, begging long and pitifully, "Masses for the *souls!*"

At the church, after he had handed his bowl to the sacristan and was taking off his surplice, he heard a feeble voice, as of faraway souls, asking him if the two milreis . . . The two milreis (said another, less feeble voice) were naturally his, who, in the first place, also had a soul, and, in the second place, had never received such a big donation. If anyone wants to give such an amount he goes to church or buys a candle, he does not just drop a banknote in the bowl for trifling alms.

If I convey a false impression, I do not do so intentionally. It is true, the words did not come forth like this, grammatical and well enunciated, neither those in the feeble voice nor those in the less feeble: they all made a humming in the ears of his conscience. I translated them into spoken language in order to be understood by those who read me. I don't know how I could transfer to paper an indistinct murmur, and another less indistinct one, one after the other, and then both jumbled together, and finally only the second one remaining: "He did not take the banknote from anybody . . . it was the owner who put it in the bowl with her own hand . . . and, besides, *he* was a soul . . ."

Outside, in the street, as he let fall the dark blue curtain edged with yellow which hung over the entrance to the sacristy, he no longer heard anything. He saw a beggar

holding out his shabby, greasy hat; he slowly put his
hand in his vest pocket (which was also shabby and
worn), and brought out a little copper coin, which he
placed in the beggar's hat, hastily, in secret, as the Gospel
commands. It was two vintens: he still had left one thousand, nine hundred and sixty *reis*. And as he quickly
walked away, the beggar sent after him these words of
thanks so like his own: "God bless you, my dear Senhor,
and grant you . . ."

IV   *The Coupé Mass*

Natividade's thoughts ran on the cabocla of the Castello,
on the prophecy of greatness and the message of the fighting. She again recalled that, really, her pregnancy had not
been easy; but, in the end, there remained only the glorious destiny, the greatness. The fighting was receding into
the past, if it had ever existed. The future, yes, that was
the main thing, or the whole thing. They went past Santa
Luzia beach without her noticing it. In the Largo da Lapa
she asked her sister what she thought of the fortuneteller.
Perpetua answered she thought well of her, that she believed in her; and both agreed that it was as if she had
been speaking of her own children, so great was her enthusiasm. Perpetua still blamed her for paying fifty milreis: twenty would have been enough.
    "It doesn't matter. Things fated to be!"
    "What things will they be?"
    "I don't know, things to be in the future."
    They again sank into silence. As they turned the corner
of the Rua do Cattete, Natividade thought of the morning
she had driven along it in that same coupé, and had con-

fided her delicate condition to her husband. They were coming back from a Mass for the dead at São Domingos' church . . .

"Today, at São Domingos' church, Mass will be said for the soul of João de Mello, who passed away in Maricá." This was the announcement that you can still read in certain newspapers of 1869. I don't remember the day, the month was August. The announcement I do remember: it was just that, with nothing more, neither the name of the person or persons who ordered the Mass to be said, nor the hour, nor was there an invitation to attend. It did not even say that the deceased had been a court stenographer—a position he gave up only because of death. Lastly, it seems that they even took away one of his names: he was, if I am correctly informed, João de Mello e Barros.

Since people did not know who ordered the Mass, no one went. The church chosen gave still less importance to the function: it was not showy, nor stiffly formal, but oldish, without pomp or congregation, tucked away in the corner of a little square, suitable for an obscure, anonymous Mass.

At eight o'clock, a coupé stopped at the church door: the footman got down, opened the carriage door, whipped off his hat, and stiffened. A gentleman got out and gave his hand to a lady; she got out and took the gentleman's arm. They crossed the bit of square, and went into the church.

In the sacristy, all was amazement. The soul that had attracted a fine carriage, blooded horses, and two such elegant persons to a place such as this, could not be like the other souls prayed for there. The Mass was heard: there were no condolences, no tears. When it ended, the gentleman went to the sacristy to leave the offering.

The sacristan, cuddling the ten-milreis note in his

pocket, concluded that it proved the sublimity of the deceased. But what kind of deceased was this? The box for the *souls* would have had the same thought, if it could have thought, when the lady's glove dropped a little silver five-tostões piece into it. There were already half a dozen ragged children in the church, and a little crowd waiting outside, and in the square. When the gentleman reached the door, he glanced carelessly around and saw that he was an object of curiosity. The lady kept *her* eyes on the ground. Both got into the carriage with the same distant air. The footman slammed shut the carriage door, and they were off.

The local population spoke of nothing else the rest of that day, and on the days following. Sacristan and neighbors kept recalling the coupé, with pride. It became "the coupé Mass." Other Masses kept coming, all on foot, some in shabby shoes, many without shoes, little old capes, worn white cottons, Masses in calico on Sunday, Masses in wooden clogs. Everything went on as before, but the coupé Mass lived on in memory for many months. Finally they no longer talked of it: it was forgotten, like a fancy ball.

Well, *this* was the coupé. The Mass was ordered by this gentleman, whose name is Santos, and the deceased was a relative of his, a *poor* relative. He too had been poor, he too had been born in Maricá. He arrived in Rio de Janeiro at the time of the *stock-buying* fever (1855); and they say that he revealed great talents for making money quickly. He soon made lots of it, and caused others to lose theirs. He married, in 1859, this Natividade, who was then in her twenties. She had no money, but she was handsome and could love passionately. Fortune blessed them with wealth. A few years later they had a fine house, a carriage, horses, and new, distinguished connections. Natividade had had two poor relations: her father died in 1866,

17

there remained only her sister. Santos had a few in Maricá, to whom he never sent money, whether from stinginess or because he was shrewd. I don't believe it was stinginess: he spent freely and gave lots of money to charity. Shrewdness? Very likely: in this way he did away with their taste for coming to the city to ask him for more.

It did not work with João de Mello. One day he appeared here and asked him for a job. He wanted to be, like him, director of a bank. Santos lost no time in getting him a position as court stenographer in Maricá, and in packing him off with some of the best advice in this world. João de Mello went back home with the stenographer's job, and also, they say, with a *grande passion*. Natividade was the handsomest woman of that time. Even at the end of her life, when her locks were almost sixty, one could easily believe in the tradition. João de Mello was bewitched when he saw her. She knew it, and conducted herself with propriety. It is true, she did not shut off her smiles in his presence; she was more beautiful smiling. Neither did she shut her eyes to him: her eyes were black and sultry. She closed her heart against him. A heart that must love like no other: that was what João de Mello concluded when he saw her going to a ball, one night, in a low-necked dress. He had an impulse to grab her, float down, soar upward, lose himself with her . . .

Instead of this, a stenographer's job in Maricá: it was a black abyss. He descended into it. Three days later he left Rio de Janeiro, never to return. At first he wrote a great many letters to his relative, with the hope that she too would read them and would understand that certain words were intended for her. But Santos never replied, and time and absence finally made of João de Mello an excellent court stenographer. He died of an attack of pneumonia.

That the motive for the little silver coin dropped by Natividade into the *souls* box was to repay the dead man's adoration . . . I do not say that it was, nor that it was not. I lack precise information. But it may very well have been, because this lady was by nature no less grateful than chaste. As for her husband's generosity, do not forget that his relative was dead, and, as a dead man, one relative the less.

V   *There Are Contradictions*
          That Can Be Explained

Don't ask me the reason for such reticent modesty in the announcement and in the Mass, and such publicity in the carriage, footman, and livery. There are contradictions that can be explained. A good author, who makes up his story, or respects the apparent logic of events, would deliver the Santoses on foot or in a cab or a hired carriage; but I, my friend, know how the things happened, and I relate them just that way. As a concession, however, I will explain them, on condition that this practice does not become a habit. Explanations eat up time and paper, delay the action, and end by boring. The best thing is for you to read attentively.

As to the contradiction we are dealing with, it is plain that in that secluded corner of a modest little square, no one would run into them, while *they* would enjoy the local astonishment. Such was Santos' idea, if one can give such a name to a vague inner urge that makes a person do one thing rather than another. As for the Mass: it was enough that the Mass be heard of in heaven and in Maricá. Quite properly, they dressed for heaven. The rich magnificence of the couple tempered the poverty of the religious service, it was a kind of respect paid the deceased. If the soul of João de Mello saw them from on high, he could not but rejoice at the *chic* with which they went to pray for a poor stenographer. It is not I who say it, it was Santos who thought it.

VI   *Motherhood*

At first they rode along in silence. Natividade *did* complain of the church, because it had soiled her dress.

"I'm covered with fleas," she went on. "Why didn't we go to São Francisco de Paula's or to the Gloria church? They are nearer, and they are clean."

Santos changed the subject, and spoke of the badly paved streets that made the carriage bump and would surely break its springs.

Natividade made no reply. She was immersed in silence as in that other chapter twenty months later when she was returning from the Castello with her sister. Her eyes did not have the starry look they had then, they were dull and somber as they had been in the morning and the day before. Santos, who had noticed this, asked her what was wrong. I don't know whether she answered in words; if she did the answer was so brief and muffled that it was completely lost. Perhaps it did not go beyond a glance, a sigh, or some such thing. Be that as it may, when the coupé was halfway up Cattete the two had their hands clasped, and the look on their faces was the look of the blest. They were not even aware of the people in the streets, they were not aware perhaps of themselves.

Reader, you are about to learn the reason for that look,

and for those interlaced fingers. It was actually told you some time back, although it would have been better to let you figure it out for yourself; but you would probably not have figured it out, not that you are short of understanding or dim of wit, but because one man is not like another, and you, perhaps, might have worn the same look, simply because you knew you were going to a dance next Saturday. Santos did not dance, he preferred cards as a diversion. The reason was a moral one, as you know: Natividade was pregnant; she had just told her husband.

At thirty years of age it was not too soon nor too late; it was unexpected. Santos felt more pleasure than she at the thought of a child. The dream of ten years was about to become reality, a being drawn from Abraham's thigh, as those good Jews used to say—the ones we later burned, and now they generously lend their money to companies and nations. They get interest for *it;* but the Hebraisms are given free of charge. This is one of them. Santos, though he knew only the money-lending part, unconsciously felt affinity for the Hebraism also and took delight in it. Emotion tied his tongue; his eyes, as he turned them upon his wife and enfolded her in their warmth, were those of a patriarch; his smile seemed to shower light upon the person of the beloved, blessed as she was and beautiful among women.

Natividade did not feel this way right off; but, little by little, she was won over, and came to have an expression of hopefulness and of motherhood. In the beginning the prospect put her out of temper. It is painful to relate, but it is true. It would be the end of balls and company, the end of freedom and fun. Natividade now moved in the highest social circle; she had entered it with such art that she seemed to have been born there. She exchanged letters with great ladies, was friends with many, on intimate terms with some. There was not only this house in Botafogo, but another in Petropolis; not only a carriage, but a box at the Theatro Lyrico, not to mention balls at the Casino Fluminense, those given by her friends, and by herself—the whole repertoire, in short, of the fashionable life. Her name was mentioned in the papers. It was one of the dozen or so planetary names that shine forth from the midst of a rabble of stars. Her husband was a capitalist and director of a bank.

In the midst of all this, why did a child have to come and deform her for months, force her into retirement, claim her nights, ruin her teeth and all that? Those were her first feelings of motherhood, and her first impulse was to crush the germ. She was irritated at her husband. Her next sensation was better. Motherhood, arriving in the noon of life, was like a fresh, young dawn. Natividade imagined her son or daughter, aged three, playing on the lawn of the *chácara* or on the lap of its nurse, and this picture would give her thirty-four years the look of scarcely more than twenty.

This is what reconciled her with her husband. I do not exaggerate. Neither do I dislike this lady. The feeling of some women would be fear; of most, love. The implication is that, one way or another, what the embryo wants is to enter life. Caesar or John Doe, the whole thing is to live, to secure the succession, and go out of the world as late as possible.

The couple rode on in silence. As they came out along Botafogo beach, the inlet brought the customary pleasure. Their house stood up in the distance, a magnificent thing. Santos reveled in the sight of it, he saw himself mirrored in it: his stature increased, he was raised aloft. The statue of Narcissus, in the center of the garden, smiled on their entrance, the sand became lawn, two swallows crossed above the pool of the fountain, marking in the air the happiness of the two human beings. The usual ceremony

22

on getting out of the carriage. Santos still stood a few seconds to watch the coupé make the turn and disappear toward the coach house. Then he followed his wife, who was already in the entrance court.

VII   *Gestation*

Waiting at the head of the stairs was Perpetua, that sister of Natividade's who accompanied her to the Castello and is waiting there in the carriage where I left the two women in order to tell the antecedents of the little sons.

"Well? Were there many there?"

"No, no one; fleas."

Perpetua had not understood the choice of church either. As for the attendance, she had thought all along there would be few, if anybody. But her brother-in-law was coming, and she said no more. She was a circumspect person, and not one to fall out of favor for a careless word or gesture. Nevertheless, she could not conceal her astonishment when she saw her brother-in-law come in and give his wife a long, tender embrace sealed with a kiss.

"What's this?" she cried out in astonishment.

Without taking notice of his wife's annoyance, Santos gave his sister-in-law a hug, and would have given her a kiss too if she had not drawn back in time, and with energy.

"But what is this? Did you win the Spanish sweepstakes?"

"No, something better, young'uns."

Santos had kept certain childish gestures and modes of speech from his earliest years; they cannot properly be called familiar, but it is not necessary to call them any-

23

thing. Perpetua, who was accustomed to them, smiled, gave him her congratulations. Natividade had already left them to go and change. Santos half regretting his expansiveness became serious and conversed about the Mass and the church. He agreed that the latter was run-down and out-of-the-way, but excused it with spiritual reasons: prayer was always prayer wherever the soul spoke to God. The Mass, in the strict sense, had no need of an altar; the rite and the priest were all that was needed for the sacrifice. Perhaps these reasons were not really his own but simply ones heard from somebody else, memorized without effort, and repeated with conviction. His sister-in-law nodded agreement. Then they spoke of the dead relative, and piously agreed that he was an ass. They did not use this word but the sum total of their appraisals was just that, with the addition that he was honest, very honest.

"He was a jewel," concluded Santos.

It was the last word of the obituary; peace to the dead.

From now on, the sovereignty of the child to be born was supreme. They did not alter their habits at first, and the visits and balls continued as before, until, little by little, Natividade closed herself up at home completely. Her women friends came to see her. The gentlemen came also, in the evening, especially to play cards with the husband.

Natividade wanted a boy, Santos a girl, and both supported their choice with such good reasons that they ended by changing sides. And she held out for the girl, dressing her in the finest laces and cambric, while he put a magistrate's robe on the young lawyer, gave him a seat in parliament, another in the cabinet. He also taught him how to get rich quick, helping him with a savings account from the day of his birth to his twenty-first birthday. Sometimes, on the nights they were alone, Santos would take a pencil and draw a picture of his son, with moustachios, or he would sketch a vaporous young lady.

"Stop it, Agostinho," said his wife one night. "Must you always be a child?"

And shortly thereafter she found herself sketching a word-picture of her son or daughter, and they both chose the color of the eyes, of the hair, the complexion, and height. You see, she too was a child. Motherhood is given to these contradictions, so is happiness, and even hope, which is the childhood of the world.

The perfect thing would be a couple. Thus the desires of both father and mother would be satisfied. Santos thought of consulting a spiritualistic medium about it. He was just being initiated into this religion, and had a novice's firm faith. But his wife opposed it. If he was going to consult anyone, rather the cabocla of the Castello, the famous fortuneteller of the time, who discovered lost articles and prophesied what was to be. But she opposed this too, as being unnecessary. Why consult an oracle about something that would be cleared up in a matter of months? Santos thought that, as to consulting the cabocla, it would be imitating the superstitions of the vulgar; but his sister-in-law interposed that it was not, and cited a recent example of a distinguished person, a municipal judge, whose appointment had been foretold by the cabocla.

"Maybe the Minister of Justice is sweet on the cabocla," suggested Santos.

The two sisters laughed at the witticism and thus the chapter of the fortuneteller was closed—to be opened later. Now, it is a question of leaving the fetus to develop, the child to move, to throw itself about, as if impatient to be born. Yes, the mother suffered a good deal during pregnancy, and especially during the last weeks. She began to think she was carrying a general who had already started his campaign of life, if it was not a married couple who were learning to fall out of love beforehand.

Neither Married Couple
nor General

Neither a married couple, nor a general. On the seventh
of April, 1870, there saw the light of day a pair of male
children, so alike that one seemed the shadow of the
other, if it was not simply the illusion of the eye, which
saw double.

They were expecting anything but twin boys. Though
their astonishment was great, their love was no less. This
can be understood without my laboring the point; just as
it will be understood that the mother gave her two sons
the "bread that is whole though divided" of which the
poet speaks, *I* add that the father did the same. He lived
those first days gazing at the babies, comparing them,
measuring them, weighing them. They had the same
weight, and they gained at the same rate. The change in
them followed a single course: the long face, chestnut
hair; the slender fingers so alike that when those of the
right hand of one were crossed with those of the other's
left, one could not tell that they belonged to two persons.
They would come to have different natures, but, for the
present, they were the same shy little things. They both
began to smile on the same day. The same day saw their
baptism.

Before their birth it had been decided to use the name
of the father or mother depending on the sex of the child.

When it turned out to be a pair of boys, and there was no masculine form of the mother's name, the father refused to let his name figure without hers; and they began a search for other names. The mother proposed French or English names, according to the novels she was reading. Certain Russian stories that were in vogue suggested Slavic names. The father accepted this one or that one, but consulted other parties, and remained undecided. Usually those consulted brought in a third name that was not acceptable at home. Finally there came the ancient catalogue of Portuguese names, with no better luck. One day, as Perpetua was reciting the Creed at Mass, she noticed the words, "the holy apostles St. Peter and St. Paul," and could hardly wait till the end of the service. She had discovered the names: they were simple and "twin." The parents agreed with her, and the debate was over.

Perpetua's joy was almost as great as that of the father and mother, if not greater. No, it was not greater, nor was it so profound, but it *was* great, even though transitory. The lucky chancing upon the names was almost as if she had given birth to the babies. A widow, without children, she felt that she might have had them, and it was something to name them. She was five or six years older than her sister. She had married a lieutenant in the artillery who died a captain in the war with Paraguay. She was rather short, and she was plump—unlike Natividade who, though not thin, still was not fat, and was tall and straight. Both radiated health.

"Pedro and Paulo," said Perpetua to her sister and to her brother-in-law, "when I recited these two names, I felt something in my heart . . ."

"You shall be godmother to one of them," said her sister.

The babies, who had been wearing a colored ribbon to

tell them apart were now given gold medals, one with the image of St. Peter, the other with that of St. Paul. The confusion did not cease right away, but much later, slowly and only in part: the resemblance remained so great that those who knew were fooled many times, or always. But, their mother did not need external signs to know who those two pieces of herself were. Their nurses, though they could tell them apart, never left off hating each other because of the similarity between "their foster children." Each maintained that hers was prettier. Natividade agreed with both of them.

Pedro was to be a doctor, Paulo a lawyer; these were the first professions selected. But soon their parents changed their careers. They thought of placing one of them in engineering. The navy attracted their mother, because of its distinguished school. Its only drawback was that first, faraway voyage; but Natividade considered invoking the protection of the Secretary of the Navy. Santos spoke of making one of them a banker, or both of them. Close friends entered into the plans. There were those who would have them cabinet members, judges of the high court, bishops, cardinals . . .

"I don't ask so much," said the father.

Natividade did not say anything before outsiders; she only smiled as if it were a St. John's eve merrymaking: a casting of dice and reading in the book of fortunes, the portrait corresponding to the number on the dice. No matter, deep inside she too coveted a brilliant destiny for her sons. She believed, she hoped, she prayed at night, she begged Heaven to make them great men.

One of the nurses, I think it was Pedro's, knowing of these anxieties and conversations, asked Natividade why she did not go consult the cabocla of the Castello. She claimed that *she* could tell everything, what was and what would come to be; she knew the number of the grand prize in the lottery but would not say what it was nor buy a ticket, so as not to rob the chosen of Our Lord. It was plain she had been sent by God.

The other nurse confirmed this information and added some bits of her own. She knew people who had lost and found jewels and slaves. Even the police, when they did not succeed in capturing a criminal, would go to the Castello to talk to the cabocla and would come back with all the information: this was the reason they did not put her out of business as the envious kept demanding. Many people never took a trip without first climbing the morro. The cabocla interpreted dreams and thoughts, and averted the evil eye.

At dinner, Natividade told her husband of the nurses' advice. Santos shrugged his shoulders. Then with a laugh he questioned the wisdom of the cabocla, especially the matter of the grand prize. It was inconceivable that, knowing the number, she should not buy the ticket. Natividade found this the most difficult thing to explain, but maybe it was something the common people made up. *On ne prête qu'aux riches,* she added with a laugh. Her husband, who had been with a high court judge the day before, repeated the judge's words, "As long as the police do not put an end to the scandal . . ." The judge had not finished the sentence. Santos finished it with a vague gesture.

"But you are a spiritualist," reflected his wife.

"Beg pardon, let us not confuse matters," he replied gravely.

Yes, he could consent to a spiritualistic consultation; he had already thought of it. A spirit could tell him the truth . . . but a low-comedy fortuneteller! . . .

Natividade defended the cabocla. People of social rank talked of her in all seriousness. She was not quite willing to admit that she believed in her, but she did. When she refused to go, before, it was probably the lack of sufficient motive that gave her the strength to say no. What use was it to learn the sex of an unborn child? But, to learn the destiny of two sons was more imperative and advantageous. Old notions that had been instilled in her in childhood now came trooping out of her brain and descended into her heart. She thought of going with the babies to the Morro do Castello, on the pretense of taking them for an airing . . . For what? To confirm her in her hope that they would be great men. A contrary prediction had never crossed her mind. Perhaps, my lady-reader, if you had been in the same situation you would have waited for destiny; but, dear lady, besides not believing (not all do), it is possible that you are no more than twenty to twenty-two years of age, and have the patience to wait. Natividade, when she was by herself, admitted to thirty-one, and she was afraid she might not see the greatness of her sons. Suppose she should see it, for people do die old and sometimes even of old age, but would she take the same pleasure in it?

Later in the evening, a subject of conversation among their guests was the cabocla of the Castello. It was Santos who introduced the topic, repeating the opinions expressed the day before, and that day at dinner. Some of the guests related things they had heard about her. Natividade did not go to sleep that night before she got her husband to promise to let her go with her sister to see the cabocla. No harm would be done; all she had to do was take the babies' pictures and a small bit of their hair. The nurses would know nothing about the adventure.

On the day of the appointment, the two women got into the carriage, between seven and eight o'clock, on the pretext of going for a drive, and off they went toward the Rua da Misericordia. And you already know that there they left the carriage between São José church and the

Chamber of Deputies, and climbed to the Rua do Carmo where it joins the steep slope of the Castello. As they were about to start up the morro they hesitated, but the mother was a mother, and on the very threshold of hearing the word of fate. You have seen that they went up the hill, that they came down, that they gave two milreis to the *souls,* that they got into the carriage and returned to Bota-fogo.

I X   *Palace View*

On the Rua Cattete a coupé and a victoria passed each other, and both stopped at once. A man jumped down from the victoria and walked toward the coupé. It was Natividade's husband, who was on his way to the office, a little later than usual because he had waited for his wife's return. He was riding along, thinking of her, of prices on the exchange, of his little sons, and of the Rio Branco law of *free birth* then being discussed in the Chamber of Deputies; his bank was a creditor of the farming interests. He also thought about the cabocla of the Castello and of what she might have told his wife . . .

As he passed the palace of the Count of Nova-Friburgo, he raised his eyes toward it with the customary desire, a greedy desire to possess it, without ever foreseeing the high destiny the palace would attain under the Republic—but who then foresaw anything? Who foresaw anything at all? For Santos the question was only to possess it, to give grand, matchless balls in it, parties glorified in the papers, talked of in the city, among friends and enemies, who would all be filled with admiration, with covert hostility, or with envy. He did not imagine the fond memories that matrons-to-be would pass on to their grandchildren, still less the books of annals to be written and printed in this other age. Santos had no imagination for posterity. He saw the present and its wonders.

He was no longer satisfied with what he had. The house in Botafogo, though fine, was not a palace; besides, it was not so exposed to public view as here on Cattete, where everyone had to pass and see the great windows, the great doors, and, above, the great eagles with outspread wings. Those who looked from the shore side would see the back of the palace, the gardens and lakes . . . Oh! infinite delight! Santos imagined the bronzes, marble, lights, flowers, dancing, carriages, music, suppers . . . All this passed through his head quickly, because although the victoria did not speed (the horses had been instructed to moderate their gait), still it did not slow its wheels so that Santos could finish his dreams. Thus it was that, before reaching the Praça da Gloria, the victoria sighted the family coupé and the two carriages stopped a short distance from each other, as already mentioned.

X   *The Oath*

It was also mentioned that the husband left the victoria and walked toward the coupé where his wife and sister-in-law, who guessed he was coming to question them, began to smile in anticipation.

"Don't tell him anything," advised Perpetua.

Santos' head soon appeared with its short side whiskers, close-cropped hair, trimmed moustache. He was a likeable fellow; in his calmer states, most presentable. His agitation, as he ran up, stopped, and spoke, took away the gravity with which he had ridden along in the carriage, his hands resting on the gold head of his cane, his cane between his knees.

"Well? Well?" he asked.

"I'll tell you later."

"But what happened."

"Later."

"Good or bad? Just say whether it was good."

"Good. Things destined to be."

"Is she a person to be relied upon?"

"Oh, yes, very reliable. See you later," repeated Natividade, holding out the tips of her fingers to him.

But her husband could not let the coupé go: he wanted to know everything, right then, the questions and answers, the people waiting to see the cabocla, and if both were to have the same destiny, or if each had his own. None of this was written as it is here, slowly so that the author's bad handwriting would not spoil his prose. No, sir, Santos' words tumbled out in a bunch, one on top of another, mixed up, without a beginning and without an end. His lovely wife, whose ears were long since accustomed to her husband's manner of speaking, especially in crises of emotion or curiosity, understood every bit of it, and kept saying "no." Her head and her finger underlined the negative. Since there was nothing he could do, Santos took his departure.

As he rode along, he reminded himself that inasmuch as he did not believe in the cabocla, it was silly to insist on hearing the prediction. It was worse, it was as good as agreeing with his wife. He promised himself not to ask a single question when he went home. He did not promise to forget, however: hence the persistence with which he

33

kept thinking of the oracle. Besides, they would tell him everything without his asking a thing, and this certainty brought him peace of mind for the rest of the day.

Do not conclude from the above that the affairs of the bank's customers suffered any inattention. All ran smoothly, as if he had no wife or sons, as if there were no Castello or cabocla. It was not only the hand that performed its function by signing, the mouth talked, gave orders, spoke names, laughed if necessary. Yet, the anxiety remained, and shapes passed and repassed before his eyes. In the interval between two letters, Santos would resolve upon one thing or the other, if not on two things at once. As he got into the carriage that afternoon, he threw himself upon the mercy of the oracle. He had his hands on the head of his cane, the cane between his knees, as in the morning, but his mind ran on the destiny of his sons.

When he reached the house, he found Natividade gazing at the babies, who were both in their cradles, their nurses close by and a little amazed at the persistence with which she had kept visiting them since morning. It was not only to gaze at them, or let her eyes wander in space and time, it was also to kiss them and hug them to her breast. I forgot to mention that, when they returned that morning, Perpetua changed her clothes before her sister, and came back to find her in front of the cradles, dressed as she had come from the Castello.

"I just knew you were with the great men," she said.

"Yes, but I do not know in what way they will be great."

"Whatever way it is, let's have breakfast."

At breakfast and during the rest of the day, they spoke many times of the cabocla and of her prophecy. Now, when Natividade saw her husband come in, she read the dissimulation in his eyes. She had made up her mind to say nothing and wait, but she was so eager to tell him everything, and she was so kind by nature, that she decided to do the opposite. Only she did not have the chance to carry out her purpose. Before she could even begin, he had already asked what happened. Natividade related the ascent, the consultation, the response, and all the rest. She described the cabocla and her father.

"And so, great destinies?"

"Things fated to be," she repeated.

"Surely, fated to be. It's only the matter of the fighting that I don't understand. Fight over what? And how? Could they really have fought?"

Natividade recounted the pains she suffered during pregnancy and admitted she had not mentioned them so as not to distress him, and probably the cabocla had divined these and interpreted them as fighting.

"But fight over what?"

"That I don't know, but I am sure it was nothing bad."

"I am going to consult . . ."

"Consult whom?"

"Somebody."

"I know, your friend Placido."

"If he were only a friend, I would not consult him, but he is my master and guide; he has clear, far-seeing vision, granted him by Heaven. I will put it to him as a hypothetical case, I won't use our names . . ."

"No! no! no!"

"Only as a hypothetical case."

"No, Agostinho, don't speak of this to anyone. Don't ask anyone anything about me, do you hear? Promise that you won't speak of this to anyone, either spiritualists or friends. The best thing is to say nothing about it. It is enough to know that their lot will be fortunate. Great men, things fated to be . . . Swear, Agostinho."

"But didn't you go in person to the cabocla?"

"She doesn't know me, not even by name. She saw me once, will never see me again. Go on, swear!"

"You are funny. All right, I promise. What difference would it make if I spoke, so, by the way?"

"I don't want it. Swear!"

"Look, is this a matter for oaths?"

"Without an oath, I don't trust you." She was smiling.

"I swear."

"Swear by Our Lord Jesus Christ!"

"I swear by Our Lord Jesus Christ."

XI   *A Unique Case!*

Santos believed in the sanctity of the oath. For this reason he resisted, but he finally gave in and swore. Still, the thought of his sons fighting in the womb would not leave him. He decided to forget it. He played cards that night as usual, the next night went to the theater, the night after to a friend's house, then back to the usual game of ombre, and the "fighting" always with him. It was a mystery. Perhaps a unique case . . . Unique! No other like it! The uniqueness of it made him hold on more than ever to the idea, or the idea to him: I can offer no better explanation for this inner phenomenon that took place where the eye of man does not penetrate, and thought and conjecture are not enough. Even so, it did not last long. On the first Sunday, Santos upped and went to Professor Placido's house, on the Rua do Senador Vergueiro, a small house with three windows and a large stretch of land on the side facing the sea. I believe it is no longer there: it dated from the time when the street was called "the old road," to distinguish it from the "new road."

Pardon me these trivial details: the action can go forward without them, but I want you to know which house it was, and on what street, and further, I will tell you that it was the home of a kind of spiritualistic club, temple, or what you will. Placido served as both priest and president. He was an old man with a great beard, a bright blue eye, and he wore a roomy silk jersey. Put a wand in his hand and you would have a sorcerer. But, the truth is, he did not wear the beard and the jersey so that they would give him that appearance. Contrary to Santos, who would have changed his face ten times over if it had not been for his wife's objections, Placido had worn the beard since youth and the jersey for ten years.

"Come in, come in," he said. "Help me to convert our friend Ayres. For a half-hour I've been trying to instil eternal truths in him, but he is resisting."

"No, no, I'm not resisting," said a man of about forty years of age, and he held out his hand to the newcomer.

XII   *This Fellow Ayres*

This fellow Ayres, who appears here, still retains some of the virtues he had at that time, and almost none of the vices. You are not to attribute this state to any plan of his, nor imagine this is homage to his moderation. No, sir, it is the actual truth and a natural development. In spite of his forty, or forty-two, years, or perhaps even because of them, he was a fine type of man. A career diplomat, he had arrived from the Pacific some days before, on a six-months' leave.

I won't take time to describe him. You need only know that he wore the protective shell of his profession, the approving smile, the bland and cautious style of speaking, the air appropriate to every occasion, just the right amount of expression, all so well distributed that it was a pleasure to hear and see him. Perhaps the skin of his smooth-shaved face was ready to show the first signs of time's passage. Even so, his moustache, still youthful in color and in the niceness with which it ended in a fine, jaunty point, would give an air of youthful vigor to his face when the half-century had come. And the same with his hair, which was vaguely grizzled and parted in the center. On the top of his head there was a bald spot. In his buttonhole an eternal flower.

Time was—it was during his previous leave and when he was only a legation secretary—time was when he too fell in love with Natividade. It was not exactly passion: he was not a man for that. He was attracted by her as by other jewels and rarities; but as soon as he saw his attentions were not accepted, he quickly changed his tune. It was not lack of energy, nor coldness. He was fond enough of women, and more than that if they were pretty. The trouble was he did not want them by force, nor did he care to persuade them. He was not a general for scaling the walls on sight, nor for long sieges; he was content with military excursions—long or short depending on the weather he ran into. In short, he was extremely sensible.

An interesting coincidence: it was at this very time that Santos got the idea of marryng him to his sister-in-law, who had recently been widowed. She seemed willing. Natividade opposed it, it was never clear why. It was not jealousy; nor do I believe it was from envy. The simple wish not to see him enter the family by the side door is a figure worth scarcely more than the two hypotheses we have rejected. It could not have been regret at losing him to another or at having their happiness constantly before her eyes, it could not have been that, although the heart is the abyss of abysses. Are we to suppose her purpose was to punish him for having loved her?

Perhaps. In any event, the major obstacle came from him. Though a widower, he had never been, strictly speaking, married at all. He was not fond of marriage. He married out of necessity, for the sake of his profession: he considered it better to be a married diplomat than an unmarried one, and proposed to the first young lady who seemed adequate to his destiny. He was mistaken: the difference in temperament and understanding was such that, though he lived with his wife, it was as if he lived alone. He was not distressed by the loss of her; he was a bachelor by nature.

I repeat, he was sensible, although this word does not exactly convey what I mean. He had a spirit ready to accept everything—not out of a love of harmony but rather because argument bored him. To understand this aversion, it was enough to have seen him enter Santos' drawing room, some nights before. Guests and members of the family were discussing the cabocla of the Castello.

"You have come at the right moment, Counselor," said Perpetua. "What do *you* think about the cabocla of the Castello?"

Ayres did not think anything, but he understood that the others thought something, and he made an ambiguous gesture. When they insisted, he did not choose either of the opposing opinions, but found another, compromise opinion that satisfied both sides, a rare thing with compromise opinions. As you know, it is their destiny to be scorned. But this Ayres—José da Costa Marcondes Ayres —held that, in arguments, a vague or compromise opinion could have the force of a pill, and he composed his in such a way that the invalid, if he did not get better, at least did not die, and that is the most one can expect of pills. Don't hold this against him: the bitter drug is swallowed quite easily, for it has a sugar coating. Ayres gave this opinion of his with delicate pauses and circumlocutions, wiping his monocle on a silk handerchief, letting drop profound or obscure words, turning up his eyes as if in search of a recollection, which he found and used to round off his opinion. One of his hearers accepted the opinion right off. Another dissented a little, but ended in agreement, so, a third, a fourth, and the whole room.

Don't imagine that he was not sincere; he was. When he did not happen to hold the same opinion and his was worth writing down he wrote it down. He used to keep a record of his discoveries, observations, reflections, criticisms, and anecdotes, using for this purpose a series of notebooks to which he gave the name of *Memorial*. That night he wrote these lines:

"Evening at the Santoses'. No ombre. We talked of the cabocla of the Castello. I suspect that Natividade or her sister wants to consult her. It will surely not be in regard to me.

"Natividade and a Padre Guedes who was there, a mellow, fat man, were the only interesting persons present. The rest were insipid, but insipid of necessity—not having it in their power to be anything else but insipid. When the *padre* and Natividade left me in the clutches of the others' insipidness, I tried to escape into my memory, recalling sensations, reliving scenes, voyages, persons. So it was that I began to think of the Capponi woman, whom I saw today from the back, on the Rua da Quitanda. I knew her, here, in the old Hotel de Dom Pedro, years ago. She was a dancer; I myself had seen her dance before in Venice. Poor Capponi! As she walked along, her left foot slipped above her shoe and showed a hole in the heel of her stocking—a dear little hole.

"Finally I returned to the everlasting insipidness of the others. I do not understand how this lady, in other respects so refined, can organize soirées like tonight's. It is not that the others did not try to be interesting, and, if intentions counted for anything, no book could do them justice; but they were not interesting, no matter how they tried. So much for them! Let us hope that other evenings will bring better subjects without any effort whatsoever. 'What the cradle holds only the grave will take away,' says one of our old proverbs. Truncating a verse of my dear Dante's, I would say of such insipid persons, 'Dico, che quando l'anima mal nata . . .' "

XIII   *The Epigraph*

Well, there is the epigraph of the book, if I should wish to give it one, and no other occurred to me. It is not only a way of rounding out the characters and their ideas, but it is also a pair of spectacles with which the reader may penetrate whatever seems not quite clear or wholly obscure.

Furthermore, there is an advantage in having the characters of my story collaborate in it, aiding the author in accordance with a law of solidarity, a kind of exchange of services between the chess-player and his men.

If you accept the comparison, you will recognize the king and the queen, the bishop and the knight, and that the knight cannot become a castle, nor the castle a pawn. There is of course the difference of color, white and black, but this does not affect the power of each piece to move, and finally one side or the other wins the game, and so goes the world. Perhaps it would have been a good idea to insert, from time to time (as in chess books), the favorable positions or the difficult ones. With no chessboard, that procedure is a great aid for following the moves, but then it may be that you have enough vision to reproduce the various situations from memory. Yes, I think so. Away with diagrams! Everything will go along as if you were actually witnessing a game between two players or, to be more precise, between God and the devil.

XIV   *The Disciple's Lesson*

"Don't go, don't go, Counselor," said Santos, taking the diplomat's hand. "Learn the eternal truths."

"Eternal truths demand eternal hours," reflected the latter, consulting his watch.

A man like Ayres was not easy to convince. Placido spoke in terms of scientific laws to avoid all taint of sectarianism. And Santos went along with him. All the spiritualistic terminology was dragged forth, and the cases, phenomena, mysteries, witnesses, verbal and written testimony . . . Santos came up with a hypothetical question: Suppose two spirits returned to this world, together; and if they had fought before they were born?

"Children don't fight before they are born," replied Ayres, tempering the affirmative sense with a doubtful intonation.

"Then you say that two spirits would not . . . ? I don't see why not, Counselor. What is there to keep two spirits from . . . ?"

Ayres saw the abyss of argument before him, and tried to ward off dizziness with a concession: "Esau and Jacob fought in their mother's womb, that's true," he said. "And we know the cause of the conflict. As for others that fight, granted they do, the whole thing is to discover the cause of the conflict, and, not being able to discover it, *why* Providence hides it from human knowledge. If the cause is a spiritual one, for example . . ."

"For example?"

"For example, if two children want to kneel at the same time to worship their Creator. Here is an instance of conflict, but of spiritual conflict, the procedures of which are beyond human wisdom. There might also be a temporal motive. Let us suppose the necessity of elbowing each other to get into a more comfortable position: it is a hypothesis that science might accept. That is, I don't know . . . There is also the possibility of their both trying for primogeniture."

"Why?" asked Placido.

"Although this privilege is nowadays limited to royal families, the House of Lords, and I do not know who else, still, it has a symbolic value. The simple pleasure of being born first, without other social or political advantage, may arise instinctively—especially if the children are destined to attain to high places in the world."

Santos pricked up his ears at this point, for he recalled the *things fated to be.* Ayres added some more fine words, and some others less pleasant, admitting that the fighting might be a foreshadowing of serious battles on earth. But he quickly tempered this idea with a second one: "No matter! Let us not forget what one of the ancients said, that 'war is the mother of all things.' In my opinion, when Empedocles refers to war he does not use the word in a technical sense. Even love, which is the first of the arts of peace, may be called a duel; not to the death, but to the life," concluded Ayres smiling gently, as he had spoken low; and he took his leave.

"Well?" said Santos. "The Counselor, instead of learning, has taught us, hasn't he? I think he presented some good arguments."

"At least, plausible ones," agreed the master, Placido.

"It's a pity he left," continued Santos, "but happily my business is with you, sir. I've come to consult you, for your knowledge is the true light of the world."

Placido thanked him with a smile. The compliment was not new to him; quite the contrary, he was so accustomed to hearing it that the smile had already become an incurable habit. He could not leave off paying his disciples in this coin.

"It is a question? . . ."

"The question is this. The hypothesis that I put just now is an actual fact. It happened with my sons . . ."

"What?"

"That is what I believe, and I came for the very purpose of having you explain it to me. I have never spoken of it before for fear that you would find it absurd; but I have been thinking, and I suspect that such a fight took place and that it is an extraordinary case."

Santos then disclosed the consultation of the fortune-teller, gravely, enlarging his eyes in a particular way he had, in order to enlarge the strangeness of his tale. He neither forgot nor concealed anything; he even old of his wife's trip to the Castello, with disdain, it is true, but point by point. Placido listened attentively, asking questions, going back, and then he meditated for several minutes. Finally he declared that the phenomenon, if it had really occurred, was rare, if not unique—but, it was possible. The very fact of their being named Pedro and Paulo indicated a certain rivalry, because these two apostles had fought too.

"Beg pardon, but the baptism . . ."

"Was later, I know, but the names may have been predestined, especially since the choice of the names came about, as you have told me, yourself, through the inspiration of the babies' aunt."

"That's right."

"Dona Perpetua is very devout."

"Very."

"I believe that the spirits of St. Peter and St. Paul themselves may have chosen her to inspire the names that are in the Creed. Remember, she had recited the Creed many times, but it was on this occasion that she noticed them."

"True, true!"

The professor went to the bookcase and took down a Bible bound in leather with great metal clasps. He opened it to the Epistle of St. Paul to the Galatians, and read the passage of Chapter II, Verse 11, in which the apostle tells how he went to Antioch, where St. Peter was, and "resisted him to the face."

Santos read it, and had an idea. Ideas like to be feted when they are fine, and inspected when they are new: his idea was at once new and fine. Dazzled by it, Santos raised his hand and brought his palm down on the page, exclaiming triumphantly, "Besides, this number *eleven* of the verse, composed of two identical digits, 1 and 1, is a twin number, doesn't it seem so to you?"

"Exactly. And further, the chapter is the second, that is two, which is the number proper to twin brothers."

Mystery begets mystery. There was more than one intimate essential, hidden link that united everything. Fighting, Peter and Paul, twin brothers, twin numbers, all were waters of mystery, which they were now cleaving, swimming, flailing with vigor. Santos went further into the depths: might it not be that the two baby boys were the spirits of St. Peter and St. Paul themselves, who were now reborn again, and *he* a father of two apostles? . . . Faith transfigures one; Santos had an almost divine air, he rose with his own bootstraps, and his eyes, ordinarily without expression, seemed to give off the flame of life. Father of apostles! and what apostles! Placido was almost, almost on the point of believing too. He found himself in a terrible, shadowy sea, where voices from the infinite mingled and were lost. But, then it occurred to him that the spirits of St. Peter and St. Paul had achieved perfection; they would not return here below. No matter: they would be great and noble men anyway. It was possible for their destinies to be brilliant; the cabocla spoke the truth, without knowing what she was saying.

"Let the ladies keep their childish beliefs," he concluded. "If they have faith in that woman on the Castello and think she is a vehicle of truth, do not disillusion them, for the present. Tell them I am in agreement with their oracle. *Teste David cum Sibylla."*

"I will, I will! Write it down."

Placido went to his secretary, wrote out the verse, and gave him the paper. But Santos had already thought better of it: to show it to his wife was to confess the spiritualistic consultation, and, of course, his perjury. He told his friend of Natividade's scruples and begged him to keep the whole matter quiet.

"When you see her, don't mention what passed between us."

He left soon after, repenting of his indiscretion, but dazzled by the revelation. He was full of Scriptural numbers, of Peter and Paul, of Esau and Jacob. The air of the street did not clear away the dust of mystery. On the

contrary, the blue sky, the lazy shore, the green mountains, only encircled and covered him with a more transparent, a more infinite, veil. The brawling of his baby
boys, a rare or unique occurrence, was a divine distinction. Contrary to his wife, who thought only of the future
greatness of her sons, Santos concentrated on the conflict
in the past.

He entered the house, ran to the babies, and fondled
them with such a strange expression that their mother
suspected something, and demanded to know what it
was.

"It's nothing," he answered laughing.

"It *is* something. Come, out with it."

"What *could* it be?"

"Whatever it is, Agostinho, tell me."

Santos begged her not to be angry, and told her the
whole thing: the great destiny, the brawling, the Scriptures, apostles, symbolism, all in such a rush of words that
she could hardly understand, but finally she did understand, and she retorted between clenched teeth, "Oh! you!
you!"

"Forgive me, my darling. I was so anxious to know the
truth . . . And, remember, I believe in the cabocla, and
so does the professor—he even wrote this in Latin," he
concluded, taking out the slip of paper and reading,
"Teste David cum Sibylla."

XVI   *Parenthoodism*

In a few minutes Santos took his wife's hand; she let it lie
limply in his. Both gazed at the little boys, forgetting
their anger, being just parents.

It was no longer spiritualism, nor any other newfangled

religion. It was the oldest of all religions, the one founded by Adam and Eve: you may call it, if you like, parenthoodism. They prayed without words, crossed themselves without fingers, a ceremony that was still and mute, that embraced the past and the future. Which of them was the priest, which the sacristan, I do not know, nor is there need to know. The Mass was the same as usual, and the Gospel began like the Gospel of St. John (emended). "In the beginning was the Love, and the Love was made flesh." But let us get to our twins.

XVII   *All That I Suppress*

The twins, having nothing else to do, went on nursing. In this function they conducted themselves without rivalry, except when the nurses were on good terms, and suckled the babies in company. Each of them then seemed to want to show that he sucked more, or better, passing his fingers over the friendly breast and sucking with all his soul. The nurses, for their part, took pride in their breasts and compared them when they were together; the babies, full at last, let go of the teats and laughed at their nurses.

If it were not for the necessity of putting the babies on their feet, grown men, I would extend this chapter. Really, the sight, though a common one, was beautiful. The young gentlemen, unlike their parents, nourished themselves without the arts of the cook, without the vision of viands and beverages placed in crystal and porcelain to offset or cheer the hard necessity of eating. With them, they did not even see the food: their mouths, fastened to the breast, did not allow the milk to be seen. Nature indicated her satisfaction with a laugh or with sleep. When it was sleep, each nurse placed her baby in its cradle and busied herself with other things. This comparison would have furnished me four whole pages.

One page would scarcely suffice for the little bells that enchanted the babies with their music as if it had been the music of heaven itself. They would smile, hold out their hands, become angry if the bells were only dangled in front of them, but quiet again as soon as they were given them, and even if they could not make them sound they did not become angry for that. And speaking of little bells, I should say that these instruments do not leave any mark on our memory. If one sees them in the hands of a child and thinks he remembers his own, he is mistaken; he will find that the recollection is more recent—some harangue of the year before ringing in his ears, if it was not the cow that brought yesterday's milk.

The process of weaning could be told in half a line, but the weeping of the nurses, the goodbyes, the gold trinkets given to each by the mother as a farewell present—all this would require a good page or more. A few lines would suffice for the nursemaids that followed, inasmuch as I would not tell whether they were tall or short, ugly or handsome. They were gentle, devoted to their duties, fond of the babies, and soon of each other. Hobbyhorses, toy flags, marionettes, soldier hats, and drums, the whole store of childhood's gewgaws, would take up much more space than the mere names.

All this I suppress merely to avoid boring my lady reader who is curious to see my babies grown gentlemen. Come, let us see them, my dear. In no time, they will be grown and strong. Then I will hand them over to themselves and let them cut their way through life and the world with sword or tongue, or simply with their elbows.

How They Grew

Here they are growing up. The resemblance, though it no longer made them indistinguishable, was still great. The same bright, observing eyes, the same lovely mouth, slender hands, and a high color in their cheeks that made you think they were painted with blood. They were healthy. Except for teething, they had no illness whatsoever —I do not count occasional attacks of indigestion from sweets that their parents gave them or that they themselves took on the sly. They both had a sweet tooth: Pedro more than Paulo, and Paulo more than anyone.

At seven years of age they were two masterpieces, or rather a single one in two volumes, if you like. In truth, there was not along all that beach, nor in the Flamengos, Glorias, Cajús and other environs, there was not one, let alone two such lovely children. And note that they were tough. Pedro would knock Paulo down with a blow of his fist; in return, Paulo would fell Pedro with a kick. They often raced through the chácara on bets and dares. Once they decided to climb the trees, but their mother would not allow it: it was not nice. They amused themselves with peeking up at the fruit, from here below.

Paulo was more aggressive, Pedro more deceitful, and, as both ended by eating the fruit of the trees, it was a slave boy who fetched it from above, whether prompted by the rap on the head of the one or by the promise of the other. The promise was never performed. The rap on the head, being paid in advance, was always performed, and sometimes with a repeat after the job was done. I do not mean by this that one and the other of the twins did not know how to be both aggressive and deceitful; it was only that each was better versed in his own peculiar specialty—something so obvious that it is not worth writing down.

They obeyed their parents without great effort, though they were stubborn. Nor did they lie more than other boys of the city. After all, lying is sometimes half a virtue. For example, when they said they had not seen the theft of a watch of their mother's given her by their father at the time of their marriage, they lied consciously, because the servant girl who took it was caught by them right in the act of stealing it. But she was so fond of them! and she begged them so tearfully not to tell anyone, that the twins denied seeing a thing. They were seven at the time. When they were nine, and the girl long since far away, they disclosed the concealed crime, apropos of I do not know what. Their mother asked why they had kept quiet about it before. They could not explain, but it is clear that the silence of 1878 was the result of their affection and pity: hence the *half a virtue,* because it is something to repay love with love. As for the disclosure of 1880, it can only be explained in terms of distance and time. Their sweet Miquelina was no longer there; perhaps she was already dead. Besides, it came up so naturally . . .

"But why haven't you told me till this moment?" persisted their mother.

Since they did not know what reason to give, one of them (I think it was Pedro) decided to accuse his brother. "It was his fault, Mama!"

"Mine?" retorted Paulo. "It was his, Mama. He was the one who wouldn't tell."

"It was you!"

"It was you! Don't lie!"

"He is the one who's lying!"

They sprang at each other. Natividade came nimbly to the rescue, not quickly enough, however, to prevent a first exchange of blows. She grabbed their arms in time to ward off further ones. And instead of punishing them or threatening them, she kissed them with such tenderness that they could think of no better time to beg her for sweets. They got the sweets; they also had a ride that afternoon in their father's carriage.

They returned friends, or reconciled. They told their mother about the ride, the people in the street, other children, who looked at them with envy, one who put his finger in his mouth, another who put his in his nose, and there were young ladies at their windows, some of whom found them handsome and nice. On this last point they differed, because each took the admiration only for himself.

Their mother intervened. "It was for both. You are so alike, it could only be for both. And do you know why the young ladies praised you? Because they saw you were friends, fond of each other. Nice boys do not fight, especially if they are brothers. I want to see you quiet and friendly, playing together without shouting or anything. Do you understand?"

Pedro said "yes." Paulo waited until his mother repeated the question, and gave the same answer. Finally, because she told them to, they embraced, but it was an embrace without enthusiasm, without energy, almost without arms: they leaned toward each other, held out their hands to the other's sides, and let them fall.

At night, in their bedroom, each concluded within himself that he owed the attentions of that afternoon—the sweets, the kisses, and the carriage—to the fight they had had, and that another fight could bring as much or more. Without words, like a ballade for piano, they resolved to fly in each other's face at the first opportunity. And this, which was to be a snare set for their mother's tenderness, brought both their hearts a private sensation that was not only consolation and revenge for the blows received that day, but was also satisfaction of a deep, inner, essential desire. They even talked without hatred, the words passing back and forth from bed to bed; and they laughed at this or that recollection from the street, until sleep entered on wooly paws and with silent beak, and took charge of the whole bedroom.

XIX   *Only Two–Forty Years–*
                                        Third Thing

One of my aims in this book is to not put tears in it. Still, I cannot pass over in silence two that welled up in Natividade's eyes once, after there had been a quarrel between the little boys. Only two, and they disappeared at the corners of her mouth. As quickly as she shed them she swallowed them, thus recalling, in reverse, the close of those stories children used to tell: "She came in one door and went out the other, our lord the king commands you to tell us another." And the second child would tell the second story, the third the third, the fourth a fourth, until there came tedium, or sleep. People who date from the time when they told stories this way, affirm that the children did not attach any monarchical idea to that formula —either absolute or constitutional: it was a means of linking together their *Decameron,* a style inherited from the old Portuguese reign when the kings commanded what they wished, and the nation said that it was good.

When she had swallowed the two tears, Natividade laughed at her own weakness. She did not call herself silly, because such admissions are rarely made, even to oneself; but in the secret part of her heart, way at the bottom where men's eyes do not penetrate, I believe she felt something of the sort. Not having clear proof, I limit myself to defending our lady.

In truth, another would tremble for the fate of her sons, knowing of their earlier brawling within her. Now the bouts were more frequent, the hands more and more quick, and everything made one fear they would end up disemboweling each other . . . But at this point there would rise in her mind the idea of their greatness and prosperity—things fated to be!—and this hope was like a handkerchief that dried the eyes of the beautiful lady. It could not be that Sibyls spoke only evil, nor the Prophets, but of good too, mostly of good.

With this green handkerchief she dried her eyes, and she must have had other handkerchiefs, in the event that one became torn or dirty: one, for example, that was not green—the color of hope, but blue—blue as her own soul. I did not tell you that Natividade's soul was blue? Well, it was. A celestial blue, clear and transparent, that sometimes clouded over, occasionally stormed, but never darkened with the night.

No, reader, I have not forgotten her age; I remember her as well as though it were today. This is how she was at forty. Never mind! The sky is older, and it has not changed color. So long as you do not attribute any romantic significance to the blueness of her soul, you follow me. On the day she attained that age, she felt a chill—nothing more. What had happened? Nothing, one day more than the last, a few hours only. All a question of number, less than number, the name of number—that word *forty,* there was the only trouble. Hence the melancholy with which she said to her husband as she thanked him for his birthday gift, "I'm an old woman, Agostinho!" Santos playfully tried to choke her.

But it would be a pity to choke her. Natividade had the

figure she had before the twins came, the same litheness, the same slender, lively grace. She had kept the queenly elegance of thirty. Her dressmaker placed in relief all the meanings still left in her figure, and even lent her a few from the sewing box. Her waist persisted in getting no bigger, the hips and bosom were the original upholstery.

There are those regions in which spring is confused with autumn, as in our land, where the two seasons differ only in temperature. In her, not even in temperature. Fall had the heat of summer. At forty she was the same green lady, with the very same sky blue soul.

She received this color from her father and from her grandfather; but her father died early, it was rather from her grandfather, who lived to be eighty-four. At that age he sincerely believed that all the delightful things of this world, from his morning coffee to his peaceful dreams, had been specially invented for him alone. The best cook on earth had been born in China for the unique purpose of leaving family, country, mother tongue, religion, everything, to come and cook him chops and make his tea for him. The stars gave *his* nights a splendid appearance, the moonlight too, and the rain, if it rained, was to give him a rest from the sun. There he is now in the São Francisco Xavier cemetery. If anyone could hear the voice of the dead within their graves, you would hear him shouting that it is time to close the gate of the cemetery and let no one else in, now that he is resting there for all eternity. He died sky blue; if he had lived to be a hundred he would not have had any other color.

Well, if nature wanted to spare this lady, wealth lent a helping hand to nature, and between them they turned out the handsomest color a human soul can have. Everything worked together, then, to quickly dry her eyes, as we have seen. If she drank those two lone tears, she may have drunk others before in the course of her life, and this is a further proof of that spiritual tint: it will show that she had few, and swallowed them to keep them.

But there is still a third thing that gave her the sensation of sky blue, a thing so unusual that it deserves to go in a chapter by itself, but it won't, for the sake of economy. It was her spiritual detachment, the having crossed through life intact and pure. The Cape of Storms turned into the Cape of Good Hope, and she triumphed over her first and second youth without having the winds overwhelm her ship or the waves suck it down. I would not deny that occasionally a strong gust may have torn loose her foresail, as in the case of João de Mello, or even worse with Ayres, but these were merely Adamastor's yawns. She quickly mended her sail, and the giant was left behind encircled by Thetis, while *she* pursued the route to India. Now she remembered the prosperous voyage. She felt honored by those vain, lost winds. Memory brought her the savor of dangers passed. Here was the hidden land: two sons born, brought up, and beloved of fortune.

XX   *The Jewel*

Forty-one did not cause her a shiver. She was already accustomed to the forties. She did feel a shock of amazement: she woke up and did not see the usual gift, the "surprise" from her husband at the foot of the bed. She did not find it on the dressing table; she opened drawers, peeked in, nothing. She thought her husband had forgotten the day, and became sad; it was the first time! She went downstairs, looking . . . nothing. Her husband was in the study—silent, withdrawn, reading the newspapers; he scarcely held out his hand to her. The boys, though it was Sunday, were studying in a corner. They came to give her the customary kiss and went back to their books. Their mother still cast a furtive glance around the study, to see if she could find some remembrance, a painting, a dress, it was all in vain. Perhaps under one of the daily papers on the chair opposite her husband there might be . . . Nothing. Then she sat down, and, opening the paper, kept saying to herself, "Can it be possible they don't remember what day it is? Can it be possible?" Her eyes began to read at random, skipping items, going back . . .

Opposite, her husband observed her attentively, without exactly paying attention to what she was reading. So passed several minutes. Suddenly Santos noticed a new expression come over Natividade's face, her eyes grew larger, her lips parted, her head came up, his too, both left their chairs, took two steps and fell into each other's arms like two lovers mad with love. One, two, three, many kisses. Pedro and Paulo stood amazed in their corner. Their father, when he could speak, said to them, "Come kiss the hand of the Baroness de Santos."

They did not understand right off. Natividade did not know what to do; she gave her hand to her sons, to be kissed, to her husband, then she went back to the newspaper to read and reread that in the imperial dispatch of the day before Senhor Agostinho José dos Santos had been awarded the title of Baron de Santos. Then she understood. This was her birthday gift; the goldsmith this time had been the Emperor.

"Go on, go on, now you may go play," said the father to his sons.

And the boys went out to spread the news throughout the house. The servants rejoiced at the advancement of their masters. Even the slaves seemed to receive a portion of liberty and decorated themselves with it: "Nhan Baroneza!" they cried, jumping about. And João pulled forth Maria, snapping his fingers, "Folks, who is this colored girl?" "I am a slave of Nhan Baroneza!"

But the Emperor was not the only goldsmith. Santos drew a little box from his pocket, in it was a brooch on which the new coronet sparkled with diamonds. Natividade thanked him for the jewel and consented to put it on that he might see it. Santos felt himself to be the author of the jewel, the creator of the form and of the stones; but he soon permitted her to take it off and put it away. He picked up the papers to show her that the notice appeared in all of them, in some with an adjective, "highly regarded" in one, "distinguished" in another, and so on.

When Perpetua came into the study, she found them walking back and forth, their arms around each other's waist, talking, saying nothing, looking at their feet. She too gave and received an embrace.

The whole house was merry. On the chácara the trees appeared more green than ever, the buds in the garden unfolded their petals, and the sun covered the earth with an infinite brightness. Heaven, to collaborate with the rest of nature, remained blue the whole day. Soon cards and letters of congratulation began to arrive. Later there were visits. Men of law, men of commerce, men of society, many ladies, a few titled persons also: they came or sent messages. Some of Santos' debtors presented themselves immediately; others preferred to continue in a state of forgetfulness. There were names that they could recognize only by dint of great research and many an almanac.

An Obscure Point

I know that there is an obscure point in the last chapter. I am writing this chapter to clarify it.

When his wife inquired about the antecedents and circumstances of the imperial dispatch, Santos gave her the explanations she asked for. Not all of them were strictly true. Time is a gnawing mouse that diminishes things, or alters them in the sense of giving them another appearance. Besides, the material lent itself so well to the fluster that might easily bring confusion to the memory. There are, in the most serious events, many details that get lost, others that the imagination invents to replace them; even so, history does not die.

It remains to discover (this is the obscure point) how it was that Santos could keep quiet for many long days an affair that was so important for him and for his wife. In truth, he was more than once on the point of telling, by word or look if he had found one, that closely guarded secret; but a greater force stopped his mouth. It would seem that it was the anticipation of a new, unexpected joy that made him possess his soul in patience. In that scene in the study, everything had been arranged beforehand— the silence, the indifference, the boys planted there, studying on Sunday—all for the single effect of that phrase, "Come kiss the hand of the Baroness de Santos!"

XXII   *Now a Leap*

That the twins shared the nobiliary honeymoon of their
parents is not anything that need be written. The love
they bore them would be enough to explain it; but, in
addition, since the title appeared to produce two different
feelings in other boys, one of respect, one of envy, Pedro
and Paulo concluded they had received with the title
some special merit. When Paulo later adopted republican
ideas, he never involved this family distinction in his con-
demnation of the institutions. The states of soul to which
it gave rise would supply material for a special chapter if I
did not prefer to make a leap at this point, and go to 1886.
The leap is a large one, but time is an invisible web on
which everything may be embroidered—a flower, a bird, a
lady, a castle, a tomb. One may also embroider nothing.
Nothing embroidered on the invisible is the most subtle
work possible in this world, and perhaps in the other.

XXIII   *When You Have Beards*

That year, one August night when there were a number
of guests at the house in Botafogo, it happened that one of
them, I do not know whether it was a man or a woman,
asked the two brothers how old they were.

Paulo answered, "I was born on the anniversary of the
day that Pedro I abdicated the throne."

And Pedro, "I was born on the anniversary of the day
His Majesty ascended the throne."

The answers were simultaneous, not one after the other, so that the guest asked them to speak one at a time. Their mother explained, "They were born on April 7, 1870."

Pedro repeated, slowly, "I was born on the day His Majesty ascended the throne." And Paulo, after him, "I was born on the day Pedro I abdicated the throne."

Natividade scolded Paulo for his subversive answer. Paulo explained his position, Pedro contested the explanation and gave another, and the room would have become a debating club if their mother had not conciliated them in the following manner: "These are schoolboy opinions. You are not old enough to speak on politics. When you have beards."

The beards refused to come, no matter how often they felt of the down with their fingers, but political, and other kinds of opinions came, and grew. They were not, strictly speaking, opinions, they did not have roots, great or small. They were, so to speak, neckties of a certain color that they tied around their necks until they grew tired of the color and took another tie. Naturally each one had his own. One may also rest assured that it more or less suited his personality. Since they received the same good marks and honors in examinations, they lacked cause for envy; and, if ambition was to divide them one day, it was not yet an eagle or a condor, or even a fledgling—at most, an egg. At the Pedro II High School all were fond of them; only their beards did not care to come. What were they to do when their beards did not care to come? Wait till they came in their own sweet time, till they appeared, grew, turned white, as is the usual way, except those that never turn white, or only partly so and temporarily. All this is well known and commonplace, but it gives me an opportunity to tell of two beards of the last type that were famous in their time, and now completely forgotten. Having no other spot where I might tell of them, I avail myself of this chapter, and the reader may turn the page if he prefers to pursue the story. I will stay behind for a few lines, recalling the two dead beards, though I do not understand them now, as we did not understand them then—the most baffling beards in the world.

The first of these beards was that of a friend of Pedro's, a Capuchin monk, an Italian, Brother ***. I could insert his name—no one would recognize it—but I prefer this triune symbol, a mystic number expressed by stars, which are the eyes of heaven. We are talking about a monk. Pedro did not know him when his beard was black, but only when it was already grizzled, long, and thick, adorning a masculine, handsome head. He had a laughing mouth, sparkling eyes. And he laughed with both eyes and mouth, so sweetly that he gathered folk to his heart. His chest was broad, his shoulders strong. His bare foot, bound to its sandal, was one to uphold the body of a Hercules. All, mild and spiritual as a page of the Gospel. His faith was alive, his love unshakable, his patience infinite.

One day Brother *** said goodbye to Pedro, went to the interior, Minas, Rio de Janeiro, São Paulo—to Paraná also, I believe—a spiritual journey, like that of his brother Capuchins, stayed away for six months or more. When he came back, he brought us all great joy, and greater astonishment. His beard was black, I do not know whether as black as it had been originally, or blacker, but very black, and very shiny. He offered no explanation for the change, and no one asked him about it. It might have been a miracle or nature's caprice; it might also have been human improvement, although this last would be harder to believe than the first. This color lasted nine months. After another journey, of thirty days, his beard seemed of silver or snow, whichever seems to you more white.

As for the second of these beards, it was still more astonishing. It was not a friar's beard but belonged to a ragged, shabby fellow who lived on his debts, and in his youth had emended an old Portuguese proverb in this manner: "Pay what you owe and see what you *do not* have left." He reached the age of fifty without money, without employment, without friends. His clothes must have had the same age, his shoes were no younger. But his beard had not reached fifty; he dyed it black—and it was a poor job, probably because the dye was not of the best quality, and because he did not own a mirror. He used to walk along by himself, often going up or down the same street. One day he turned the corner of Life and fell in Death's square, with his beard streaked, for the simple reason that there was no one to dye it in the charity hospital.

"Well, *bene*," as my Capuchin would say, why is it that his beard and the ragged fellow's turned from grizzled to black? Let my lady reader figure it out if she can: I give her twenty chapters to do it in. Perhaps I too, at that point, may spy some explanation; but at the moment I know of none, nor do I hazard a guess. Let spiteful people attribute some profane passion to Brother ***; even so, one cannot understand why he would give himself away in that manner. As for the ragged fellow, what ladies would he hope to please to the point of frequently exchanging bread for dye? It may be that the one and the other yielded to a desire to lay hold of fleeing youth— maybe so. The monk, learned as he was in the Scriptures, knowing that Israel wept for the onions of Egypt, may also have wept and his tears may have fallen black. It may be, I repeat. This desire to take Time captive is a necessity of the soul and of the jowls; but God grants Time a writ of *habeas corpus*.

The opinions of Pedro and Paulo grew until one day they became affiliated with something. They were going along the Rua da Carioca. There was a glazier's shop there, with mirrors of various sizes, and besides the mirrors it also had old portraits and cheap prints, framed and unframed. They stopped a while, gazing at random. Then Pedro saw a picture of Louis XVI hanging in the shop. He went in and bought it for eight hundred reis. It was a simple print, fastened to the display rack by a cord. Paulo determined to enjoy a similar fortune, but one suited to his opinions, and discovered a Robespierre. As the shopkeeper asked twelve hundred reis for this, Pedro grew somewhat heated.

"So, Senhor, you sell a king for less—a martyred king?"

"You must forgive me, but, the fact is, that other print cost me more," returned the old shopkeeper. "We sell according to what we have to pay. See: it is newer."

"Oh, no it isn't," interjected Paulo. "They are the same age; but the point is this man is worth more than that one."

"I have heard it said that he also was a king . . ."

"What do you mean 'king?'" both retorted.

"Or tried to be one, I don't know much about it . . . All the history I know is the history of the Moors that I learned in my country from my grandmother, some scraps of verse. But there *are* handsome Moorish women, for example this one: in spite of her name, I believe she was a Moor, or still is, if she is alive . . . May her husband have little joy of her!"

He went to a corner and brought out a picture of Madame de Staël with the famous turban on her head. O the power of beauty! The young men forgot their political opinions for a moment and stood gazing at the person of Corrine. The eyes of the shopkeeper, in spite of his seventy years, grew moist with amorous passion. He took pains to point out her figure, her head, the mouth that was rather coarse but expressive, and he kept saying that it was not dear. As neither was disposed to buy it, perhaps because there was only one, he told them that he had another, but that she was "a shameless hussy"—may the gods forgive him when they learn that he was only trying to whet the appetite of his patrons. He went to a cupboard, took from it and brought to them a Diana, naked as she lived here below in other days, in the woods. Even so he did not sell it. He had to content himself with political portraits.

He decided to pick up some extra money selling them a framed portrait of Pedro I that was hanging on the wall. But Pedro refused because he did not have the money with him, and Paulo said he would not give a vintem for "that traitor's mug."

It would have been better if he had said nothing! The moment the shopkeeper heard his response he shed his obsequious manners, clothed himself in an air of indignation, and cried out yes, sir, the lad was right. "You are quite right. He was a traitor, a bad son, bad brother, bad everything. He did all the harm he could in this world; and in hell, where he surely is if religion does not lie, he must be harming the devil. This young man spoke a moment ago of a martyred king," he went on, showing them a portrait of Dom Miguel de Bragança, half profile, frock coat, hand on the chest, "this man was truly a martyr of that fellow, who robbed him of his throne—it was not his—to give it to someone to whom it did not belong; and my poor king and lord went to starve, in Germany, they say, or God-knows-where. Ah, the turn-coats! Sons of the devil! You can't imagine, gentlemen, what that gang of liberals was. Liberals! Liberal with other men's property!"

"All from the same dough," reflected Paulo.

"I don't know whether they were of dough, I know they got many a beating. They won, but they paid dearly for it. My poor king!"

Pedro, as an answer to his brother's insinuation, offered to buy the portrait of Pedro I. The shopkeeper regained his self-control, and began to negotiate the sale; but they could not come to an agreement on the price. Pedro wanted to pay eight hundred reis, as for the other picture; the shopkeeper was asking two thousand reis. He pointed out that it was framed, and Louis XVI was not; besides, it was newer. He brought it to the door, to get a better light, called attention to the face, especially the eyes—what a fine expression they had! And the imperial cloak . . ."

"How could you lose if you pay two thousand reis?"

"I'll give ten tostões for it. Will that do?"

"No, it won't. It cost me more than that."

"Well, then . . ."

"Look. It's easily worth *three* thousand reis. The paper is not discolored; the engraving is excellent."

"Ten tostões is my limit."

"No, Senhor. Look, for ten tostões you may have this one of Dom Miguel; the paper is in excellent condition, and for very little extra you can have it framed. There, only ten tostões."

"Oh, I'm sick of the whole business . . . Ten tostões for the Emperor."

"Oh, *no!* It cost me seventeen hundred, three weeks

ago; I make only some three hundred reis, almost nothing. I make less with the Dom Miguel, but you will agree that he is in less demand. This one of Dom Pedro I, if you come by tomorrow you will very likely not find it here. What do you say?"

"I'll come by some other time."

Paulo had already gone on ahead, admiring his Robespierre. Pedro overtook him.

"Look, take the Dom Miguel for seven tostões."

Pedro shook his head.

"Six tostões?"

Pedro, now beside his brother, unrolled his print. The old shopkeeper was going to shout after him, "Five tostões!" but they were now far off and it was hard to do business at such a distance.

XXV   *Dom Miguel*

"Well, in any case," the old man mused, "I'll never sell it if I keep it rolled up and put away. I am going to have it framed, some narrow bit of old wood . . ."

Dom Miguel turned toward him eyes that were reproachful and troubled with sadness: so it appeared to the glazier, but it may have been an illusion. Be that as it may, it also seemed to him that the eyes in the picture returned to their customary gaze, to the right, far into the distance . . . toward what? Toward a place where there is eternal justice, the owner probably thought. As he stood in the doorway contemplating the picture, a man stopped, came in, and looked with interest at the portrait. The shopkeeper noted his expression: he might be a Miguelist, but he might also be a collector . . .

"How much are you asking for that, Senhor?"

"This? You must excuse me; you want to know how much I'm asking for my precious Dom Miguel? I'm not asking much, it is a little soiled, but the drawing is still fine. How superb it is! It's not dear; I'll give it to you for cost. If it were framed it would be worth four thousand reis. You may have it for three."

The customer calmly took the money out of his purse while the old man rolled up the portrait, and, exchanging one for the other, they took leave of each other, both courteous and satisfied. The shopkeeper, after following him to the door, went back to his customary chair. Perhaps he was thinking of the misfortune he had so narrowly escaped: if he had sold the portrait for ten tostões. In any event, he sat gazing outside, into the distance, to a place where there is eternal justice . . . Three thousand reis!

XXVI   *The Fight Over the Portraits*

It is perhaps unnecessary to tell the fate of the portraits of king and Conventionist. Each of the boys hung his at the head of his bed. This state of affairs did not last because both played tricks on the poor prints, which were not to blame for anything, but had to suffer dunce caps, bad names, and animal drawings, until one day Paulo tore up Pedro's and Pedro Paulo's. Naturally they took their revenge in blows, their mother heard the noise and ran upstairs. She separated them, but they were already scratched up when she found them, and she went away sad. Would that curse of rivalry never end? She asked this question without words, stretched out on the bed, her face in the pillow. This time the pillow remained dry, but her soul wept.

Natividade had faith in training, but training, no matter how she perfected it, only took the edges off the boys' natural bent: the essential character remained. The passions that had been present in the embryo struggled to live, grow, burst forth, just as she had felt the two of them struggling in her own womb . . . She recalled the pain of those days, and ended by cursing the cabocla of the Castello. Really, she should have kept silent. Evil that is kept silent is still evil, but one does not know about it. Now, it may be that this not keeping silent will confirm the general opinion that the cabocla had been sent by God to tell men the truth. And, after all, what *did* she say to Natividade? It was no more than a mysterious question, and yet the prediction was luminous and clear . . . Once more the words of the Castello sounded in the mother's ears, and imagination did the rest. Things fated to be! Behold her sons great and glorious. A few fights as boys? What matter? Natividade smiled, got up, went to the door, and there was her son Pedro, who had come to make excuses.

"Mama, Paulo is awful. If you heard the terrible things he said you'd die of fright, Mama. It's all I can do not to keep from punching him in the nose. I could have knocked his eye out."

"O my boy, don't talk like that, he's your brother."

"Then let him leave me alone, let him stop bothering me. And the swear words he used! When I was praying for the soul of Louis XVI, just to annoy me *he* began to pray for Robespierre. He made up a long mumbo jumbo to his 'saint' Robespierre; he mumbled it under his breath so that you and Papa couldn't hear him. All the same I gave him a couple raps on the head with my knuckles . . ."

"There, you see!"

"But he's the one that hit me first, because I put a dunce cap on Robespierre . . . Was I to take it and say nothing?"

"Neither saying nothing nor saying something."

"How then, just go on letting him hit me, huh?"

"No, sir! I won't have fighting. You must forget all this and love each other. Don't you see how your parents love each other? There will be no more fights. I don't want to hear any muttering or complaints. After all, what do you care about a good-for-nothing fellow who died so many years ago?"

"That's what *I* say, but *he* won't change his ideas."

"He will change. His studies will make him forget this foolishness. You too, when you are a doctor you'll have your hands full fighting disease and death—something much better than going about hitting your brother . . . Here, here! I won't have threats, Pedro! Be quiet, and listen to me."

"You are always against me, Mama."

"I'm not against either of you, I'm for both of you, you are both my sons. And besides, twins. Come, Pedro. Don't imagine I disapprove of your political opinions. I even like them: they are mine, they are ours. Someday they will be Paulo's also. At his age one accepts all kinds of nonsense. Time will change him. Look, Pedro, what I hope is that you will be great men, but on condition that you also be great friends."

"I'm willing to be a great man," conceded Pedro with an ingenuous air of resignation.

"And a great friend too."

"If he will, I will."

"Great men!" cried Natividade giving him two hugs, one for him and one for his brother when he should come.

But Paulo came at once and received the hug himself, whole and real. He too came to complain, and kept muttering and growling, but his mother would not listen to him and again spoke the language of greatness. Paulo also consented to be great.

"You will be a doctor," said Natividade to Pedro, "and you a lawyer. I want to see who will cure more illnesses and who will win the hardest cases."

"I," they answered in unison.

"Simpletons! Each will have his own career, his own profession. Are your noses better? Yes, the bleeding has stopped. Now the first one who strikes his brother will be in disgrace."

Separating them was an ingenious remedy: one would stay in Rio studying medicine, the other would go to São Paulo to study law. Time would do the rest, not counting the fact that each would marry and go his own way with his wife at his side. It would be everlasting peace; later would come everlasting friendship.

XXVII   *Concerning an Untimely Observation*

And now there comes an observation by my lady reader: "But if two old prints can bring them to blows and blood, are they going to be content, each with a wife of his own? Won't they both set their hearts on having the same woman?"

What you want, my dear Senhora, is to come at once to the chapter of love, or love affairs, which is your main interest in books. Hence the cleverness of your query, as if you said, "Look, sir, you have not yet shown us the lady, or ladies, that are to be loved, or fought over, by these two young enemies. I am tired of being told that the young men don't get along, or get along badly. It is the second or third time I have witnessed their mother's coaxing or friendly scoldings. Let's get on to their ladylove, to both of them, if it is not one alone, the person . . ."

Frankly, I do not like people who are always figuring things out and putting together a book that is being written with method. My lady reader's insisting that there is only one woman amounts to an impertinence. Suppose that the young men are actually in love with only one woman, will it not appear that I relate what my lady reader has told me to—when the truth is that I only write what actually happened and can be corroborated by dozens of witnesses? No, my dear Senhora, I did not take up my pen with the idea of lying in wait for people with suggestions. If you want to write the book, here is the pen, here is paper, here is your humble admirer; but, if you only want to read, keep quiet, and go from line to line, I will grant you permission to yawn through a couple of chapters, but wait for the rest, have faith in the narrator of these adventures.

XXVIII *The Rest Is Certain*

Yes, there was a "person," younger than they, by one or two years, who had fettered them through force of habit, or of nature, if it was not both. Before her, it may be that there were others, older than they, but there is no mention of them in the notes out of which this book is made. If they fought over them, there is no record of it; but it is possible they did, if their inclination happened to be the same, or even if the contrary was true and like knights of old each defended his lady.

All conjectures!

It was natural that handsome as they were, perfectly matched, elegant, given to life and society, to conversation and dancing, and, lastly, being heirs to a fortune—it was natural that more than one young lady should take a fancy to them. The girls that saw them go by on horseback, along the shore, or up the street, fell in love with that perfect order of form and motion. Their very horses were exactly alike, almost twins, and beat their hooves in the same rhythm, with the same vigor, with the same grace. Don't go imagining that the tossing of their tails and of their manes was simultaneous: it is not true, and might make one doubt the rest. But the rest is certain.

XXIX   *The Young Person*

The young person will not enter even in this chapter, for an excellent reason, which is—the propriety of presenting her parents first. It is not that she could not be presented very well without them. She could, the three are different, almost contradictions of one another. And no matter how peculiar it seems to you, it is not necessary that the parents be present. Children do not always reproduce their parents. Camoens claimed that from a certain father one could only expect a son of the same sort, and science confirms this poetic rule. For my part I believe in science as in poetry, but there are exceptions, my friend. It happens at times that nature does something quite different, and not for this reason do the plants stop growing and the stars shining. What one must believe without fail is that God is God, and if an Arabian girl is reading me let her put "Allah" in the place of "God." All languages lead to heaven.

XXX

The Baptistas

The Baptistas made the acquaintance of the Santoses on some plantation or other in the province of Rio. It was not in the township of Maricá, although that was where the twins' father had been born: it could have been in *any* other locality. Wherever it was, it was there that the two families became acquainted, and as they lived not far apart in Botafogo, cordiality and inclination strengthened the hand of chance.

Baptista, the damsel's father, was a man of forty or so, an attorney in private practice, former governor of a province, and a member of the conservative party. The object of his trip to the plantation had been a political meeting, with electoral ends in view, but it proved so sterile that he came back without even a sprig of hope. In spite of having friends in the government, he had obtained nothing—neither the post of deputy nor a governorship. His career had been at a standstill ever since he was relieved of his office "at his request," said the decree, but the protests of the "relieved" would lead one to think otherwise. In reality he had been responsible for the loss of the elections, and it was to this political accident that he attributed his being "relieved" of his office.

"I don't know what more he expected me to do," said Baptista, speaking of the Minister. "I persecuted churches, no friend asked for the use of the police but what I granted it, I brought some twenty persons to trial, others went to jail without trial. Was I supposed to *hang* people? As it was, there were two deaths in Riberão das Moças."

This last was an exaggeration: the deaths were not *his*

doing. All he did was to hush up the investigation—if one can call a friendly conversation about the ferocity of two dead men an investigation. In short, the elections were bloodless.

Baptista said that it was this matter of the elections that had cost him the governorship, but there was another version current, a transaction in water supply, a concession granted to a Spaniard at the solicitation of the brother of the Governor's wife. The part about the brother-in-law's solicitation was true, the imputation of a pay-off was false. Nevertheless, there was enough that the opposition newspaper could say this had been a good "family arrangement"—adding that, as water was involved, it was no doubt a clean deal. The administration paper retorted that if there *was* water it was not enough to wash away the soot of a coal deal left by the liberal administration of the Governor's predecessor—enough to supply a palace. It was not strictly true; the opposition journal resurrected the trial and showed that the defense had been perfect and complete. It could have stopped here, but it continued, "as we were now in Spanish territory, the Governor improved upon the Spanish poet, author of that epitaph,

> Brothers-in-law friends and at peace,
> It's certain they're deceased;

and he emended the poet in order not to have to kill anyone, rather he gave life to himself and his, saying in our language,

> Brothers-in-law friendly and close,
> Alive for sure and very much with us!"

Baptista hastened to set everything to rights, declaring the concession canceled, but this only gave the opposition powder for fresh attacks. "We have the confession of the accused!" was the title of the first article. Their correspondents had already sent articles to Rio de Janeiro telling of the concession, and the Administration ended by removing its representative from office. Actually, no one but politicians paid any attention to the business. Dona Claudia mentioned the campaign of the press, which had been extremely violent.

"It wasn't worth the trouble of leaving here," said Natividade.

"Oh, no, Baroness!" Dona Claudia maintained that it *was* worth the trouble. Life was painful, but one must be patient. It was so good to arrive in the province, all announced, the visits aboard the ship, the landing, the investiture, the officials' greetings, magistrates, civil service, officialdom, many a bald head, many white hairs, the flower of the countryside in short, with their infinite bowing—on a curve or at an angle, and the eulogies printed in the papers. Even the vilification by the opposition was agreeable. To hear her husband called tyrant, when she knew he had a pigeon's heart, did her soul good. The thirst for blood that they attributed to him, when he did not even drink wine, the mailed fist of a man that was a kid glove, his immorality, barefaced effrontery, lack of honor, all the unjust, but strong, names she loved to read as if they were eternal truths . . . where were they now? The opposition newspaper had been the first thing she read each morning at the Governor's mansion. She too would feel the sting of the whip, and it gave her a voluptuous thrill of pleasure as if it fell on her own flesh: her breakfast tasted the better for it. Where were the scourges of those times? Now, she could scarcely find his name in print—at the bottom of some legal report, or in the list of persons who had waited upon the Emperor.

"Not every time," explained Dona Claudia. "Baptista is very reticent. He goes to São Christovam at rare intervals, in order not to make it appear that he is asking to be remembered, as though that were a crime. On the other hand, never to go might look like pique. Mind you, the Emperor has never failed to receive him with great kindness, and me also. He has never forgotten my name. I hadn't been there for two years and when I appeared, he immediately said to me, 'How are you, Dona Claudia?' "

Aside from these regretful memories of power, Dona Claudia was a happy soul. The liveliness of her speech and manners, her eyes that seemed to see nothing because they never stopped moving, her kindly smile, and constant wonder, everything about her was calculated to cure people's melancholy. When she kissed her friends, or looked at them, it was as if she wanted to eat them alive, to consume them with love, not with hate, to put them inside her, deep down inside.

Baptista did not have this expansiveness. He was tall, and his undisturbed air gave him a fine, governmental aspect. All he lacked was vigor of action, but his wife could inspire him with it; he never failed to consult her in the crises of the governorship. Even now, if he had listened to her, he would have already gone to ask something of the government, but on this point he was firm, with a firmness born of weakness. "They will send for me, just you wait," he would say to Dona Claudia each time an office fell vacant in the provinces. It is certain that he felt the need of returning to active life. With him, politics was not so much a conviction as an itch: he felt a need to scratch himself often and hard.

XXXI

Flora

Of such sort was that pair of politicians. A son, if they had had a male child, might have been a fusion of their opposite qualities, and perhaps he would have been a statesman. But Heaven denied them this dynastic consolation.

They had an only daughter who was the exact opposite of them. Neither Dona Claudia's passion nor Baptista's governmental aspect distinguished the soul, or the body, of young Flora. One who knew her in those days might have compared her to a fragile vase, or to a flower of a single morning, and had matter for a tender elegy. Even then she had those great, clear eyes, not yet so knowing, but already possessed of a special way of moving. It was not the darting glance of her mother's eyes, nor the faded expression of her father's, but rather something sweet and thoughtful, so full of grace it would have softened a miser's face. Give her an aquiline nose, sketch in a half-laughing mouth, all in a slender face, smooth auburn hair, and there you have the maiden Flora.

She was born in August, 1871. Her mother, who dated things by ministries, never denied her daughter's age. "Flora was born in the Rio Branco administration, and she was so quick at learning that in the Sinimbú administration she could already read and write fluently."

Flora was retiring and modest, averse to social gatherings; it was only with great difficulty that she could be persuaded to learn to dance. She loved music, piano better than singing. At the piano, withdrawn within herself, she could go without eating the whole day long. There is a bit of exaggeration here, but hyperbole is the way of the world, and people's ears are so clogged already that it is only by force of strong rhetoric that one can penetrate them with a whisper of truth.

So far, there is nothing that greatly distinguishes this girl from others her age, since modesty goes with charm, and at a certain age reverie is as natural as mischief. At fifteen, Flora was given to withdrawing within herself. Ayres, who met her about this time, at the home of Natividade, believed she would turn out to be "a mystery."

"How do you mean?" asked her mother.

"I don't really mean anything," Ayres hastened to add, "but if you'll allow me to say so, I would say that this young lady sums up and epitomizes her mother's rare gifts."

"But I am not mysterious," replied Dona Claudia with a smile.

"Quite the contrary, my dear Senhora. Everything, however, depends on how we define the word. Perhaps there is no exact definition possible. Let us imagine a person for whom perfection does not exist on this earth, a being who judges that the most beautiful soul is no more than a point of view, if it does not change with the point of view, perfection . . ."

"Perfection is hearts," insinuated Santos.

It was an invitation to a game of ombre. Ayres was reluctant to accept, so disquieted did Flora appear, with her eyes on him, questioning, curious to know why she was, or would come to be, "a mystery." Besides, he preferred the conversation of women. It was he who said, in his *Memorial,* "In woman, sex corrects banality, in man it aggravates it."

It was not necessary either to accept or to refuse Santos' invitation. There arrived two devotees of the sport, and with these and Baptista, who was in the sitting room close

by, Santos went to his regular nightly pastime. One of
the players was old Placido, professor of spiritualism, the
second was a stockbroker named Lopes who loved cards
for the sake of cards and was less pained to lose money
than tricks. Off they went to ombre while Ayres stayed in
the drawing room, in a corner, listening to the ladies, and
never once did Flora take her eyes off him.

XXXII   *Retired*

Even then this ex-diplomat was retired. He had come
back to Rio de Janeiro, after a last look at the familiar
sights, to live out the rest of his days here. He could have
done it in any city, he was a man of many climes, but he
had a special love for his own land, and it happened he
was tired of other places. He did not associate so many
disasters with *it*. Take yellow fever, for example: as a
result of denying the truth of it, all those years abroad, he
had come to disbelieve in it himself, and here back in the
country again, when he read the cases published in the
paper, he was already infected with the belief that all
diseases were just so many names. Perhaps it was because
he was a healthy man himself.

He had not altogether changed. He was the same, or
nearly so. True, he was a little more bald, thinner, had a
few wrinkles. In short, a hardy old age of sixty. His
moustache still terminated in two elegant points. His step
was firm, his aspect grave, with that touch of gallantry he
never lost. In his buttonhole the same eternal flower.

Nor did the city seem to him to have changed much. He
found a little more bustle, a few less operas, heads grown
gray, dead people, but the old city was the same. His

house in Cattete was well preserved too. Ayres gave his tenant notice as politely as if he were paying his respects to the minister of foreign affairs, and installed himself in it, alone with one servant—no matter how his sister tried to carry him off to Andarahy.

"No, Rita, no, my little sister, let me stay in my corner."

"But I'm your only living relative," she said.

"In blood and in spirit. It's true," he agreed. "And you can add, the best of them all, and the kindest, and the godliest. Where is that long hair? . . . You needn't lower your eyes. You cut it off to put in your husband's coffin. These locks are silver, but the ones you cut were black, and more than one widow would have kept them for a second marriage."

Rita liked to hear him say this. In time gone by, when she was first a widow, no: she was ashamed of an act of such sincerity, it seemed ridiculous—cutting off her hair because she had lost the best of husbands. But, as time went on, she began to see that she had done right, to accept what people said, and to recall their words in secret. Now, she seized upon the allusion to retort, "If I am all that, why do you prefer to live with strangers?"

"What do you mean, *strangers?* I'm not going to live with anyone. I'll be living with Cattete, the Largo do Machado, Botafogo beach, and Flamengo, I'm not talking about the people who live there, but of the streets, the houses, the fountains, and the shops. There are strange things there, but could I find a topsy-turvy kind of house like mine in Andarahy? Let's be content with what we know. There in my old neighborhood my feet walk of themselves, and things are petrified, and men immortal —like that famous Custodio of the pastry shop, remember?"

"I remember, the Imperial Pastry Shop, *Confeitaria do Imperio*."

"It was forty years ago that he set up shop. It was in the days when carts still paid toll. The old devil! he's old but there's no end to him. He'll bury me yet. He looks like a boy. Comes to see me every week."

"You too look like a boy."

"Don't joke, little sister, I'm finished. I'm an old dandy, perhaps, but it's not to impress the girls, it's because that's the way I am. And, why don't *you* come and live with me?"

"Ah! I too like to be in my own nest. I'll visit you from time to time, but now I'll never move from here till it's time to go to the cemetery."

They arranged to visit each other. Ayres would have dinner with her on Thursdays. Dona Rita again spoke of his health. Ayres replied that he never got sick, but if he did he would come to Andarahy. Her heart, he said, was the best hospital in the world. Perhaps in all these refusals there was also the need to avoid controversy, because his sister had a way of inventing reasons for disagreement. That very day (it was at breakfast) he found the coffee delicious, but his sister said it was vile, and so forced him to the great effort of reversing himself and declaring it abominable.

At first, Ayres stuck by his solitude, cut himself off from society, shut himself up at home, accepted no invitations—or very few, and at rare intervals. He really was tired of men, and of women, of parties and late nights. He set a schedule for himself. As he was given to reading literary classics, he found in Padre Bernardes this translation of the famous psalm, "I fled afar off and dwelt in solitude." It became his device. If Santos had taken it for his, he would have had it chiseled over the entrance to the drawing room, to regale his numerous friends. Ayres let it remain within himself. Now and again he liked to say it over under his breath, partly for the sense, partly for the old-style language: "I fled afar off and dwelt in solitude."

This is the way it was in the beginning. On Thursdays he went to take dinner with his sister. At night he walked along the beach, or through the streets of his neighborhood. Most of his time was spent in reading and rereading, or in composing the notebook he called his *Memorial,* or in looking over what he had written, in order to once more call to mind things past. They were many, and of divers moods, from gay to melancholy, diplomatic funerals and receptions—an armful of dry leaves that now seemed green to him. Sometimes persons were designated by an *X* or ***, and he did not immediately recollect who they were, but it was sport to search for them, to find them, to complete them. He had a glass cabinet made, in which he placed the relics of his life: old portraits, gifts from governments and individuals, a fan, a glove, a ribbon, and other feminine mementos, medals and medallions, cameos, bits of Greek and Roman ruins, an infinity of things that I will not name, so as not to fill up space. The letters were not *there.* They lived on inside an old suitcase, catalogued alphabetically by cities, languages, and sexes. Fifteen or twenty of them would fill as many chapters, and would be read with interest and curiosity. One note, for example, a note that was dingy and bore no date, young, as only old notes are, and signed with initials, an *M* and a *P* that Ayres translated with nostalgic longing. It's not worth the trouble to tell you the name.

Solitude Wearies Too

But everything grows wearisome, even solitude. Ayres began to feel a twinge of boredom: he yawned, nodded, got a thirst for live people, strangers, no matter who, gay or sad. He began to poke his nose into out-of-the-way neighborhoods, climb the morros, go to old churches, up new streets, to Copacabana and Tijuca. The sea out there, here the wilderness, and the sight awoke an infinite number of echoes in him that seemed the very voices of the past. All this he would write down, in the evenings, to strengthen his purpose for a solitary life. But no purpose can stand against Necessity.

Strangers had the advantage of drawing him out of his solitude without subjecting him to conversation. The formal calls he made were few, short, and scarcely a word said. These were the first steps. Little by little he came to have a relish for the old habits, a nostalgia for drawing rooms, a yearning for laughter, and it was not long before the retired diplomat was reinstated in the profession of sociability. Solitude, in the Biblical text as well as in the Padre's translation, was archaic. Ayres changed a word of it, and the sense: "I fled afar off, and dwelt among people."

So much for the schedule of the new life! It was not that he no longer believed in it, or no longer found it congenial, or that he did not still practice it at times, once in a great while, as one makes use of a remedy that obliges one to stay in bed or in the bedroom, but he would quickly get well and go outdoors again. He wanted to see other people, hear them, smell them, taste them, feel them, apply all his senses to a world that could kill time, deathless time.

XXXIV   *Mysterious*

Thus we left him, only two chapters ago, in a corner of the drawing room at the Santoses', in conversation with the ladies. You will recall that Flora had not taken her eyes off him, for she was anxious to know why he found her mysterious. The word tore at her brain, wounding without penetrating. A mystery—what was it? Something that cannot be explained; but why can it not be explained?

She wanted to ask him, but could not find an opportunity, and he left early. The first time, however, that he came to São Clemente, Flora frankly asked him to favor her with a fuller definition. Ayres smiled, took her hand —she was standing—and quickly invented this reply:

"Mysterious is the term we might apply to artists that paint without ever finishing the painting. They slap on color, more color, another color, much color, little color, fresh color, and it never seems to them that the tree is a tree or the cottage a cottage. If it's people they're painting, good night! No matter how much the portrait's eyes may speak, such painters always imagine they don't say anything; and they retouch with so much patience that some of them die between two eyes, others kill themselves in despair."

Flora found the explanation obscure, and you, my dear lady, if you happen to be older and more astute than she, will perhaps find it no clearer. But Ayres did not add

85

another word, so as not to be included in the class of artists he had described. He patted the palm of Flora's hand in a fatherly manner and asked after her studies. Her studies were going well. Why shouldn't studies go well? And, seating herself beside him, she confided that she had actually had the idea of learning to draw and paint, but, if she was doomed to put on too much paint or too little and end by not painting anything, it would be better to stick with her music. She and music got along together, French too, and English.

"Then only music, English, and French—nothing more," agreed Ayres.

"But do you promise not to think me a mystery?" she asked softly.

Before he could answer, the twins came into the room. Flora forgot one subject for another, and the old man for the young men. Ayres waited only long enough to see her laugh with them, and to feel within himself a twinge of something like regret. Regret at growing old, I think.

XXXV
Attendance Upon the Young Lady

The two brothers were already in the university: one at the School of Law in São Paulo, the other at the Medical School in Rio. It would not be long before they sallied forth with their degrees: one to defend the rights and wrongs of humanity, the other to help it live and die. Man is a thing of contrasts.

Politics was not so important as to make them forget Flora, nor Flora so important as to make them forget politics. Both interests together were not great enough to interfere with their studies and their pursuit of pleasure.

They were at an age when everything combines without destroying the essence of any one thing. That they should come to love the girl with equal force may be readily admitted. There was no need for her to set out to attract them. No, Flora laughed with both of them without especially rejecting either one or the other. It may even be that she did not notice anything. Paulo was away most of the time. When he returned for holidays, he seemed to find her more full of charm. At these times, Pedro multiplied his attentions, so as not to be outdone by his brother, who was prodigal with *his*. And Flora received them all with the same friendly expression.

Please note—and this point should be emphasized—the twin brothers continued to be alike, growing taller and more handsome all the time. Perhaps they lost somewhat being together, because then the resemblance lessened in each their individual style. Besides, Flora sometimes pretended to mistake one for the other in order to laugh with both.

She would say to Pedro, "Dr. Paulo!" and to Paulo, "Dr. Pedro!"

It was no use for them to change from left to right and from right to left. Flora changed their names as well, and the three ended up laughing. Intimacy excused this play and increased with it. Paulo liked conversation more than piano: Flora conversed. Pedro got along better with piano than with conversation: Flora played. Or she would do both, play as she talked, giving free rein to her fingers and to her tongue.

Such arts placed at the service of such charm were really cause to inflame the brothers, and that is what happened, little by little. Flora's mother, I think, noticed something, but at first she did not give it much thought. She too had been gently brought up and girlish. She too had distributed herself without giving any of herself to anybody. It may even be that from her point of view it was a necessary exercise for the eyes of the spirit as well as for those in one's face. The whole thing is that they should not become infected nor run after "sweet singing," as the country folk say, meaning by this the enchantments of Orpheus. On the contrary, it was Flora who played the role of Orpheus, she was the sweet singer. In due time, her mother thought, she would choose one of them.

The intimacy of the three young people was broken by long interruptions besides the enforced absences of Paulo. Though Pedro did not leave the city, he did not come to see her all the time, and many times she did not go to the house on the beach. They would not see each other for days and days. That they thought of each other is possible. But I do not have the slightest proof of it. The truth is that Pedro had his classmates, affairs of the heart—mundane and romantic—jaunts to Tijuca and the like. Further, the twin brothers were still at a stage where they spoke of her in their letters, praised her, said a thousand tender things, without jealousy.

XXXVI   *Discord Is Not So Black*
                                       As It Is Painted

Discord is not so black as it is painted, my friend. It is neither ugly nor sterile. Count the books alone it has produced, from Homer to the present, not to mention . . . Not to mention what? I was going to say, *this one,* but Modesty motioned me from afar to stop there. I will stop, and long live Modesty, who can hardly endure the capital letter I gave her, the letter and the vivas, but she will have to put up with it, and with them. Long live Modesty, and we will omit mention of this book. We will stick with the *great* books, epic and tragic, to which Discord has given life; and you tell me if such great results do not prove the greatness of the cause. No, discord is not so black as it is painted.

I emphasize this in order that sensitive souls may not begin to tremble for the lady and for the young men. There is no need to tremble, especially since the brothers' discord began with a frank accord that very night. They were going along the beach, silent, alone in their thoughts, until each of them, as if speaking to himself, uttered this one sentence, "She's getting mighty pretty."

And each, turning to the other, "Who?"

Both smiled, savoring the simultaneity of the reflexion and of the response. I know, this phenomenon is exactly the same as that of Chapter XXV [XXIII—tr.] when they described their age, but don't blame me: they were twins, they could have had twin speech. The point is, they were not vexed. It was not yet love that they felt. Each expressed his opinion about the young lady's charms, her expression, voice, eyes, and hands, all with such a friendly air that it excluded the idea of rivalry. At most, they differed in the choice of her best point, which for Pedro was her eyes, for Paulo her figure, but, as they ended finding a harmonious whole, it was plain they would not fight over this. Neither of them imagined in the other the vague thing, or whatever it was, that they had begun to feel, and they seemed more aesthetes than lovers. Even politics left them in peace that night. They did not fight for its sake. It is true, a feeling of contentiousness came over them at the sight of the shore and of the sky, which were delightful. The moon was full, the water still, confused, scattered voices, an occasional tilbury going slow or at a trot, depending as it was vacant or had a fare. Now and then a fresh breeze.

Imagination carried them into the future, to a brilliant

future, as the future is at that age. Botafogo would play a historic role, an imperial bay for Pedro, a republican Venice for Paulo, without doge or council of ten, or perhaps a doge under another title, a simple president who would marry this little Adriatic in the name of the people. Perhaps he himself would be the doge. This possibility, in spite of his tender years, puffed out the sails of his soul. Paulo saw himself at the head of a republic in which the ancient and the modern, the future and the past mingled —a new Rome, a National Convention, the French Republic, and the United States of America.

Pedro, for his part, constructed something halfway, with one palace for national representation, another for the Emperor, and he saw himself as Minister and President of the Council. He made speeches, silenced the tumult and opinions, wrested a vote from the Chamber of Deputies or put through a decree of dissolution. It is a trifling detail, but it deserves to be included: though Pedro retained the status quo in his dream, his thoughts ran on motions for dissolution. He saw himself at home, with the act signed, referendumed, copied, sent to the newspapers and to the Chambers, read by the secretaries, filed in the archives, and the deputies departing crestfallen, some of them grumbling, others irate. Only *he* remained tranquil, in his study, receiving friends that came to congratulate him and ask for messages to the country at large.

Such were the bold brush strokes made by their imaginations. The stars in heaven accepted all their thoughts, the moon went its quiet way, and the wave stretched itself along the shore with its customary indolence. When they came to, they were in front of the house. Some impulse or other tried to push them into an argument about the weather, the night, the temperature, and the quiet inlet. A faint murmur, it may be, made them move their lips and start to break the silence, but the silence was so august that they acquiesced in respecting it. And then they found within their hearts that the moon was splendid, the inlet beautiful, and the temperature divine.

XXXVII   *Disaccord in Accord*

I must not forget to mention that in 1888 a grave, very grave, question made them agree again, although for different reasons. The date explains the event: it was the emancipation of the slaves. They were at that time far apart, but their opinion united them.

The only difference in their opinion was in respect to the significance of the reform, which for Pedro was an act of justice, and for Paulo was the beginning of the revolution. He himself said so in concluding a speech in São Paulo on the twentieth of May: "Abolition is the dawn of liberty, we await the sun: the black emancipated, it remains to emancipate the white."

Natividade was thunderstruck when she read this. She took her pen and wrote a long, maternal letter. Paulo answered with thirty thousand expressions of tenderness, declaring at the end that he could sacrifice everything for her, including life and even honor, but not his sentiments. "No, Mama, not my sentiments."

"Not my sentiments," repeated Natividade as she finished reading the letter.

Natividade could not understand her son's feelings, she who had sacrificed her "sentiments" to her principles, as in the case of Ayres, and continued to live without stain. Not sacrifice? But why? . . . She found no explanation. She reread the sentence in the letter, and that of the speech. She was afraid he would ruin his political career, if it was politics that was to make him a great man. "The black emancipated, it remains to emancipate the white," it was a threat against the Emperor and the Empire.

She did not guess . . . Mothers don't always. She never guessed that the phrase in the speech was not really her son's; it was nobody's. Someone said it one day, in a speech or a conversation, in an article, or during a journey over land or sea. Another repeated it, until many people made it their own. It was fresh, it was forceful, it was expressive, finally it became public property.

There are felicitous phrases like that. They are born in modest circumstances, like poor people. When they least expect it, they find themselves ruling the world, under the guise of ideas. Even ideas do not always keep the name of their father; many appear to be orphans, born of nothing and begotten by no one. Each man lays hold of them, improves them as he can, and carries them to market, where all take them as their own.

XXXVIII   *Opportune Arrival*

At two o'clock in the afternoon of the following day, when Natividade got on the streetcar to go shopping in the Rua do Ouvidor, she still carried the phrase with her. The sight of the bay did not take her mind off it, nor did the people they passed, nor happenings in the street, nor anything. The phrase went before her and inside her with its threatening tone and aspect. At Cattete someone jumped on without stopping the car. Can you guess who it was? The Counselor. Guess also that his foot on the step, he caught sight of our friend up front, rapidly went toward her, and accepted the edge of bench she offered him. After the first greetings:

"You looked startled," said Ayres.

"Naturally. I never imagined you were capable of such a feat of gymnastics."

"Matter of habit. My legs jump by themselves. Someday they will let me fall, and I shall be run over."

"Well, however it was, you arrive at an opportune moment."

"I always arrive at an opportune moment. I heard you say that once many years ago, or was it your sister . . . Wait . . . I have not forgotten the circumstance. I believe you were talking about the cabocla of the Castello. Don't you remember there was some cabocla or other who lived on the Morro do Castello and divined the destinies of people? I was here on leave, and heard wonderful stories of her marvels. As I had always had faith in Sibyls, I believed in the cabocla. What became of her?"

Natividade glanced at him, as if fearful that he divined she had consulted the cabocla. She decided he had not. She smiled and called him an unbeliever. Ayres denied he was an unbeliever: on the contrary, being broad-minded, he professed practically all beliefs in this world. And he concluded, "But, after all, why have I arrived at an opportune moment?"

Either the past, or the person, with his discreet manners and poise, or all this together, gave this man, in the eyes of this lady, reliability that she did not now find in anyone else, or in very few. She spoke to him of a confidence, something she did not want to confide to her husband.

"What I want is counsel, Counselor. Besides, why trouble my husband? I may tell my sister Perpetua. I think it's best not to say anything to Agostinho."

Ayres agreed that it was not worthwhile bothering him

if it came to that, and waited. Natividade, without mentioning the cabocla, first told him about the antagonism that existed between her sons, now shown in the matter of politics, and speaking particularly of Paulo she repeated the sentence from his letter and asked what would be the best thing to do. Ayres felt that it was youthful enthusiasm. She should not oppose him. If she did, he would change the words but not his sentiments.

"Then you think Paulo will always be like this?"

"I don't say 'always'; neither do I say the contrary. You demand definite answers, Baroness, but, tell me, what is there that's definite in this world—except your husband's game of ombre? Even that is not sure. How many days is it that I haven't had to be excused? It's true, I have not been there. And anyway the pleasure of conversation easily outweighs that of cards. Though I have an idea the married men who go to your house are of another opinion."

"Perhaps."

"Only bachelors can appreciate women's ideas. A childless widower, like me, is as good as a bachelor. No, I'm wrong, at sixty years of age, like me, he is worth two or three bachelors. As for young Paulo, don't think any more about the speech. I too made speeches when I was a young man."

"I have been thinking of getting them married."

"Marriage is a good idea," assented Ayres.

"I don't mean right away, but in two or three years. Perhaps I'll take them on a trip abroad first. What do you think? Now don't answer me by repeating what I say. I want your honest opinion. Do you think a trip . . . ?"

"I think a trip . . ."

"Go on."

"Trips do one good, especially at their age. They'll get their degrees in the coming year, won't they? Well, then! Before beginning any kind of career, married or not, it's a

94

good thing to see other lands . . . But why need you go with them, Senhora?"

"Mothers . . ."

"But I too (pardon my interrupting), I too am your son. Don't you think that habit, kindness, indulgence, affection, and all the other homely virtues that adorn you, constitute a kind of motherhood? I tell you, I would be an orphan."

"Then come with us."

"Ah, Baroness, for me there is no longer any part of the world that is worth the price of the ticket. I have seen everything, in various languages. Now, my world begins here on the Gloria docks, or on the Rua do Ouvidor, and ends at the São João Baptista Cemetery. I hear there are dark seas out there by Point Cajú, but I am an old unbeliever, as you yourself said, Senhora, just a few minutes ago, and I do not accept these reports without complete, visual proof, and I lack the legs to investigate."

"Always joking. Didn't I see them climb on the car just now? Your sister said to me the other day that you are the same as you were at thirty."

"Rita exaggerates. But coming back to the trip, you have not yet bought your tickets?"

"No."

"Nor even ordered them?"

"No."

"Then, let us think of something else. Each day brings its own problem, not to mention the weeks and months. Let us think of something else, and leave Paulo to ask for the republic."

Natividade believed in her heart that he was right. She thought of something else, the idea she had had in the beginning. She did not immediately say what it was; she preferred to converse for a few minutes. It was not difficult with this fellow. One of his talents was talking to women without either lapsing into banality or rising into the clouds. He had a special way, all his own: I do not know whether it was in the idea, in the gestures, or in the words. It is not that he spoke evil of anyone, yet if he had, it would have been amusing. I am inclined to believe he spoke no evil, out of indifference or from caution: provisionally, let us call it charity.

"But, Senhora, you have not yet told me what you wished of me, besides counsel. Or don't you wish anything further?"

"I am afraid to ask it of you."

"Ask anyway."

"You know that my twins do not agree in anything, or in very little, for all I have done to bring them into harmony. Agostinho is no help: he has other concerns. And I no longer feel that I have the strength. And then it occurred to me that a friend, a man, a moderate man, a man who is sociable, adroit, refined, cautious, intelligent, well educated . . ."

"I, in short?"

"You guessed."

"No, I didn't guess: it is my portrait cap-a-pie. But, what do you think *I* can do?"

"You can give them good manners, bring them together, even when they disagree. And make them stop disagreeing. You have no idea, they seem to do it on purpose. They don't disagree about the color of the moon, for example, but when they were eleven, Pedro decided that the shadows on the moon were clouds, and Paulo, that they were flaws in our vision, and they jumped at each other's throats; I had to separate them. Imagine, in politics . . ."

"Imagine what it will be in love affairs, you should say. But it is not actually for such a contingency . . ."

"Oh! no!"

96

"For the other things, it will be equally useless, but I was born to serve, even to no purpose. Baroness, your request is the same as appointing me tutor or pedagogue . . . Don't protest, I don't consider myself lowered. As long as you pay my salary . . . Don't be alarmed, I don't ask much. Pay me in words: your words are golden. I have already told you my efforts will be useless."

"Why?"

"It's useless."

"A person of authority like you, Senhor, can accomplish a great deal if you love them, because they are really good, believe me. Do you know them very well?"

"Not very."

"Know them better and you will see."

Ayres consented with a laugh. For Natividade it was one more attempt. She relied on the Counselor's efforts, and to tell the whole truth . . . I don't know whether I should say it . . . Yes I will. Natividade counted on the old diplomat's former weakness for her. His white hair would not have taken away his desire to serve her. I do not know who is reading me on this occasion. If it is a man, perhaps he will not immediately understand, but if it is a woman, I think she will understand. If no one understands, never mind; it is enough to know that he promised what she asked. He also promised to say nothing about it: this was a condition she made. And through it all he remained polite, sincere, and skeptical.

A Thief

They came to the Largo da Carioca, got off, and said goodbye. She went up the Rua Gonçalves Dias, he down the Rua da Carioca. Halfway down the street, Ayres came upon a group of people standing still, then they began to walk in the direction of the square. He thought of going back, not from fear but from aversion, he had a horror of crowds. He saw that the group was small, fifty or sixty people, and he heard shouting against the imprisonment of someone. He stepped into a doorway to wait for the group to pass. Two policemen were conducting the arrested man by the arm. From time to time he resisted, and then they had to pull him or force him in some other way. It was a matter, it seemed, of the theft of a wallet.

"I didn't steal anything!" shouted the man, checking his step. "It's false! Let me go! I am a free citizen! I protest! I protest!"

"Come along to the station!"

"I won't go!"

"Don't go!" shouted the anonymous crowd. "Don't go! don't go!"

One of the policemen tried to convince the crowd that it was true, that the fellow had stolen a wallet, and the disturbance subsided somewhat, but when the policeman returned to walk with the other policeman beside the arrested man—each holding one of his arms—the crowd began again to shout against the unjust violence. The arrested man took heart: now pitiful, now defiant, he called for protection. It was then that the other policeman unsheathed his sword to clear a passage. The people flew not gracefully, like a swallow or a dove to its nest or after food; it was a flying herd, a leap here, a leap there, a leap yonder, in every direction. The sword returned to its scabbard, and the arrested man went along with the police. But soon throats took vengeance for the affront to their legs, and a great, free outcry, of vindication, filled the street and the soul of the arrested man. The crowd once more closed ranks and marched off in the direction of the police station. Ayres went on his way.

The sound of the voices died away little by little, and Ayres went into His Imperial Majesty's Secretariat. It would appear he did not find the Minister in, or else the conference was short. At any rate when he came out into the square, he met some of the crowd on its way back commenting on the arrest and the robber. They did not say "robber," but "thief," believing that this word was more mild. And, as they had shouted a short while before against the action of the police, now they laughed at the groans of the arrested man.

"Aw, the crazy guy!"

"But? . . ." you will ask. Ayres did not ask anything. After all, there was a core of justice in that twofold and contradictory manifestation: that is what he thought. Besides, he figured that the cry of the protesting crowd was the daughter of an ancient instinct of resistance to authority. He reminded himself that man, once he was created, immediately disobeyed his Creator, who, what is more, had given him a paradise to live in. But there is no paradise to equal the pleasure of opposition. That man accustom himself to the laws, well and good. That he bend his neck to force and to a whim, very well. It is what the plant does when the wind blows. But that he bless the force and keep the laws always, always, always, is a violation of primitive liberty, the liberty of ancient Adam. This is what Counselor Ayres was thinking.

99

Don't attribute to him a belief in all these ideas. His thoughts ran thus as if he had been speaking aloud, at someone's dinner table or in a drawing room. It was a gentle, delicate criticism, and so convincing to all appearances that a hearer in search of ideas might be tempted to lift one or two . . .

He was about to go down the Rua Septe de Septembro, when the recollection of the shouting brought back the echo of another, greater, more remote shout.

XL   *Memories Spanish Style*

This other, greater, more remote shouting would not be fitted in here if it were not for the necessity of explaining the sudden gesture with which Ayres stopped dead on the sidewalk. He stopped, came down to earth, and went on walking, with his eyes on the ground and his soul in Caracas. It remained in Caracas, where he had served as an attaché of the legation. He was at home, chatting with a popular actress, a witty, gallant girl. Suddenly they heard a great outcry, confused, agitated voices, vibrating, growing louder . . .

"What is that noise, Carmen?" he asked between two caresses.

"Don't be alarmed, my darling; it's only the government falling."

"But I hear cheering."

"Then it must be the new government that's coming into power. Don't worry. Tomorrow will be plenty of time to pay your respects."

Ayres let himself drift with that old memory that now rose up out of the shouting of some fifty or sixty persons.

This sort of remembrance had more effect on him than the other kinds. He reconstructed the hour, the place, the person of the Spanish girl. Carmen was from Seville. The ex-dandy still remembered the popular ballad that he used to hear her sing when she left—after she adjusted her garters, smoothed her skirts, stuck the comb in her hair, at the moment she threw her mantilla around her, gracefully swaying her body:

> The girls of Seville
> On their mantilla
> Have a sign that reads
> Viva Sevilla!

I cannot give you the tune, but Ayres still had it by heart, and gently hummed it to himself as he walked on. And he mused over his lack of diplomatic vocation. The rise of a government—no matter what the political system—with its new ideas, its fresh, untarnished men, laws, and cheers, was worth less to him than the laughter of the young comedienne. Where would she be? The shade of the girl swept away everything else, the street, the people, the thief: it alone remained before old Ayres, swaying its hips and trolling the Andaluzian air:

> The girls of Seville
> On their mantilla . . .

XLI   *Incident of the Donkey*

If Ayres had followed his inclination, and I him, he would not have gone on with his walk; nor would I have begun this chapter: we would still be in the last one, without ever finishing it. But there is no memory that lasts if some more urgent business draws our attention, and a simple donkey made Carmen and her song disappear.

It happened that a donkey cart had stopped in the narrow entrance of the cross street Travessa de São Francisco and would not let a carriage get by: the donkey driver was wildly beating his donkey. A common occurrence, yet this sight made our Ayres stop, no less sorry for the donkey than for the man. The effort spent by the latter was great because the ass continued to ruminate over whether he should abandon his position; but, notwithstanding its superiority, he was getting a devil of a beating. There were already several people standing around watching. This situation lasted five or six minutes. Finally the donkey chose walking in preference to blows, drew the cart from its position, and went on his way.

In the animal's round eyes Ayres saw a profound expression of irony and patience. It seemed to him to be the grand look of an invincible spirit. Further, he read in them this dialogue: "Go on, Boss, heap up the cart, earn money to get me fodder. Earn your living going barefoot on the rough ground to buy me iron shoes. Even so you can't stop me from calling you a bad name. But I don't call you anything. You will always be my darling boss. While you work yourself to the bone to earn a living, I keep thinking that your power is not worth much, since you can't take from me my freedom to be stubborn . . ."

"It's almost as if I heard him meditating," Ayres observed to himself.

Then he quietly laughed at himself, and went on his way. He had made up so many lies in the diplomatic service that perhaps he made up the donkey's monologue. That's what it was: he did not read anything in its eyes, except irony and patience, but he could not help giving these the form of speech, with its rules of syntax. Even the irony was most likely in his own retina. The eye of man serves to photograph the invisible, just as his ears record the echo of silence. The important thing is that the owner of eyes and ears have a spark of imagination to help the memory forget Caracas and Carmen, his own kisses and political experience.

XLII   *A Hypothesis*

Visions and reminiscences were thus consuming time and space for the Counselor, to the point of making him forget Natividade's request. But he did not totally forget it: the words exchanged a short while before rose to his ears from the cobblestones of the street. He supposed he would not lose much by studying the young men. And then he came upon a hypothesis, a kind of swallow that flies among the trees, below, above, lights here, lights there, darts away again, and pours itself out in constant motion. This was the confused and bright-colored hypothesis, to wit, that if the twins had been begotten by him they would not have differed, much or little, thanks to his equilibrium of spirit. The old man's soul began to sough in the branches, whispering retrospective desires, as it gazed on that hypothesis: a far different Caracas, a far different Carmen, he a father, these boys his, a beautiful swallow that dispersed and vanished in a wordless rustle of gestures.

XLIII   *The Speech*

As for Natividade, her fancy did not wander in any direction whatsoever. She was all wrapped up in her sons, and now especially with the letter and the speech. She began by making no reply to Paulo's political effusions; it was one of the Counselor's bits of counsel. When her son returned for the holidays he had forgotten the letter he wrote.

The speech he did not forget, but who is there who forgets the speeches he makes? If they are good, memory engraves them in bronze. If they are bad, they leave a certain bitterness that lasts a long time. The best remedy, in the second instance, is to assume they are excellent, and, if reason will not accept this fancy, to consult persons who *will* accept it and believe *them*. Opinion is an old oil that never grows rancid.

Paulo had talent. His speech may have sinned here and there in being overemphatic or in some of its ideas being ordinary and outworn. Paulo had talent. In short, the speech was good. Santos thought it excellent, he read it to his friends and decided to have it printed in the newspapers. Natividade was not opposed but she believed a few words should be cut.

"Cut? Why?" asked Santos, and waited for an answer.

"Don't you see, Agostinho? These words contain republican sentiment," she explained, reading the sentence that distressed her.

Santos listened to her read them, read them to himself, and did not deny that she was right. Still, he was unwilling to suppress them.

"Then the speech must not be printed."

"Oh, no! The speech is magnificent and must not be allowed to perish in São Paulo. The Court city must read it, and the provinces also. I wouldn't mind seeing it translated into French. In French it'll very likely be even better."

"But Agostinho, it may harm the boy's career. It may be the Emperor won't like it . . ."

Pedro, who had been present during the last few minutes of the argument, gently intervened to say that his mother's fears were groundless; it would be best to keep the whole sentence, and, strictly speaking, it was not much different from what the liberals were saying in 1848. "A liberal monarchist might very easily put his name to that passage," he concluded after rereading his brother's words.

"Exactly!" agreed his father.

Natividade, who saw the enmity of the brothers in everything, suspected it was Pedro's design to compromise Paulo. She looked at him to see if she could discover any such perverted intention, but her son's face wore an expression of enthusiasm. Pedro read passages of the speech, accentuating the felicitous phrases, repeating the more original ones, mouthing the full periods, rolling them on his tongue—all this with such a friendly air that his mother lost her suspicion, and the reprinting of the speech was agreed upon. There was also an edition in the form of a booklet, and the father had seven copies richly bound and took them to the ministers, and another copy, still more richly bound for the Princess Regent.

"Tell her," advised Natividade, "that our Paulo is an ardent liberal . . ."

"An 1848 liberal," Santos completed the phrase, recalling Pedro's remark.

Santos carried out everything to the letter, and in record

time. The presentation was made of course, in the Isabel palace, the definition "1848 liberal" came out louder than the other words, either to lessen the revolutionary odor of the phrase that had been condemned by his wife, or because it had historical value. When he returned home the first thing he said was that the Princess had asked after her; but in spite of being flattered by the compliment, Natividade tried to find out what impression the speech had made on her, if she had already read it.

"Apparently a good impression. She told me she had already read the speech. Nevertheless, I mentioned to her that Paulo's sentiments were loyal, and that if one noted a certain passion in them one could also sense that they were the sentiments of an 1848 liberal . . ."

"You said that, Papa?" asked Pedro.

"Why not, if it's the truth? Paulo is what may be called an 1848 liberal," repeated Santos in an attempt to convince his son.

XLIV   *The Salmon*

It was during the holidays that Paulo learned of the interpretation his father had given the Princess of that passage of his speech. He protested against it at home; he was determined to do the same in public, but Natividade intervened in time. Ayres poured oil on the troubled waters.

"It's not worth the trouble, lad," he said to the future advocate. "What's important is that each man have his own ideas and fight for them until they win out. But if people happen to misinterpret them, that's nothing to be distressed about."

"Yes, it is, Senhor. It may appear that it is as they

say . . . I am going to write an article on something or other, and I'll leave no doubts."

"To what purpose?"

"I don't want them to suppose . . ."

"But who doubts your sentiments?"

"They may."

"Aw, nonsense! In any case, first, come have breakfast with me someday . . . Look, come Sunday, and bring your brother Pedro. We'll be three at table, a stag party. We'll open a special bottle of wine that the German Minister gave me . . ."

On Sunday, the boys went to Cattete, less for the breakfast than for the host. They were both fond of Ayres, and liked to hear him and ask him questions: they would beg him for political anecdotes of former days, descriptions of parties, society news.

"Hello! My two young men!" said the Counselor. "Two young men that don't forget their old friend. How is Papa? and Mama?"

"They're fine," said Pedro.

Paulo added that they both sent their regards.

"And Aunt Perpetua?"

"She's fine too," said Paulo.

"With her homeopathy and her stories of Paraguay," added Pedro.

Pedro was in good spirits, Paulo preoccupied. After the first exchange of greetings and news, Ayres noted this difference, and thought it was good, in that it took away the monotony of their resemblance; but, after all, he did not want gloomy faces, and he asked the law student what was wrong.

"Nothing."

"Come now, you have a half-lugubrious air. I woke up in a laughing mood, and want you both to laugh with me."

Paulo growled out something that neither of them understood and pulled a bunch of papers out of his pocket. It was an article . . .

"An article?"

"An article in which I remove all doubts in respect to my sentiments, and I beg you to hear me, Senhor, it is short. I wrote it last night."

Ayres suggested hearing it after breakfast, but the young man begged him to hear it at once, and Pedro agreed, suggesting that on top of breakfast it might disturb their digestion, like the bad medicine it was. Ayres brought the matter to a head by consenting to hear the article.

"It's short, seven pages."

"Fine writing?"

"No, Senhor, so-so."

Paulo read the article. It had as an epigraph this verse from *Amos:* Hear this word, ye fat cows that are in the mountain of Samaria . . ." The fat cows were the personnel of the present government, Paulo explained. He was not attacking the Emperor, out of consideration for his mother; but with the social system and its personnel he was violent and harsh. Ayres felt that he had what was called in former days the "bump of combativeness." When Paulo finished, Pedro said with a mocking air, "I've heard all that before, they are Paulist ideas."

"Yours are colonial ideas," retorted Paulo.

Worse words might have sprung from this beginning, but luckily a servant came to the door to announce that breakfast was served. Ayres got up and said he would give his opinion at table.

"Breakfast first, for we have a salmon, something not to be neglected. Let us go to him."

Ayres was truly eager to perform the task he had been given by Natividade. Who knows if the idea of spiritual father of the twins, father in desire only, a father that he never was, that he might have been, did not give him a particular affection and a higher sense of duty than simply that of a friend? Neither is it beyond possibility that he was only looking for new material for the blank pages of his *Memorial*.

During breakfast they went on talking of the article, Paulo with love, Pedro with disdain, Ayres with neither the one nor the other emotion. The breakfast was serving its purpose: Ayres studied the two young men and their opinions. Perhaps the latter were no more than an adolescent skin eruption. And he smiled, got them to eat and drink, even spoke of girls, but in this matter the young men, embarrassed and respectful, did not go along with the ex-Minister. The political conversation died down, although Paulo still maintained that he could overthrow the Monarchy with ten men, and Pedro that he could wipe out the seed of republicanism with a single edict. But the ex-Minister, with no more edict than a stewpan, and with no more men than his cook, wrapped up the two social systems in the same delicious salmon.

XLV   *Sing, My Muse*

At the conclusion of breakfast Ayres favored them with a quotation from Homer, or rather two, one for each of them. He said the old poet had sung of them, separately, Paulo at the beginning of the *Iliad:* "Muse, sing the wrath of Achilles, Peleus' son, ill-boding wrath for the Greeks, that sent to Pluto's house many strong souls of heroes and gave their bodies to be a prey to birds and dogs . . ."

Pedro was in the beginning of the *Odyssey:* "Muse, sing that clever hero who wandered so many years after the destruction of sacred Ilium . . ."

It was a way of defining the character of each, and neither of them took the interpretation amiss. On the contrary, the poetic quotation was as good as a special certificate of merit. They both smiled with belief, acceptance, thankfulness, without uttering a word or syllable that questioned the aptness of the verses. After quoting them in our prose, the Counselor repeated them in the Greek text itself, and the two brothers felt still more epic, so certain is it that translations are not worth as much as originals. What each did was give a disparaging sense to the part that applied to his brother:

"You are right, Counselor," said Paulo, "Pedro is a tricky dog . . ."

"And you are a hothead . . ."

"In Greek, boys, in Greek and in verse, which is better than our tongue and the prose of our time."

X L V I   *Between the Acts*

These breakfasts were repeated, the months passed, the holidays arrived, the holidays ended, and Ayres kept penetrating deeper into the minds of the twins. He wrote them into the *Memorial,* where one may also read of the consultation of old Placido and what he said about them, and of the trip to the cabocla of the Castello and their fighting before they were born—old obscure bits that he recalled, pieced together, and deciphered.

While the months pass, consider that you are at the theater, chatting, between the acts. Backstage they are setting up the scenery, and the artists are changing their costume. Don't go back there! Let the lady, in her dressing room, laugh with her friends over what she wept over out here with the spectators. As for the garden that is in the making, you must not see it from behind. It is nothing but old, unpainted canvas; it is only the side toward the audience that has greenery and flowers. Stay out here in this lady's box. Look into her eyes: there are the tears the lady of the play drew from them. Talk to her about the play and the artist. Remark that it is obscure, that they don't know their parts, or that everything is sublime. Take your binoculars and run them over the boxes, dispense justice, call the pretty women pretty and the plain ones plain, and don't forget to tell anecdotes that disfigure the pretty women, and virtues that pretty up the plain ones. The virtues must be great, and the anecdotes amusing. There are also banal ones, but even banality in the mouth of a good raconteur becomes rare and valuable. And you will see how the tears dry up entirely, and reality takes the place of fiction. I am speaking in metaphors: you know that everything here is the pure truth and without tears.

XLVII   *St. Matthew IV:1-10*

If there is much laughter when one party rises to power, there is also much weeping in the party that falls; and of laughter and tears is made the first day of the situation, as in Genesis. Let us get to the evangelist who serves as the title of this chapter. The liberals had come into the power that the conservatives had been forced to abandon. There is no need to tell you that Baptista's dejection of spirits was enormous.

"Just at a time when I had high hopes," he said to his wife.

"Of what?"

"Aw, of what! Of a governorship. I didn't say anything because it wasn't absolutely certain, but it was practically certain. I had two meetings, not with ministers, but with an influential person who was in the know, and it was a matter of waiting a month or two . . ."

"A good governorship?"

"A good one."

"If you had really worked on it . . ."

"If I had really worked on it, I might now be in office, but we would be under fire."

"That's true," agreed Dona Claudia, looking to the future.

Baptista walked back and forth, his hands behind his back, his eyes on the ground, sighing, with no clear view of the time when the conservatives would return to power. The liberals were strong and resolute. The same ideas hovered in Dona Claudia's head. It was only in will power that this man and wife differed. Their ideas were often such that if they had appeared outside their owners' heads no one would have been able to say which were his, and which were hers: they seemed to come from a single brain. At that moment, neither saw immediate or remote possibilities. A single, vague idea . . . And it was at this point that Dona Claudia's will sank its feet into the ground and grew. I am not speaking in metaphors: Dona Claudia rose rapidly from her chair and fired this question at her husband, "But, Baptista, what can you expect of the conservatives?"

Baptista stopped with a dignified air and answered simply, "I expect them to get back into power."

"And if they do? You'll have to wait eight or ten years, to the end of the century, won't you? And then how do you know you'll be given a post? Who will remember you?"

"I can found a newspaper."

"Oh, forget about newspapers. And if you die?"

"I shall die in a position of honor."

Dona Claudia looked fixedly at him. Her sharp little eyes bored deep into him like two persistent augers. Suddenly, raising her upturned hands, "Baptista, you never *were* a conservative!"

Her husband turned pale and recoiled, as if he had heard an ungrateful reproach from his own party. He had never been a conservative? But what was he then, what else could he be in this world? What had caused him to have the esteem of the heads of his party? This was all that was needed . . .

Dona Claudia paid no attention to his outburst. She repeated what she had said, and added, "You were with them, like people at a ball, where it is not necessary to have the same ideas to dance the same quadrille."

Baptista smiled a fleeting smile: he loved graceful metaphors, and that one seemed to him most graceful, so graceful that at first he agreed. Then his star inspired him with a prompt refutation: "Yes, but people don't dance with ideas, they dance with their legs."

"Dance with what you please, the fact remains that all your ideas tend toward the liberal side. Remember how your opponents in the province accused you of supporting the liberals . . ."

"It was false! It was the government that advised me, they recommended moderation. I can show the letters."

"What do you mean moderation! You are a liberal."

"I a liberal!"

"A great liberal. You were never anything else."

"Think what you're saying, Claudia. If someone should hear you he might believe it and spread it around . . ."

"What difference does it make if someone spreads it around? He would be spreading the truth, he would be spreading justice, because your true friends will not leave you.out in the street, now that everything is being organized. You have personal friends in the administration; why don't you go and see them?"

Baptista recoiled in horror. To mount the stairways of power and tell them he was at their service! It was not even conceivable. Dona Claudia admitted it was not, but a friend could take care of it, an intimate friend of the government who would say to Ouro Preto, "Viscount, why don't you send for Baptista? He was always liberal in his ideas. Give him a governorship, no matter how small, and . . ."

Baptista made a gesture with his shoulders, another with his hand for her to hold her tongue. His wife did not hold her tongue, she went on saying the same things, louder and more emphatically. The catastrophe in her husband's soul was already great. On further consideration he would not refuse to cross the Rubicon; all he lacked was the necessary strength. He *wanted* to be willing. He wanted to see nothing, neither the past nor the present, nor the future, to know nothing of men, nothing of things, to yield to destiny's die—but he could not.

To do him justice, when he thought only of loyalty to his friends he felt better: the same trust was there, the same habit, the same hope. The trouble came when he looked beyond. And it was Dona Claudia who pointed with her finger to career, happiness, life, the long, steady march, the governorship, the ministry . . . He turned away his eyes and stood still.

When he was alone Baptista gave much thought to his personal and political situation. He probed himself spiritually. Maybe Claudia was right. What was there really conservative about him, except the instinct that helps every living thing to endure this world? He could see that he was conservative in politics because his father was, and his uncle, and their friends, and the parish priest, and he had begun in school to curse the liberals. And then, he had not really been a conservative but a *saquarema,* as the liberals were *luzias.* Baptista now fastened on these obsolete, degrading names that had changed the nature of the parties, so that now there was no longer the great abyss between them that there had been in 1842 and 1848. And he recalled the Viscount de Alburquerque or some other senator who had said in a speech that there was nothing more like a conservative than a liberal, and vice versa. And he evoked examples, the progressive party, Olinda, Nabuco, Zacharias. What were they but conservatives who had understood the changing times and had removed from liberal ideas the bloodiness of revolution and given them a lively but serene complexion? The world had no place for obstinate mossbacks . . . At this point a chill went along his spine. And, at the same moment, Flora appeared. Her father hugged her with enthusiasm and asked her if she would like to go to one of the provinces if he should be made governor.

"But didn't the conservatives fall from power?"

"Yes, they did, but suppose that . . ."

"Oh, no, Papa!"

"Why not?"

"I don't want to leave Rio de Janeiro."

Perhaps Rio de Janeiro for her was Botafogo, and more particularly the home of Natividade. Her father did not inquire into the reasons for her refusal. He supposed they were political and found new strength for resisting the temptations of Dona Claudia: "Get thee hence, Satan: for it is written, Thou shalt worship the Lord thy God, and him only shalt thou serve." And it went on, as in the Scriptures: "Then the devil leaveth him and, behold, angels came and ministered unto him." The angels were only one, but she was worth a hundred. Her father kissed her tenderly and said, "All right, my child, quite all right."

"It is, isn't it, Papa?"

But it was not the daughter that prevented the father's defection. On the contrary, if it had been a question of yielding, Baptista would have yielded to his wife or to the devil—synonyms in this chapter. He did not yield from weakness. He did not have the necessary vigor to betray his friends, no matter how much they seemed to have abandoned him. There are these virtues sprung of meanness of spirit and timidity, and not for this reason are they less lucrative, morally speaking. It is not only stoics and martyrs that have value. Feeble virtues are still virtues. It is true, however, that his language in relation to the liberals was no longer that of hatred or impatience: he had arrived at tolerance, and was edging towards fair play. He agreed that change in the parties was a principle of public necessity. His job was to encourage his friends. They would soon return to power. Dona Claudia was of a contrary opinion. As far as she was concerned, the liberals would last to the end of the century. She *did* admit that now, when they were first taking over, was not the right time for a last-minute conversion: it was necessary to wait a year or two, for a vacancy in the Chamber of Deputies, a commission, the lieutenant-governorship of Rio . . .

XLVIII   *Terpsichore*

None of these things bothered Natividade. She would sooner be concerned with the ball on the Ilha Fiscal, which took place that November to honor the Chilean officers. It was not that she still danced, but she took delight in seeing the others dance, and she was now of the opinion that dancing is a pleasure of the eyes. This opinion is one of the effects of that bad habit of growing old. Never get that habit, my dear lady. There are other terrible habits, but none worse, this is the worst. Let philosophers say what they please about old age being a fine, useful state, what with its experience and other advantages. Don't grow old, my dear, no matter how the years invite you to leave the spring. At most, accept summer. Summer is good. It is warm. The nights are short, it is true, but the dawns bring no fog, and the sky is a sudden blue. Thus you will dance forever.

I know there are people for whom dancing is primarily a pleasure of the eyes, and the ladies on the ballroom floor no more, for them, than professional ballerinas. I too, if it is permissible for someone to quote himself, I too consider dancing a pleasure of the eyes rather than of the feet, not only because of my long, hoary years, but for another reason that I won't bother to mention. After all, I am not telling the story of *my* life nor *my* opinions, nor anything except what concerns the persons that enter this book. They are the ones I must place here, with all their virtues and imperfections, if they have them. This should be clear without my having to point it out, but nothing is lost by repeating it.

For example, Dona Claudia. She too thought about the ball on the Ilha Fiscal, without the least idea of dancing, nor for the aesthetic reason given by Natividade. For her the island ball was a political action, it was the dancing of the Ministry, it was a liberal festivity that might open the gates to some governorship or other for her husband. She could already see herself with the imperial family. She heard the Princess say, "How are you, Dona Claudia?"

"Perfectly splendid, Your Serene Highness."

And Baptista would be conversing with the Emperor in a corner, before envious eyes that tried to hear what they were saying by staring at them from a distance. It was her husband who . . . I do not know what to say about her husband in relation to the ball on the island. He expected to go, but not to find it to his taste. Perhaps people would interpret his presence as a half-conversion. It was not that there would be only liberals at the ball, there would also be conservatives, and here is where Dona Claudia's aphorism fits in nicely: "It is not necessary to have the same ideas to dance the same quadrille."

As for Santos, he had no need of ideas in order to dance. He did not dance, however. As a young man he had danced a lot, quadrilles, polkas, waltzes, and the "leaping waltz," as they called it then. I do not know the exact difference between the two. I presume that in the first one's feet never left the ground and in the second they never came down out of the air. This is the way it was until he was twenty-five. Then business caught him up and set him down in that *contredanse* in which the dancer does not always return to the same place, or he may never leave it. Santos left it and we already know where he is. Lately he had taken a fancy to the idea of becoming a deputy. Natividade shook her head, no matter how much he explained that he did not want to be an orator or a minister but only to use the Chamber as a stepping stone to the Senate, where he had friends, persons of note, and that would last forever.

"Forever?" she asked with a thin, colorless smile.

"For life, I mean."

Natividade thought differently: his proper position was commercial and financial. She added that politics was one thing and commerce another. Santos answered by citing the Baron de Mauá, who blended the two. Then his wife

118

asserted in a dry, hard manner that no one became a deputy for the first time at the age of sixty.

"But its only a temporary step; senators are elderly."

"No, Agostinho," concluded the Baroness with a gesture of finality.

I am not counting Ayres, who probably would dance in spite of his years; neither do I mention Dona Perpetua, who would not even go. Pedro would go, and most likely he would dance, and a great deal, notwithstanding his passionate attachment to his studies. He was under the spell of medicine. Up in his room, besides the bust of Hippocrates, he had portraits of a number of European medical authorities, lots of engravings of skeletons, paintings of diseased parts, breasts cut vertically to show the veins, exposed brains, a cancer of the tongue, several cripples—all, things that his mother, for her part, would have had thrown out, but it was her son's "science" and that was enough. She contented herself with averting her eyes.

As for Flora, she was yet green and tender for the gyrations of Terpsichore, she was shy, or terrified, as her mother said. And this was the least; the worst was that with very little she would become weary, and if she could not go home right away would be ill the rest of the time. One will note that on the island she would have the sea around her, and the sea was one of her delights; but if she thought of the sea and began to console herself with the hope of gazing on it, there also occurred the thought that the dark night would take away her consolation. What a multitude of dependencies there are in life, sir! Things spring one from the other, intertwine, separate, mingle, lose themselves, and Time goes marching on without ever losing himself.

But where would Flora's boredom come from, if, indeed it came? With Pedro at the ball, no: he was, as you know, one of the two persons she was very fond of. Unless she was fonder of the one who was in São Paulo. A doubtful conclusion, since it is not at all certain that she preferred one to the other. If we have already seen her speak to both of them with the same affection, as she did now to Pedro in the absence of Paulo, and would do to Paulo in the absence of Pedro, there will be some lady among my readers, it never fails, who will suspect that there is a third . . . A third person would explain everything, a third who did not go to the ball, some poor student, with no other friend and with no more jacket to keep him warm than his green young heart. No, not even such a one, my curious lady, neither a third person, nor a fourth, nor fifth, nor anyone else. A funny girl, as her mother called her!

Never mind. The funny girl went to the ball on the Ilha Fiscal with her father and mother. Likewise Natividade, her husband, and Pedro; likewise Ayres, likewise the rest of the people invited to the great party. It was a fine idea of the government's, sir. Within and without, from the sea and from land, it was like a Venetian dream. That society lived several sumptuous hours, new for some, full of memories for others, for all fraught with the future—or at least for our friend Natividade, and for Baptista, the conservative.

Natividade pondered over the destiny of her sons, "things fated to be!" Pedro might well be the minister who would inaugurate the twentieth century and the Third Empire. She imagined another, greater, ball on that same island. She envisioned the decorations, saw the people, and the dancing, saw a whole great festival that would become a part of history. She too would be there, seated in a corner, not minding the burden of her years when she beheld the greatness and prosperity of her sons. It was thus that she peered into the time beyond, borrowing now on the felicity of the future, in case she should happen to die before the prophecies fell due. She had the same sensation that she had had earlier in the evening when she first saw that basket of lights in the tranquil darkness of the sea.

Baptista's imagination went less far than Natividade's. I mean, it stopped short of the beginning of the new century. God knows if not before the end of the year. At the sound of the music, at the sight of the gala dress, he heard some Carioca witches who resembled their Scotch sisters: At least the words were like the ones with which they greeted Macbeth: "All hail, Baptista, ex-Governor of a province!" "All hail, Baptista, next Governor of a province!" "All hail, Baptista that shall be Minister hereafter!" The language of these prophecies was liberal, without a hint of bad grammar. It is true, he was ashamed of listening to them, and he struggled to translate them into the old conservative idiom, but he did not seem to have any dictionaries handy. The first phrase still had the old-time accent, "All hail, Baptista ex-Governor of a province!" but the second and the last were both in that new, liberal tongue, which seemed to him like a colored man's dialect. Finally, his wife, like Lady Macbeth, told him with her eyes what the Scotch woman had said with her lips, that is, that she already felt within her those future greatnesses. She repeated the same thing to him the next morning, at home. Baptista, with a dissembling smile, denied the witches; but his memory echoed the words of the island: "All hail, Baptista, next Governor!" To which he replied with a sigh, "No, no, daughters of the devil . . ."

Contrary to what was said a while back, Flora did not grow bored on the island. My guess was bad; I hasten to correct myself. She might have grown bored for the reasons that were given, and for others I have spared the busy reader, but the truth is she passed a pleasant evening. The novelty of the festival, the sea close by, the ships lost in shadow, the city opposite on the mainland with its gas street lamps, below and above, along the shore and on the hillsides: here were new sights to enchant the swiftly passing hours.

She did not lack partners, nor conversation, nor joy in others and in herself. She shared the happiness of others with her whole heart. She saw, heard, smiled, then forgot all else to withdraw within herself. And she envied the Crown Princess who would one day become Empress, with absolute power to dismiss ministers and ladies, visitors and petitioners, and remain alone in the most hidden corner of the palace, taking her fill of contemplation or of music. This was the way Flora defined the function of governing. These were the ideas that flitted across her mind, and then returned. Once someone said to her, "Every free soul is an empress!"

It was not like the voice of the witches that spoke to her father, nor like the voice that spoke within Natividade about her sons. No, there may be many mysterious voices hereabouts, which, besides being wearisome and repetitious, may belie the reality of what actually happened. The voice that spoke to Flora came out of the mouth of old Ayres, who had come to sit beside her and had asked her, "What are you thinking about?"

"About nothing," answered Flora.

The Counselor had seen the look of something on the girl's face and insisted. Flora told him, as well as she could, the envy she felt at sight of the Princess, not because the Princess would one day glitter in the world but because she would be able to flee the glitter and the power whenever she wished to become the subject of herself. It was then that he murmured, "Every free soul is an empress." The phrase was apt, sonorous, and appeared to contain the greatest amount of truth there is on earth and among the planets. It was worth a whole page of Plutarch. If some politician had heard it, he could have kept it for his days of opposition to the government, when the Third Empire arrived. That was what Ayres wrote in his *Memorial,* along with this note: "The dear little thing thanked me for those five words."

XLIX   *The Old Signboard*

Everyone came back from the island with thoughts of the ball in their heads, many dreamed of it, some slept badly, or not at all. Ayres was one of those who awoke late: it was eleven o'clock. At noon he had breakfast, then he wrote his impressions of the evening before in his *Memorial:* he remarked upon certain lovely shoulder blades, made observations of a political nature, and ended with the words that closed the preceding chapter. He smoked, read, finally made up his mind to go to the Rua do Ouvidor. When he reached the front window he saw a strange figure in the door of the pastry shop opposite. It was old Custodio, and he was the picture of melancholy. It was such an unusual sight, that Ayres stood stock still several moments. During that brief time the owner of the shop raised his eyes and caught sight of him between the curtains, and, while Ayres went back inside, Custodio crossed the street and came to the front door.

"Have him come up," said the Counselor to his servant.

Custodio was received with the customary affability and a good bit more interest than usual. Ayres wanted to know what made him sad.

"I came to tell you just that, Your Excellency. It's the sign."

"What sign?"

"Will Your Excellency please see for yourself," said the shop owner, begging Ayres to do him the favor of going to the window.

"I don't see anything."

"Exactly! That's it. People kept advising me to have the sign fixed till I finally gave in and had it taken down by two of my employees. The whole neighborhood came out into the street to assist with the work, and they seemed to be laughing at me. I had already spoken to a painter on the Rua da Assembleia; we had not agreed on a price, because he wanted to see the job first. Yesterday afternoon off goes my clerk to the painter! And do you know, Your Excellency, what the painter told him to tell me? That the board is old and I need a new one, the wood won't hold paint. Off I go at full speed! I couldn't persuade him to paint over the same wood. He showed me where it was split and eaten away by bugs. Well, you couldn't see it from down below. I insisted that he paint over it anyway. He said he was an artist and would not turn out work that would be ruined right away."

"Then have it all done over. New paint on old wood isn't worth anything. This way, you'll see, it will last the rest of our lives."

"The old one would last too; all it needed was to have the letters touched up."

It was too late, the order had been dispatched: the wood was to be bought, sawed, and nailed, and the background painted on so that the title could be sketched in and painted. Custodio did not tell how the artist had asked him what color he wanted the lettering, whether red, or yellow, or green, on white—or vice versa, and how he had cautiously inquired as to the price of each color, in order to choose the cheapest. It is no concern of ours to know what color he chose.

Whatever the colors, they were new paint, on new boards, a renovation that he, more for the sake of economy than because of affection, had refused to make—but affection had a lot to do with it. Now that he was going to change the sign he felt as if he was losing some of his own flesh—a thing that other members of the same, or of a different, branch of commerce would not understand—such pleasure do they find in making over their faces and letting their renown grow with the new face. It is a question of one's nature. Ayres began to think of writing a Philosophy of Signs, in which he would put these and other observations, but he never got started on the work.

"Your Excellency will forgive me the bother I've caused you, coming and telling you this, but Your Excellency is always so kind to me, you speak with me in such a friendly manner, that I was bold enough to . . . You'll forgive me, won't you?"

"Of course, my friend."

"Although Your Excellency approves the replacing of the sign, you will feel with me the loss of the old one, the old friend that never failed me, that I displayed to the eyes of all on the nights of St. Sebastian and other festivals when the city was lighted up. And, when you retired, Your Excellency, you came home and found it in the same place as you had left it when you received your appointment. And I had the heart—the soul—to part with it!"

"That's all right! So it's gone! Now you must accept the new one, and you'll see, in a little while you'll be friends."

Custodio backed out of the room, as was his habit, and went haltingly down the stairs. In front of the pastry shop he paused a moment to look at the place where the old sign had been. He really did miss it.

". . . This event proves that anything can be loved, and dearly, even a piece of old wood. Believe me, it was not only the expense, which, of course, he felt, but it was also remembrance, heartache. No one tears himself loose like *that* from an object that was so intimate so integral a part of his business, of his very skin, because the sign had never once been lowered, for a single day. Custodio had no way of knowing that it had rotted away. It was always there, like the front door and the wall."

It was at dinner, in Botafogo. Just four persons, the two sisters, Santos, and Ayres. Pedro had gone to dine in São Clemente, with the Baptista family.

Dona Perpetua approved the pastryman's feelings. She cited the inkwell of Evaristo. Her sister smiled at her husband, and he at his wife, as if to say, "Here it comes!" It was an inkwell used by the famous journalist of the First Empire and of the Regency, a simple work, made of clay, the same as the inkwells that ordinary folk used to buy in stationery stores in those times, and still do to this day. Dona Perpetua's father-in-law had given it to her as a souvenir, he himself had had one of the same period, material and style.

"So it passed from hand to hand until it came to mine. It's not nearly so fine as Agostinho's and Natividade's inkwells, which are costly and fine, but it has great value for me."

"Of course," agreed Ayres, "political and historical value."

"My father-in-law used to say that out of it had come

the great articles of the *Aurora*. To tell the truth, I never read any of those articles, but my father-in-law was a truthful man. He knew all about Evaristo through hearing of it from others, and he used to praise him, endlessly . . ."

Natividade tried to turn the conversation to the ball of the evening before. They had already talked about it but she could think of no other diversion. Nevertheless, the inkwell lasted a while longer. It was not only one of Dona Perpetua's remembrances, a family heirloom, it was also one of her ideas. She promised to show it to the Counselor. He said he would see it with great pleasure. He confessed he had veneration for objects that had been used by great men. Finally dinner was over, and they went into the drawing room.

Ayres, speaking of Botafogo bay, said, "Here is a work that is older than Evaristo's inkwell and Custodio's signboard, and yet it appears to be younger, doesn't it, Dona Perpetua? The night is clear and warm, it might be foggy and cold and the effect be the same. The inlet does not differ from itself. Perhaps one day men will fill it up with earth and rocks, and build houses on top of it, a new neighborhood, with a big circus for horse racing. All is possible beneath the sun and the moon. Our good luck, Baron, is that we will die before then."

"Don't speak of death, Counselor."

"Death is a hypothesis," retorted Ayres, "perhaps a folktale. No one dies of good digestion, and your cigars are superb."

"These are new ones. You like them?"

"Superb."

Santos rejoiced in this praise: he considered it a judgment aimed straight at his person, his merits, his name, the position he held in society, his house, his estate, his Bank, his waistcoats. That is perhaps too much: it will serve as an emphatic way of explaining the strength of the bond between him and his cigars. They had as great value as the signboard and the inkwell, with the difference that the board and the inkwell signified only affection and veneration, whereas the cigars, valuable for their flavor and price, had the superiority of a miracle that reproduced itself daily.

These were the suspicions that roamed about through Ayres' brain, as he gazed mildly at his host. Ayres could not close his eyes to the aversion this man inspired in him. Not that he wished him any harm exactly. He might even have wished him well, if there had been a wall between them. It was his person, his feelings, his remarks, his gestures, his laugh, the whole soul of the fellow that offended him.

LI   *Here Present*

About nine o'clock or soon after, Pedro arrived with the Baptistas and Flora.

"We have brought your little boy home," Baptista said to Natividade.

"Thanks, Doctor," put in Santos, "but he is not of an age to go astray in these streets. And if he does go astray he'll soon find his way back to the straight and narrow," he added with a smile.

Natividade did not like the witticism, since it was about her son and spoken in her presence. It was perhaps an excess of modesty. That feeling tends to be excessive, and the sensible thing is to forgive it. There are also excesses in the other direction, in facile acquiescence, persons who enter with pleasure into an exchange of spicy allusions. They too must be forgiven. In short, forgiveness mounts to high heaven. Forgive others is the law of the Gospel.

The young man himself heard none of this. He had interrupted the conversation he was carrying on with Flora, and after exchanging a few words, the two young people retired to a corner where they again picked up the thread of their discourse. Ayres noticed their attitude; no one else paid any attention to them. Finally their conversation became an undertone; you could not hear it. She was listening, he was speaking; then it was the opposite: it was she who spoke and he was the one who listened—so absorbed in each other that they seemed unconscious of anyone else, but they were conscious. They possessed the sixth sense of conspirators and lovers. That they were talking of love is possible; that they were conspiring is certain. As for the matter of the conspiracy, you will learn of it later, shortly, a chapter from now. Ayres himself found out nothing, however much he tried to fill his eyes with that dialogue of mysteries. He was persuaded it was not serious because they smiled often; but it might have been intimate, secret, personal, or, even something external to them: say a string of anecdotes or a long story that did not really concern them, because there are states of soul in which the matter of the story is nothing, the pleasure of telling and of hearing it is everything. Yes, it may have been so.

But see how nature guides the least or the greatest things, especially if fortune lends a hand. The conversation, to all appearance, so smooth, began with something unpleasant. The cause was a letter from Paulo to his brother that Pedro showed Flora, mentioning to her that he had shown it to his mother and it had made her very angry.

"With you?"

"With Paulo."

"But what did the letter say?"

Pedro read her the principal point, which was almost

the whole letter: it concerned the military question. Even in those days there was the "military question," a conflict of generals and ministers, and Paulo's verbiage was against the ministers.

"But why did you show the letter to your mother?"

"Mama wanted to know what he said."

"And now she's angry, there you are, she'll probably scold him."

"So much the better. Paulo needs to mend his ways. But, tell me, why do you always defend my brother?"

"So as to have the right to defend you too, sir."

"Then he has already said something bad about me?"

Flora started to say "yes," then "no," in the end she said nothing. She broke off, changed the subject by asking why they were always at sword's points. Pedro denied that they were. On the contrary, they got along well together. They might not have the same opinions, and it might be too that they did have the same taste . . . From here to saying they were both in love with her was a comma; Pedro was slow about working up to the final period that would close the sentence. This cunning fox was also timid. Later, he saw that he had done well in keeping still, and he gave himself credit for the decision, but it was not true, he had not made any decision. I don't say this to his discredit: no, because fear often acts judiciously, it is my duty to set down this reflection at this point.

Then came wrath. Flora said no further word, and if the choice had been hers she would not have dined, such pity did she feel for the absent brother. Luckily, the absent one was this one before her, here present with eyes that were present, hands that were present, words that were present. It was not long before wrath fled away before charm, gentleness, and adoration. Blessed are those who remain, for they will be compensated.

A Secret

Here is the matter of the conspiracy. In the street, coming from São Clemente, after the best part of the time had been wasted on the letter, and at dinner, Paulo got a chance to reveal a secret to her.

"Aunty told us that Dona Claudia had told her in secret (don't mention it) that your father is going to be named governor of a province."

"I don't know anything about it but I don't believe it, because Papa is a conservative."

"Dona Claudia told Aunty he is a liberal, almost a radical. It seems the governorship is certain. She made Aunty promise not to mention it, and when Aunty told us she made us promise not to speak of it either. And I beg *you* not to say anything about it, but it's true."

"How could it be? Papa doesn't have anything to do with liberals. You have no idea how conservative Papa is. If he defends the liberals it's because he is tolerant."

"If the province were Rio de Janeiro I'd like it, because you wouldn't have to move to Praia Grande, and even if you did, the trip is only a half-hour and I could go there every day."

"You think you could?"

"Want to bet?"

After a moment, Flora said, "What's the use, if there's no governorship?"

"But suppose there is?"

"It's a lot to suppose—that there is a governorship and that it is Rio de Janeiro. No, no, there's nothing."

"Then suppose only half—that there is a governorship and that it is Matto Grosso."

Flora shivered. Without admitting the appointment possible, she trembled at the name of the province. Pedro went on to mention Amazonas, Pará, Piauhy . . . It was the infinite, especially if her father gave a good administration, because then he would not return to Rio so soon. Already she was offering fewer objections, finding it possible, and abominable, but this she said only to herself, within her own heart.

Suddenly Pedro stopped in his walking: "If he goes, I will apply for the position of secretary and go too."

The intermittent light from the shops, shining on the young girl's face, as they passed by, added to that of the street lamps and showed the emotion caused by that promise. It was plain that Flora's heart must have been beating hard. Soon, however, she began to think of something else. Natividade would never consent to it; besides, a student . . . No, it was out of the question. She conjured up a scandal. That he would flee, take ship, go after her . . .

All this was seen or thought in silence. Flora was not surprised at thinking such things, and so boldly: it was like the weight of her body, which she did not feel: she walked and thought, as she breathed. She did not even count the time she was wasting in building up ideas and demolishing them. That it gave her more pleasure than displeasure is sure. At her side, Pedro walked along thoughtfully, attentively, with his eyes on his feet, his feet in the clouds. He did not know what to say in the midst of such a long silence. Meantime he decided there was but one solution. He was no longer thinking about the governorship of Rio. He wished himself away with her to the most remote corner of the Empire, without his brother. The hope of exiling himself from Paulo put forth green leaves and flourished in Pedro's soul. Yes, Paulo would not go along, their mother would not be forsaken. To lose one son, no matter, but both . . .

If anyone should find the end of this monologue egotistical, I beg him by the souls of his relatives and friends that are in heaven to weigh the causes. Consider the young man's state of soul, the nearness of the young lady, the roots and blossoms of passion, the very age of Pedro, the evil of the earth, the good of the same earth. Consider further the will of Heaven, which watches over all its creatures that they may love one another—except if one loves with an unrequited love, for then heaven is an abyss of misery, and this image does not apply. Consider everything, friend, and let me go on telling the story by myself, telling it badly—what took place in that short trip between the two houses. When they arrived they were talking with their lips.

There inside, as you have seen, they went on talking until the subject of the governorship came up again. Flora then noted the cautious insistence with which Ayres kept looking in their direction as if he were trying to divine the subject of their conversation. She was sorry that he was not there with them, listening, speaking, finally promising to do something for her. He could—he was her friend, and all held him in high regard—he could intervene and demolish the project of the governorship.

Without willing it, without knowing it, she said this very thing to the old diplomat with her eyes. She withdrew them, but they went of themselves and repeated the monologue and perhaps asked something that Ayres did not hear and that would have been interesting. It may have been that they reflected the anguish, or whatever it was that caused the pain there inside. It may have been. The truth is that Ayres began to be curious, and the moment Pedro left his place to answer a call from his mother, *he* left Natividade to go speak with the young lady.

Flora had already risen to her feet; there was scarcely time to exchange two words, of the kind that cannot be broken off without sadness, or at least without impatience. Ayres asked her if he had ever told her that he had psychic powers.

"No, Senhor."

"Well I have. I divined just now that you want to tell me a secret."

Flora was astonished. Unwilling either to deny it or to confess the truth of it, she answered that he had divined but half.

"And the other half . . . ?"

"The other half is to ask a favor of you as a friend."

"Ask."

"No, not now, we're leaving. Mama and Papa are already saying goodbye. Only if it is in the street. Would you like to accompany us to São Clemente?"

"With the greatest of pleasure."

LIII   *Confidences*

You understand of course that it was not. It was not with pleasure great or small. It was a burden imposed by society, once Flora had made the request—I do not know whether discreetly or not. If you add to this a sort of desire to know a certain secret, I am not one to deny it, nor are you, nor even he. After a few moments, Ayres began to feel that this girl awoke gentle voices within him, voices that were dead or sleeping or unborn, paternal voices. The twins had given him the same feeling one day, only because they were the sons of Natividade. Now, it was not the mother, it was Flora herself, her gesture, her speech, and perchance, her inescapable fate.

"I really believe that this time she is caught, she has finally made up her mind," thought Ayres.

Flora spoke to him of the governorship, but she did not ask him to keep it secret, as the others had done. She confessed she did not want to go away from here, no matter where. And she ended by saying that everything was in his hands. Only *he* could dissuade her father from accepting the governorship. Ayres found her request so absurd that he almost burst out laughing, but he restrained himself. Flora spoke gravely and sadly. Ayres gently replied that he could do nothing.

"You can, you can. Everyone pays attention to your counsel."

"But I don't give counsel to anyone," he said. " 'Counselor' is a title the Emperor conferred on me because he thought I deserved it. But it does not obligate me to give counsel—he's the only one I'll give it to, if I'm asked for it. Now just imagine if I went to a man's house or ordered him to come to mine to tell him that he should not be a governor. What reason would I give him?"

The young lady did not have reasons, she had need. She appealed to the talents of the ex-Minister to find a proper reason. But there was no call for reasons, it was enough if he spoke, used the art that God had given him to please everybody, to pull them his way, to influence them, to get what he wanted. Ayres saw that she was exaggerating to draw him in, and he found it not unpleasant. Nevertheless, he disclaimed having such accomplishments and virtues. God had not given him any art at all, he said, but the young lady kept insisting that he had, until Ayres stopped demurring and made a promise.

"I'll think about it. Tomorrow or the day after, if I come upon an idea, I'll have a try at the business."

It was a palliative. It was also a way of putting an end to the conversation, for the house was nearby. He had not counted on Flora's father, who needs must show him, at that hour, a *novelty*—in other words, an old thing, a document of diplomatic value.

"Come, come on up; it won't take more than five minutes, Counselor."

Ayres sighed in secret, and bowed his head to Fate. One can't struggle against Fate, you will say: the best thing is to let her take us by the hair and drag us which way she pleases, whether to exalt us, or to hurl us headlong. Baptista did not even give him time to reflect. He was all apologies.

"Five minutes and you will be free of me, but, you'll see, it will be worth the sacrifice."

The study was small, few books but good ones, solemn furniture, a portrait of Baptista in his governor's uniform, a calendar on the desk, a map on the wall, a number of souvenirs of his administration of the province. While Ayres cast his eyes about, Baptista went to get the document. He opened a drawer, took out a portfolio, opened the portfolio and took out the document, which was not alone, but with other documents. One recognized it at once by the old, yellowed paper, in places eaten away. It was a letter from the Count de Oeyras to the Portuguese Minister in Holland.

"It's antiques day," thought Ayres, "the signboard, the inkwell, this autograph . . ."

"The letter is important, but lengthy," said Baptista. "We can't read it now. Would you like to take it along?"

He did not give Ayres time to answer, but took a large envelope, put the manuscript in it, and wrote this note on the outside, "To my very distinguished friend, Counselor

136

Ayres." While he was doing this, Ayres let his eyes wander over the backs of some of the books. Among them, there were two handsomely bound *Reports* of Baptista's administration.

"Don't attribute such extravagance to me," said the ex-Governor. "It was a present from the Governor's Secretariat. They had never done this for anyone. They were a very distinguished staff." And he went to the bookcase and took down one of the reports for better viewing. When it was opened it showed the imprint and the vignettes; if it were read it would show the style on the one hand, and on the other the prosperous state of the finances. Baptista limited himself to the total figures: expenditures, one thousand, two hundred and ninety-four contos, seven hundred and ninety milreis; receipts, one thousand, five hundred forty-four contos, two hundred and nine milreis; balance, two hundred and forty-nine contos, four hundred and nineteen milreis. Verbally, he explained the balance, which he obtained by a modification of certain services and by a slight increase in taxes. He reduced the province's debt, which he had found in the three hundred and eighty-four thousands and left in the three hundred and fifty thousands. He constructed new works and made important repairs, began a bridge . . .

"The binding befits the contents," said Ayres by way of concluding the visit.

Baptista closed the book and retorted that he could not leave without granting him a conference. "Everything topsy-turvy," he concluded. "In the morning *I* grant conferences, now, at night, it is I who seek them."

This was the introit, but it is a long way from the introit to the Creed, and for him the main part of the Mass was the Creed. Not having a prayer-book text handy, he explained a seal, a gold pen, a copy of the Penal

Code. The Code though old, was worth thirty new ones, not that it was any better to all outward appearances, but because it contained annotations written in the hand of a great jurist, So-And-So. Having passed a large part of his life outside the country, Ayres scarcely recognized the name of the author of the notes, but as soon as he heard him called *great* he assumed the appropriate expression. He picked up the Code with care, read some of the notes with veneration.

During all this time Baptista was gathering wind. He had framed a sentence with which to initiate the conference, and was only waiting for Ayres to close the book in order to utter it, but the Counselor kept lingering over his examination of the Code. It might have been a touch of malice, but it was not. Ayres' eyes had a strange power—not so strange as one would think, because others possess it though they may not mention it. It happened that his eyes did not leave the page, but in reality they had already withdrawn their attention from it: time, people, life, things past, rose up to peer at him from behind the book that had been their contemporary, and Ayres again saw a Rio de Janeiro that was not this one, or only faintly suggested it. Do not imagine that it was only criminals and judges, there were walks and pleasure trips, streets, merrymaking, gay old dogs, old and dead, fresh young blades now rusty as himself. Baptista coughed, Ayres came back to earth and read some of the notes that Baptista must have known by heart, how profound they were! Finally, he admired the binding, found the book well preserved, closed it and restored it to the library.

Baptista did not lose an instant, he came immediately to the point, for fear of seeing Ayres pick up another book.

"I admit I am of a conservative temperament."

"I too hang on to old presents."

138

"It's not that: I am referring to a political temperament. There really are opinions, and . . . temperaments. A man may very well have a temperament that is contrary to his ideas. My ideas, if one compares them with the political programs of the world, are more liberal than not, some of them are *very* liberal. Universal suffrage, for example, is for me the cornerstone of a good representative government. The liberals, on the contrary, demanded, and forced through a bill, that the vote be given only to taxpayers. Today I am more progressive than they are. I accept what we now have, for the present, but before the end of the century it will be necessary to revise some of the articles of the Constitution—two or three."

Ayres concealed his amazement . . . Invited, thus, at this hour . . . A profession of political faith . . . Baptista kept insisting on the distinction between his *temperament* and his *ideas*. Certain old friends, who were familiar with this moral and mental duality of his, persisted in wanting him to accept a governorship. He didn't want to. Frankly, what did the Counselor think?

"Frankly, I think you are wrong."

"Wrong in what?"

"In refusing."

"Strictly speaking, I did not refuse . . . It's a difficult decision, and my wish is," he added with more clarity, "that my good and sagacious friends tell me if such a thing would be wise. It doesn't seem to me that it is . . ."

"I think it is."

"So that if you, sir, were in this position . . ."

"With me it could not happen. As you know, I am no longer of this world, and, politically speaking, I never had a part in anything. Diplomacy has the effect of separating its functionary from the parties and keeping him so far from them that it is impossible to express an opinion with verity, or at least with assurance."

"But didn't you say you thought . . . ?"

"I did."

". . . that I could accept a governorship, if they offer it to me?"

"You can; a governorship is not something to be turned down."

"You shall know the whole thing. You are the only one of our acquaintance to whom I have unbosomed myself so frankly. The governorship *was* offered to me."

"Accept, accept."

"I have."

"Already?"

"The appointment is to be signed Saturday."

"Then accept my congratulations as well."

"Confidentially, it was not the Minister's idea; on the contrary, the Minister did not reach a decision until he knew whether I had actually waged a campaign against the liberals, some years ago. As soon as he learned, however, that it was for not persecuting them that I was dismissed, he accepted the recommendation of the heads of the party, and soon after I received this note."

The note was in his pocket, inside his billfold. Another man, flustered at the prospect of the nomination, would have taken time in finding the note among the other papers, but Baptista was an old hand. He took out his billfold, calmly opened it, and with his fingers drew out the Minister's note inviting him to an interview. In the course of the interview, everything had been settled.

LIV   *Finally, Alone!*

Finally, alone! When Ayres found himself in the street, alone, free, loose, handed over to himself, without let or hindrance, he breathed deep. He started a monologue, which he shortly interrupted as he remembered Flora. Everything she had determined should not happen was going to happen: there was her father on his way to the governorship, and she with him, and her recent fondness for Pedro would be over before it had half begun. Nevertheless, he did not repent what he had said, and still less what he had not said. The die was cast. Now it was a matter of turning his attention to other things.

LV   *"Woman Is Man's Undoing"*

On taking leave, Ayres had made a reflection that I will place at this point, in case one of my readers has also made it. The reflection was the result of astonishment, and the astonishment arose out of seeing how a man, so difficult when it came to yielding to his wife's promptings (Get thee behind me, Satan, etc., Chapter XLVII), could so easily toss overboard all his previous convictions. He could think of no explanation, nor would he ever have found one if he had not learned, as they told him later, that the initial steps of the husband's conversion had been taken by the wife. "Woman is man's undoing," said some socialist philosopher, I believe it was Proudhon. It was she, the widow of the governorship, who by various secret means schemed to enjoy a second marriage. By the time *he* learned of the courtship, the banns had already been published: there was nothing left but consent and marry also.

Even so, it was hard for him. The outcry of his party dinned in his ears beforehand, his soul wandered blind and dizzy; but his wife served as guide and staff, and, in a few hours, Baptista saw clearly and stood firm.

"We are on the threshold of the Third Empire," Dona Claudia said thoughtfully, "and surely the liberal party will not soon fall from power. Its men are powerful, the inclination of the times is toward liberalism, and even you . . ."

"Yes, I . . ." sighed Baptista.

Dona Claudia did not sigh; she sang the victory song, her husband's ellipsis was the first figure in the dance of acquiescence. She did not say this bluntly and to his face, neither did she show unseemly joy. She continued to speak the language of cold logic and of inflexible will. Baptista, sensing the support, walked straight toward the abyss and made the leap into the dark. He did not do it without grace, nor with grace. Though the will he had put on was a borrowed one, he was not lacking in desire —to which his wife's "will" gave life and soul. Hence the authority in which he clothed himself and so made his confession.

This was Ayres' conclusion, as one may read it in the *Memorial*. This will be the reader's, if he cares to conclude. Note that I have spared him Ayres' work; this time I did not oblige him to find out everything for himself as he has been obliged to do on other occasions. For, the attentive, truly ruminative reader has four stomachs in his brain, and through these he passes and repasses the actions and events, until he deduces the truth which was, or seemed to be, hidden.

LVI   *The Blow*

The following day brought the maiden Flora the great news. The appointment was to be signed on Saturday; the province was in the North. Dona Claudia did not see her grow pale, nor feel her cold hands, and went on talking of the event and of the future, until Flora, in an attempt to sit down, almost fell.

Her mother ran to her side: "What is it? What's the matter?"

"Nothing, Mama. It's nothing."

Her mother helped her into the chair.

"A dizzy spell. It's gone."

Dona Claudia gave her some vinegar to smell, rubbed her wrists. Flora smiled.

"This Saturday?" she asked.

"The appointment? Yes, this Saturday. But don't tell anyone yet. State secrets. It's all arranged; finally, someone has done right by us, probably the Emperor. Tomorrow you will go shopping with me. Make a list of what you need."

Flora needed not to go and thought only of this. Now that the appointment was about to be signed there was no use arguing against it; the only thing now was for her to stay behind. But how? All dreams are found in the slumber of a child. It was not easy, but it would not be impossible. Flora believed in everything. She had not withdrawn her hopes from Ayres, and there was Natividade. The two of them could do it, or rather the three of them if you counted the Baron, and, if his sister-in-law came along, four. Join to these four the five stars of the Southern Cross, the nine muses, angels and archangels, virgins and martyrs . . . Join them all, and together they could accomplish this simple act of preventing Flora from going to the province. These were the vague, momentary hopes that came to take the place of the sadness in the young girl's face, while her mother, attributing the effect to the vinegar, replaced the glass stopper and put the bottle back on the dressing table.

"Make a list of what you need," she repeated to her daughter.

"No, Mama, I don't need anything."

"Yes, you do, I know what you need."

LVII   *Shopping*

I would not write this chapter if it was really about shopping, but it is not. Everything is an instrument in the hands of Life. The two ladies left the house, one sprightly and cheerful, the other melancholy, and off they went to select a quantity of articles for traveling and for personal use. Dona Claudia was thinking about dresses for the first reception and for calls, she also designed, in her mind's eye, an outfit for the disembarkation. Her husband had asked her to buy him some ties. Hats, however, were the principal article on her list. The woman's hat, in Dona Claudia's opinion, is what gives the true stamp of the taste, manners, and culture of a society. It's not worth the trouble to accept the office of governor and then wear hats that have no charm, she would say—without conviction, however, because deep in her heart she knew that the office conferred charm on everything.

It was while they were sitting in the hat shop, Rua do Ouvidor, their eyes far away, that the true subject matter of this chapter appeared, the twin, Paulo. He had arrived on the night train, and, learning that they had gone out shopping, had come to look for them.

"You!" they exclaimed.

"I arrived this morning."

Flora had risen, from excitement caused by the unexpected sight of Paulo. He hurried toward them, grasped their hands, asked after their health, and observed that they looked well and happy. His impression was correct: Flora now had a liveliness that contrasted with her low spirits all that sad morning, and wore a smile that made her gay.

"I have had news of you, ladies, that Mama sent me, and Pedro too sometimes. From you, Senhora, I received two letters. How is the doctor?"

"Well."

"At last, here I am!"

And Paulo divided his eyes between them, but the greater share naturally went to the daughter. Soon it was practically all for her, and little for the mother. Dona Claudia returned to the selection of hats, and Flora, who till then had expressed her opinion with her head, forgot to make even that gesture. Paulo took the chair an employee brought him, and sat looking at the girl. They spoke of trivial things, about others or about themselves, anything that served to hold them in a veiled contemplation of each other. Paulo was the same as he had always been, the same as Pedro, and yet with a certain individual stamp that she could not make out clearly, still less define. It was a kind of mystery; Pedro had his.

Dona Claudia interrupted them, from time to time, apropos of a choice; but everything ends, even the choosing of hats. They went from there to dresses. Paulo, though he had not heard of the governorship, thought highly of it for the opportunity it gave him of accompanying them from store to store. He related anecdotes of São Paulo, which held no great interest for Flora. The news she gave him about girls of her acquaintance was more or less dispensable. Any subject was good enough for their purpose. The street fostered this reciprocal absorption: the people who came and went, ladies or gentlemen, whether they stopped or not, served as the point of departure for a digression. The digressions finally began to turn to silence, and the young man and woman went their way with bright eyes and heads high, but he more so than she, because a shade of melancholy had begun to drive the hour's happiness from the young girl's face.

On the Rua Gonçalves Dias, as they went toward the Largo da Carioca, Paulo saw two or three politicians from São Paulo, republicans, and, if one could judge, planters. As he had left them there, he expressed surprise at seeing them here, without reflecting that the last time he had seen them was some time past.

"Do you know them?" he asked the two ladies.

No, they did not know them. Paulo told them their names. The mother perhaps would have asked some question of a political nature, but then she noticed she had neglected to buy a certain article and suggested they go back. The two young people agreed with docility in spite of the veil of sadness that was closing over the girl's face. Those purchases were like one-way tickets, the steamship would not be long in coming, they would make haste with their baggage, the arrangements, the farewells, hasten to their cabins, to seasickness, and to that other sickness, that surfeit of sea and land that would surely kill her, thought Flora. Her silence grew; Paulo had more and more difficulty in breaking through it; and yet she enjoyed being with him, liked to hear him tell various things, some new, others old, recollections from the time before he had left here and gone to São Paulo.

So they let themselves go on, piloted by Dona Claudia, who had almost forgotten about them. In the midst of that fragmentary conversation, which was sustained by him rather than by her, Paulo felt an impulse to ask her, secretly in her ear, there in the street, if she had thought of him, or at least dreamed of him sometimes at night. If she should say no he would give way to a burst of anger, would utter the most abusive and insulting reproaches. If she should run, he too would run and catch her by the ribbons of her hat, or by the sleeve of her dress, and, instead of strangling her, he would dance a waltz with her, a Strauss waltz, or a polka by ***. Then he would laugh at these delusions, because, in spite of the girl's melancholy, the eyes she raised to him were the eyes of one who has dreamed and thought much about a person and is trying to discover if he is the same as the one in the dream and in her thoughts. So it seemed to the law student, for when he turned away his face and then looked back again, it was again to see her eyes keenly regarding him with the same critical air of infinite scrutiny. As for the time the three of them spent in that activity of purchases and choices, visions and comparisons, there is no record of it, nor is one necessary. Time is properly the function of a watch, and not one of them consulted his watch.

LVIII   *To Kill the Longings*
of the Heart

Now you have seen how Flora received Pedro's brother, just as she would have received Paulo's. Both were apostles. Paulo found her prettier than she had been some months before and he told her so that same afternoon, in São Clemente, with these simple and heartfelt words, "You have become quite elegant and grown-up, Senhora."

Flora thought the same thing about the law student but she did not give voice to her impression. Either her present unhappiness, or some other personal feeling, made her shy at first. It was not long, however, before she once more found the brother in his twin, and both he and she began to kill their hearts' longings.

How one kills the heart's longings is not a thing that can be explained in a clear, straightforward manner. One does not use either fire or sword, rope or poison, and yet the longings expire, to rise again, sometimes before the third day. There is many a person who believes that, even though dead, they are sweet, more than sweet. This point, in the present instance, cannot be gone into; nor do I ever intend to enlarge upon it, as perhaps I should.

The longings died, not all of them, nor right away, but part of them and so slowly that Paulo accepted an invitation to dinner. It was the day of his arrival: Natividade had intended to have him at home for dinner, along with Pedro, to cement the peace proceedings initiated by absence. Paulo did not even take the trouble to send home word. He stayed on with the beautiful young woman, between her father and her mother who were thinking of another matter, near in time and remote in space. Knowing what it was, Flora passed from contentment to annoyance, and Paulo did not understand this alternation of mood. From time to time, when he saw her mother disturbed and uneasy, but with a different expression, he questioned the daughter. Instead of making some casual explanation, once, Flora passed her hand before her eyes and remained several seconds without uncovering them. The response of the law student should have been to pull away her hand, bring his eyes close to hers, closer, very close, and repeat the question in such a way that the eloquence of the gesture would remove the necessity for words. If he had any such idea, it did not emerge into the light of day, nor did it allow him more time than it took to ask, "What's wrong?"

"Nothing," answered Flora.

"There is something," he insisted, intending to take her hand.

He did not finish the gesture, he did not even begin it; he barely opened and closed his fingers. Meanwhile Flora smiled to shake off her sadness and went on killing her longings.

LIX   *Night of the 14th*

Everything was explained that night, at the home of the Santos family. The ex-Governor of a province confessed his hopes of a new investiture; his wife affirmed the imminence of the act. Hence the publishing of the news, which, a little while before, Dona Claudia would tell only in secret. There were no longer any secrets to keep silent.

Paulo learned of the whole thing for the first time. Pedro, who was familiar with some of the preliminaries, finally learned the rest. Both, naturally, were saddened by the coming separation. Pain made them friends for a matter of seconds; it is one of the advantages of that great and noble sensation. I no longer remember who it was that affirmed, on the contrary, that a common hatred is what binds two persons most tightly together. I believe this is so, but I do not disbelieve in my postulate, because one thing does not prevent the other, and both can be true.

Besides, the pain was not yet despair. There was even a consolation for the twin brothers, that is, the girl would be far from both. Neither of them would have the favored place beside her door. There is no evil that does not have its good side, and it is for this reason that evil is useful, many times indispensable, on occasion delightful. Both young men had hoped to speak to their dear little friend in private, in order to sound her out about this separation, now that it was certain, but neither got his wish. They kept an eye on each other, yes indeed. When they talked to her it was always together, and of familiar, ordinary things. Flora's looks did not betray her state of soul: it might have been joyful, melancholy, or indifferent, it did not come through. In truth, she spoke little. Her eyes did not say much either. More than once, Pedro caught her gazing at Paulo and groaned at the preference, but later he too was the favored one, and he felt compensated; then it was Paulo who ground his teeth, figuratively speaking. Natividade, busy with her reception, which was the last of the season, did not closely follow the spiritual restlessness of that trio. When she noticed it, she too felt the same trouble.

Little by little the party was breaking up. It was not large, and a note of intimacy prevailed. When most of them had gone, there remained only the *most* intimate group: three or four men in one corner of the drawing room, telling, and laughing over, witty remarks and anecdotes. They were not talking about politics, though matter was not lacking. The young ladies, for the second or third time, were exchanging their impressions of the recent *grand ball*. They also talked of orchestras and theaters, of the coming festivities at Petropolis, of those who would go that year and of those who would not go until January. Natividade divided herself among them all; finding a few seconds for Ayres, she confided to him her fear about her sons' affections, and at the same time the pleasure she felt at the hope of a long separation from Flora. Ayres did not gainsay her fear, nor her hope.

"It's a blessing that Baptista should be appointed and take his daughter away from here," she said.

"To be sure, but . . ."

"But what?"

"To be sure, he will take her; it may be that you do not know that girl very well, Senhora."

"I think she is good and kind."

"I think so too. Goodness, however, and kindness have nothing to do with the rest of the person. Flora is, as I said some time ago, a mystery. It's getting late or I'd explain the basis of my impression, some other time perhaps. Remember, I am very fond of her, I find a particular charm in her, in the contrast of a person at once so human and so far from the world, so ethereal and so ambitious at the same time, with a hidden ambition . . . you'll pardon these muddled words. Till tomorrow," he ended, holding out his hand to her. "Tomorrow I'll come back and explain them."

"Explain them now, the others seem to be busy laughing at a funny story."

It is true, the men were laughing at some witticism or pun. Ayres started to speak but checked his tongue and excused himself. The explanation would be long and difficult, and it was not urgent, he said.

"I myself don't know if I understand myself, Baroness, nor if what I think, is the truth; it may be. In any case, my dear friend, till tomorrow, or until Petropolis. When do you expect to go up?"

"Toward the end of the year."

"Then we'll still see each other a few times."

"Yes, and if you do not come to see me, I want you to see my boys, to receive them and hold them dear. They hold you in great esteem, though they do you no more than justice. Pedro considers that you are the finest, and Paulo that you are the most vigorous, intellect in our land . . ."

"Just see how you have brought them up, Senhora,

teaching them to think wrong," said Ayres with a smile and a gesture of thanks. "I vigorous?"

"The most vigorous and the finest intellect in the land."

The last of the habitual guests had come to say good night to their hostess. Ten minutes later Ayres took his leave of the Santoses.

The night was clear and tranquil. Ayres recast a part of the evening, preparatory to writing it down in his *Memorial*. A few lines, but interesting ones, in which Flora was the principal figure. "May the devil understand her if he can. I, who am less than he, can never hit upon understanding her. Yesterday I thought she was in love with one, today it was the other. A little before she left tonight it was both. I've seen this kind of alternating, and simultaneous, emotions before; I myself have been one thing, and its opposite, and yet I always understood myself. But that child-woman . . . The circumstance of their being twins may perhaps account for the double inclination. It may be too that some quality is lacking in one and running over in the other, and vice versa, and she, because of her love for both, cannot make up her mind. It is fantastic, I know. It would be less fantastic if they, doomed to enmity, should find in this one woman a narrow field of hate, but this would explain them, not her . . . Be that as it may, our political organization is useful: the governorship of a province, by taking Flora away from here for a certain time, will remove her from the situation in which she finds herself like Buridan's ass. When she comes back, the water will have been drunk and the barley eaten. An appointment will lend a hand to nature."

This done, Ayres got into bed, recited an ode of his beloved Horace by way of a prayer, and closed his eyes. Still, he did not fall asleep. He tried a page of his beloved

Cervantes, then one of his beloved Erasmus, closed his eyes once more, until he fell asleep. It was not for long: at twenty minutes to six he was up. In November, you have no doubt that it is day.

L X   *Morning of the 15th*

Whenever the thing just described happened to him, it was Ayres' habit to take an early walk, for amusement and a breath of air. He did not always meet with these, however. This time he went to the Passeio Publico. He arrived at half past seven, entered, went up on the terrace and looked out to sea. The sea was rough. Ayres began to walk back and forth the length of the terrace, listening to the waves, and coming close to the edge from time to time to see them break and recede. He liked them so, he found in them a kind of strong soul that made them move and throw fear into the land. The water, spiraling back on itself, gave him the feeling, more than of life, of a being that was not without nerves or muscles, and a voice to roar its anger.

Finally he grew tired, went down the steps, walked toward the lake, to the grove of trees, wandering at random, reliving men and things, till he finally sat down on a bench. He noticed that the few people who were there were not seated, as they usually were, gazing at random, reading magazines or sleeping off a night spent out of bed. They were standing, talking among themselves, and to others that came up and joined in the conversation without knowing the speakers, so it seemed to him at least. He heard an occasional word, *Deodoro, battalions, Campo, ministry,* etc. Some of the words, uttered in a loud voice, were perhaps sent in his direction to see if they would awake his curiosity and obtain one more ear for their news. I do not swear this was so, because the day was long ago, and the people were strangers to me. Ayres himself, if he suspected such a thing, did not mention it to anyone, nor did he strain his ears to catch the rest. On the contrary, he happened to think of some personal matter and wrote a note in pencil in his memorandum book. It was enough to scatter the group of curious bystanders, though they did not leave without first uttering laudatory epithets, some for the government, others for the army: he might be a friend of one or the other.

When Ayres went out of the Passeio Publico, he suspected something, and walked on as far as the Largo da Carioca. Little talking, and in subdued tones, astonished faces, people just standing, figures that turned in their path and hurried away, but no news that was clear or complete. In the Rua do Ouvidor, he learned that the military had carried out a revolution: he heard descriptions of the march, of the leaders, and contradictory reports of the outcome. He went back to the square, where three tilburies fought over him; he got into the nearest one, and told the driver to take him to Cattete. He did not ask the driver anything: *he,* however, told him the whole thing and a lot more. He told of a revolution, of two ministers killed, one gone into hiding, the rest thrown in jail. The Emperor had been seized in Petropolis and was being brought down the mountainside.

Ayres glanced at the driver, whose words came forth sweet with news. He was not unknown to him, this person. He had seen him before, without his tilbury, in the street or in the drawing room, at church, or on board ship; he was not always a man, sometimes he was a woman, dressed in silk, or in calico. He decided to learn more, assumed an expression of interest and curiosity, and finally asked him if what he said had really happened. The driver related how he had heard the whole story from a man he picked up on the Rua dos Invalidos and took to the Largo da Gloria, and the fellow was terrified, could hardly speak, asked him to hurry, said he would pay him double—and he did.

"Perhaps it was someone mixed up in the business," suggested Ayres.

"That could be, because his hat was mashed in, and, at first, I thought he had blood on his fingers, but I looked more closely and saw that it was clay, he must have climbed over a wall. But, now that I think of it, I believe it was blood: clay doesn't have that color. The fact is, he paid double the regular price, and rightly, because the city is not safe, and a person runs great risk carrying people from one end of it to the other . . ."

At this point they arrived at Ayres' door: he ordered the driver to stop his vehicle, paid the regular fare, and got out. As he climbed the stairs, he was probably speculating as to what really happened. At the top, he found his servant, who had heard about the whole thing and asked him if it was certain . . .

"What is there that is not certain, José? It's more than certain."

"That they killed three ministers?"

"No, there was only one . . . wounded."

"I heard that there were even more people, they mentioned ten dead . . ."

"Death is a phenomenon like life: perhaps the dead live. In any case, don't pray for their souls, because you are not a good Catholic, José."

How is it that Ayres, having heard reports of the death of
two or three ministers, confirmed only the wounding of
one minister in putting his servant's information straight?
It can only be explained in two ways—either as proceed-
ing from a noble sentiment of pity, or from the opinion
that all public report magnifies the event by two-thirds at
least. Whatever may have been the reason, his version of
the wounding was the true one. A little while later there
passed along Rua do Cattete the stretcher on which was
borne one, wounded, minister. Learning that the others
were alive and sound, and that the Emperor was expected
from Petropolis, he did not believe in the change of government he had heard about from the cab driver and
from his servant José. He reduced it all to a disturbance
that would end in a simple change of personnel.

"We shall have a new cabinet," he said to himself.

He breakfasted tranquilly, reading Xenophon: "One
day I considered how many republics had been overthrown by citizens who wanted another form of government, and how many monarchies and oligarchies are destroyed by the uprising of the people; and of all the men
that rise to power how some are soon overthrown, others,
if they endure, are admired as clever and fortunate. . . ."
You know the author's conclusion, as he seeks to prove
the thesis that man is hard to govern; but soon the figure
of Cyrus demolishes that conclusion, showing a single
man who ruled millions of other men who not only
feared him but even strove against one another to do his
will. All this in Greek, and with so many pauses that he

reached the end of his breakfast without reaching the end of the first chapter.

LXII   *"Stop on the* d"

"But, His Excellency is having breakfast," the servant was saying on the landing to someone who wanted to speak to the Counselor.

It was false, Ayres had just finished his breakfast, but the valet knew that his employer liked to enjoy an after-breakfast cigar without interruption. He was on the settee in the front room and heard the dialogue on the stairs. The man insisted on having a few words with Ayres.

"Impossible."

"All right, I'll wait. As soon as His Excellency finishes . . ."

"The best thing is to come back later. Don't you live just across the street? Well then, come back in an hour or two . . ."

It was Custodio and he went home, but the old diplomat, when he knew who it was, did not wait to finish his cigar: he sent word for him to come over. Custodio came out of his place, ran across the street, up the stairs, and entered with a look of terror.

"What's this, Senhor Custodio?" asked Ayres, "Are you mixed up in revolutions?"

"I, Senhor? Ah! Senhor! If Your Excellency only knew . . ."

"If I knew what?"

Custodio explained. We will abridge his explanation.

On the day before, since he had to go downtown, Custodio went to the Rua da Assembleia, where his sign was being painted. It was already late in the day; the painter had stopped work. Some of the letters had been painted —the word *Confeitaria* and the letter *d*. The letter *o* and the word *Imperio* were only outlined in chalk. He liked the paint and the color, was reconciled to the shape; it was only the expense he found hard to forgive. He recommended speed. He wanted to inaugurate the sign on Sunday.

When he awoke in the morning he did not learn right away of what had taken place in the city, but little by little the news began to reach him, he saw a battalion go by and began to believe that those who claimed there was a revolution and hinted at the Republic were telling the truth. At first, in his astonishment, he forgot about the sign. When he remembered it, he saw that it was necessary to hold up the painting. He hastily wrote a note and sent a clerk to the painter. The note said only this: "Stop on the *d*." Indeed there was no use painting the rest, which would be wasted, nor to waste the beginning, which could be used. There would be some word that could take up the space of the remaining letters. "Stop on the *d*."

When the messenger returned he brought word that the sign was already finished.

"Did you see it and it was already finished?"

"I did, Boss."

"It had the old name?"

"Yes, it did, sir: *Confeitaria do Imperio*."

Custodio slipped into an alpaca coat and flew off to the Rua da Assembleia. There was the signboard, and it was covered with a piece of calico. Some young men who had seen it as they were going down the street decided to break it to pieces. The painter, after defending it with eloquent words, concluded it would be more expedient to cover it. When the curtain was drawn, Custodio read,

Confeitaria do Imperio. It was the old name, the proper, the celebrated name, but it was ruination now. The sign would not last one day, even in a dark alley, let alone on the Rua do Cattete . . .

"You will paint out all this, Senhor," he said to the painter.

"I don't understand. You mean that you will pay for this job and then I will paint something else."

"But what will you lose by replacing the last word with another one? The first word can stay, and even the *d* . . . Didn't you read my note?"

"It came too late."

"And why did you paint it, after such grave events?"

"You were in a hurry, Senhor, and I got up at half past five to accommodate you. When they brought me the news, the sign was already finished. Didn't you tell me you wanted to hang it Sunday? I had to put a lot of drier in the paint, and besides the paint, I spent time and effort."

Custodio tried to refuse the work, but the painter threatened to put the number of the pastry shop and the name of its owner on the sign and display it so that the revolutionaries would go and break his windows in Cattete. There was nothing for it, he had to capitulate. He told the painter to wait, he was going to think about a substitution, in any case he would like some little reduction in the price. He got a promise of the reduction and went home. On the way, he thought of what he would lose by changing the name—such a well-known shop, for so many years! Devil take the revolution! What name would he give it now? And then he thought of his neighbor Ayres and hurried over to get his opinion.

When he had reported the above, Custodio disclosed all
the money he had lost on the name and the other expenses, the trouble that the preservation of the shop's
name would cause him, the impossibility of finding another name, an abyss of woe in short. He did not know
where to turn, he did not have any ideas or any peace of
mind. If he could, he would liquidate the pastry shop.
And, after all, what did he have to do with politics? He
was a simple maker and seller of sweets, esteemed, with a
host of customers, respected, and especially a respecter of
public order . . .

"But what's the trouble?" asked Ayres.

"The Republic has been proclaimed."

"There's already a government?"

"I think there is. But tell me, Your Excellency, have
you ever heard anyone accuse me of attacking the government? Nobody ever has. And yet . . . A cruel stroke of
Fate! Come to my rescue, most honored sir! Help me to
get out of this difficulty. The sign is finished, the name all
painted, *Confeitaria do Imperio,* the paint is bright and
nice. The painter insists on my paying for the work before
he does any more. If the sign were not finished I would
change the name, no matter how painful it would be for
me, but must I lose the money I've spent? Do you believe,
Your Excellency, that if *Imperio* remains, they will
come and break my windows?"

"Well, I don't know."

"Really, there is no reason why they should. It's the

name of the shop, has been for thirty years, no one knows it by any other name . . ."

"But you could call it *Confeitaria da Republica* . . ."

"This occurred to me, on my way home, but it also occurred to me that if in a month or two from now there is a counter-revolution, I'll be in the same spot I'm in today, and once again lose money."

"You are right . . . Sit down."

"I'm all right."

"Sit down and have a cigar."

Custodio refused the cigar, he did not smoke. He accepted the chair. They were in Ayres' study, where there were curiosities that would have attracted his attention, if it had not been for his distraught state of mind. He went on imploring his neighbor to rescue him. His Excellency, with the great intelligence that God had given him, could save him. Ayres proposed a middle term, a name that would fit both contingencies, *Confeitaria do Governo.*

"It will serve as well for one political system as another."

"I don't say that it won't, and, if it weren't for the money I've lost . . . There is, however, one thing against it. Your Excellency knows that there is no government that doesn't have an opposition. When members of the opposition come down the street they may pick a fight with me, get the idea that I am defying them, and break up my signboard, while all I want is the respect of everybody."

Ayres understood very well that fear went hand in hand with avarice. To be sure, his neighbor did not want rows at his shop door, nor gratuitous ill will, nor the hatred of no matter whom, but he was no less terrorized by the expenditures he would have to make from time to time if he did not find a name that was definitive, popular, and impartial. In losing what he had, he had already lost celebrity, besides losing the cost of the painting and having to pay more money to boot. No one would buy a condemned, criminal signboard from him. It was bad enough to have his name and the name of his shop in the Laemmert *Almanac* where some busybody might read it and come with others to punish him for what had been printed way back at the beginning of the year . . .

"Oh, no, Senhor," interrupted Ayres, "there is no need for you to withdraw the whole edition of an almanac from circulation."

And after several moments: "Look, I'll give you an idea that may prove useful, and if you do not think it good I have another ready, and it will be the last. But I believe that either of them will serve. Leave the signboard painted as it is, and, to the right, on the lower edge below the name, paint in these words to explain the name, Founded in 1860. Wasn't it in 1860 that you opened the shop?"

"It was," answered Custodio.

"Well then . . ."

Custodio reflected. One could read neither *yes* nor *no* in him. Astonished, mouth half open, he kept looking not at the diplomat, nor at the floor, nor at the walls or furniture, but at the air. As Ayres insisted, he came to and admitted that it was a good idea. As a matter of fact, it would keep the name and take from it its seditiousness, which had increased with the fresh paint. Still, the other idea might be as good or better, and he wanted to compare the two of them.

"The other idea does not have the advantage of showing the date of the founding of the house, but only that of defining the name, which will remain the same, but in a manner unconnected with the monarchy. Let the word *imperio* stand and add below it, in the center, these two words that need not be large, *das leis—of law*. Look, like this," concluded Ayres, seating himself at the secretary and writing what he had said on a strip of paper.

Custodio read it, reread it, and thought the idea practical: yes, it was not bad. He saw only one defect in it: Since the letters below were smaller, they might not be seen so quickly and easily as those above, and it was these that hit a person in the eye as he walked along the street. And so, some politician, or even a personal enemy, might not understand right away, and . . . The first idea, when he came to think of it, had the same drawback, and besides this additional one: it might appear that the pastryman, in marking the date of the establishment, was making a trademark of being old. Who knows if it was not worse than nothing?

"Everything is worse than nothing."

"Let's try to think of something else."

Ayres thought of another name, the name of the street, *Confeitaria do Cattete,* without noticing that since there was another pastry shop on the same street, it meant assigning the local designation exclusively to Custodio's. When his neighbor made this weighty observation Ayres found it just and rejoiced to see the fellow's delicacy of feeling, but he soon discovered that what made Custodio speak out was the idea that the name would be common to the two shops. Many people would not bother to look for the sign but would buy at the first shop they came to, so that he alone would have the expense of painting the sign, and on top of it would lose customers. On perceiving this, Ayres was no less struck with admiration at the sagacity of the fellow, who, in the midst of so many tribulations, was able to calculate the bad results of an ambiguous word. Then, he told him, the best thing was to pay the expense he had incurred and not put up anything, unless he preferred his own name: *Confeitaria do Cus-*

todio. Many people, surely, did not know the shop by any other name. A name, the owner's own name, did not have any political significance or historical aspect, hatred or love; it had nothing to attract the attention of the two rival political systems and consequently put his St. Clare turnovers in jeopardy, not to mention the lives of the proprietor and his employees. Why didn't he adopt this proposal? He would spend something on the changing of one word for another, *Custodio* in place of *Imperio,* but revolutions always entail expense.

"Yes, I'll think about it, most honored sir. Perhaps it will be best to wait a day or two, to see where the fad will end," said Custodio, and he expressed his thanks.

He bowed, backed away, and left. Ayres went to the window to see him cross the street. He imagined that he would carry away from an ex-minister's house a special glow that would momentarily make him forget the crisis of the signboard. Expenses are not everything in life, and the glory of one's connections can soothe the roughnesses of this world. It did not happen this time. Custodio crossed the street without stopping or looking back, and disappeared into the pastry shop with all his despair.

LXIV   *Peace!*

That, in the midst of such grave happenings, Ayres could summon the repose and lucidity to imagine he would find such a thing in his neighbor can be explained only by the incredulity with which he had received the news. Even Custodio's distress did not cause him to have faith. He had been in at the birth, and at the death, of many a false rumor. One of his maxims was that man lives to be the first to spread idle gossip in the street, and that anything will be believed by a hundred persons together, or separately. It was only at two o'clock in the afternoon, when Santos entered his house, that he gave credence to the fall of the Imperial Monarchy.

"It's true, Counselor. I saw the troops march down the Rua do Ouvidor, I heard the cheers for the Republic. The shops are closed, the banks also, and the worst is if they never open again and we fall into public disorder. It's a disaster."

Ayres tried to calm him. Nothing would change; the administration yes, it was possible, but one can also change one's clothes without changing one's skin. Business is a necessity. Banks are indispensable. By Saturday, or at the latest by Monday, everything would return to what it was the day before, minus the Constitution.

"I don't know, I am fearful, Counselor."

"Have no fears. Does the Baroness know what has happened yet?"

"When I left the house, she didn't, but now she probably does."

"Then, go calm her fears. She is probably beside herself with anxiety."

Santos was worried about firing squads: if they should shoot the Emperor and with him society people? He cited the Terror . . . Ayres took the Terror out of his head. It's the occasion that makes the revolution, he said, without intending to rhyme, but he was pleased to have made the rhyme: it gave a fixed form to the idea. Then he mentioned the gentle nature of the people. The people would change governments without hurting anyone. There would be acts of generosity. To prove what he was saying, he related a story that had been told him by an old friend, Marshal Beaurepaire Rohan. It was in the time of the Regency. The boy-emperor had gone to the Theatro de

São Pedro de Alcantara. After the show, Ayres' friend, then a young man, heard a great uproar from the direction of the church of São Francisco, and ran to find out what it was. He spoke to a man who was roaring with indignation and learned that the Emperor's coachman had not taken off his hat when the former had come to the door to get into the coach. And the man added, "I am a *ré* . . ." In those days, the republicans, for the sake of brevity, were so called. "I am a *ré,* but I will not tolerate any lack of respect to that boy!"

Not one of Santos' features evinced the slightest appreciation or comprehension of that anonymous act of heroic generosity. On the contrary, his whole being appeared to be submerged in the present, in the moment, in the closing down of business, in the banks without operations, the fear of a total suspension of commerce for an indefinite time. He crossed and uncrossed his legs. Finally he got up and sighed.

"Then, you think? . . ."

"That you should relax."

Santos approved of the advice; but he did not approve of following it, and his outward appearance was quite different from the state of his heart. His heart was beating. His whole head was crumbling to dust. He tried to leave, but he made two or three sallies before he managed to set foot outside the study and start toward the stairs. If he could only be sure! Although he had seen and heard the Republic, it might be . . . In any case, peace was what was needed, and would there be peace? Ayres inclined to think so and again urged him to relax.

"See you later," he said.

"Why don't you come have dinner with us?"

"I have to dine with a friend, in the Hotel dos Estrangeiros. Afterwards perhaps, or tomorrow. Go on, go reassure the Baroness and the boys. Will the boys be at peace?

They are fighting, no doubt. Go and straighten them out."

"You could help me in this, Senhor. Come over tonight."

"Maybe, if I can I will. Tomorrow for sure."

Santos went out. His carriage was waiting, he got in, and drove off toward Botafogo. He did not have peace within him, he could not take it to his wife nor to his sons. He was anxious to get home, because of his fear of the street, but he also wanted to remain in the street because he did not know what to say to those at home, or what advice to give them. The space in the carriage was small, yet enough for one man, but, after all, he could not stay there all afternoon. And yet, the street was quiet. He saw people at the doors of shops, in the Largo do Machado people laughing, others silent; there was astonishment but not what one would call alarm.

LXV   *With the Sons*

When Santos got home, Natividade was uneasy, and without exact and definite news of what had happened. She did not know about the Republic. She did not know the whereabouts of her husband nor of her sons. He had left the house before the first report of anything; the boys had made ready to do the same as soon as the rumors began to arrive. The mother's first impulse was to keep her sons from leaving, but it was too late. Since she was not able to stop them, she begged the Virgin Mary to spare them, and waited. Her sister did the same. It was almost noon, and then the minutes began to seem like centuries.

The anxiety of the mother was naturally greater than that of the aunt. Natividade saw time drag by with leaden feet. There was no excitement, no commotion, to tie a pair of wings to those long hours on the hall clock nor on the watch at her waist or at her sister's: time limped by on all the minute hands and hour hands. Finally she heard carriage wheels on the gravel of the drive: it was Santos.

She ran to the landing. Santos came up, both stretched out their hands and grasped the other's hands. Their long life together had made tenderness a grave and spiritual thing. And yet, it seemed as if the husband's gesture was not original, but secondary, the son or echo of the wife's. It may be that the cord of sensibility on his lyre was less vibrant than hers, even though, many years before, that other gesture, in the coupé, when they were returning from the Mass at São Domingos', remember? . . . I have just written a few lines on this, which would not be bad if I finished them, but I checked myself in time and scratched them out. It is not worth the trouble to try to read words that have been scratched out. It is less worthwhile to complete them.

Let the four clasped hands suffice. Natividade asked about her sons. Santos told her not to worry. There was nothing, everything seemed to be as it had on the day before, the streets were quiet, faces calm. There would be no bloodshed, business would go on as usual. All of Ayres' animation had now burgeoned in him, with the same green vigor, and the same style.

The sons did not get home till late, at different times— Pedro earlier than Paulo. The melancholy of one was in harmony with the soul of the house; the joy of the other sounded a discordant note. But such was one and the other—melancholy and joy—that, in spite of the expansiveness of the second, there was no repression, no fighting.

At dinner they spoke little. Paulo related the events, with a lover's eloquence. He had talked with some of his coreligionists and learned what had taken place during the night and in the morning, the joining of the battalions on the Campo, Ouro Preto's words of command to Marshal Floriano, and the reply of the latter, the acclamation of the Republic. His family listened and asked questions, they did not argue, and this moderation contrasted with Paulo's jubilation. Pedro's silence especially was like a challenge. Paulo did not know that his mother had begged it of his brother, with many kisses—a reason that, at such a moment, harmonized with his heaviness of heart.

Paulo's heart, on the other hand, was liberated, it let his joy circulate with his blood. His republican sentiments, on which his principles were overlaid, were now so strong and ardent, that they scarcely permitted him to see Pedro's dejection and the constraint of the others. At the close of dinner he drank to the Republic, but quietly, without ostentation, only looking toward the ceiling and raising his glass just a bit higher than usual. No one replied with either gesture or word.

To be sure, young Pedro would have put in a loyal word of pity relative to the Imperial Monarch and the persons of the Braganças, but his mother never took her eyes off him, as if imposing silence, or begging him not to speak. Besides, he did not believe that anything was changed: in spite of the decrees and proclamations, Pedro imagined that everything could remain as before, with only a change of government personnel. "It won't be much trouble," he said in a low tone to his mother, as they left the table, "it's only a matter of the Emperor speaking to Deodoro."

Paulo went out right after dinner, promising to come home early. His mother, who was afraid of his getting

mixed up in some row, did not want him to leave, but
another fear made her consent—this fear was that the two
brothers would fight after all. Thus one fear conquers another, and we end up giving what we have refused. It is
no less certain that she weighed the arguments for several
minutes before making a decision in the same way that I
have written a page before the one I am going to write
now; but both of us, Natividade and I, after all, let the
action take place, without opposition from her, or comment from me.

LXVI   *The Ace of Clubs and*
                            the Ace of Spades

The usual guests came, bringing news and rumors. These
did not change much and in general there was no real
opinion as to the outcome. No one knew whether the
success of the revolt was a good or an evil, they only knew
that it was a fact. Hence the ingenuousness with which
someone proposed the usual game of ombre, and the
alacrity with which the others accepted the proposal. Santos, although he declared he would not play, had the
cards and the counters put out; but the others said they
still lacked a player, and it was no fun without him. He
tried to stand fast: it was not seemly on the very day the
Monarchy had fallen, or was going to fall, to indulge in
social pleasures . . . He did not utter this opinion in a
loud voice nor in a low one, but to himself, and perhaps
he read it in his wife's face. He could have found an
excuse for standing fast, if he had looked for one, but
friends and cards would not let him look for anything.
Santos finally gave in. Perhaps it was his inner desire all

along. There are many such desires that have to be enticed outside in the form of a favor or concession of the person. In short, the ace of clubs and the ace of spades performed their function that night, in the same way as the moths and the mice, the winds and the waves, the light of the stars and the sleep of the citizens.

LXVII *The Whole Night Long*

When he left the house, Paulo went to a friend's and together they went in search of others their age and of their circle. Then they went to the newspapers, to the barracks on the Campo, and spent some time in front of Deodoro's house. It delighted them to see the soldiers, on foot or on horseback, they asked leave, spoke to them, offered them cigarettes. It was the soldiers' only concession, accepting the cigarettes: none of them told what had taken place, not all of them knew anything.

No matter, the young men were filled with self-importance. Paulo was the most enthusiastic and the most convinced. The others had only their youth, which is a program, but Santos' son had firm belief in all the ideas of the new system and he himself had still other ideas that did not seem to have been accepted: he would fight for them. He even wished someone in the street would let out a yell, now seditious, so that he could break the man's head with his cane. It might be remarked that he had forgotten, or lost, his cane. He did not notice that he did not have it; if he had, he would have been satisfied with his arms and hands.

He proposed singing the *Marseillaise:* the others refused to go to such lengths, not out of fear but from exhaustion. Paulo, whose resistance to fatigue was greater than theirs, suggested they wait for the dawn.

"Let's wait for it on the top of a morro, or on Flamengo beach. We'll have time to sleep tomorrow."

"I can't," one of them said.

The others repeated the refusal, and they agreed to go to their several homes. It was nearly two o'clock. Paulo went with them, and only after seeing the last one home did he set out alone for Botafogo.

When he went in the house he found his mother waiting for him, uneasy and sorry that she had let him go out. Paulo could think of no excuse, and reproved his mother for waiting up for him. Natividade said she could not sleep before she knew that he was home safe and sound. They spoke in a low tone and but little; having exchanged a kiss before, they kissed again afterward, and said good night.

"Look," said Natividade, "if you find Pedro awake, don't tell him anything nor ask him any questions. Go to sleep, and tomorrow we'll find out everything that happened tonight."

Paulo entered the bedroom on tiptoe. It was still that vast room in which the two brothers had fought over the two engravings, Robespierre and Louis XVI. Now there was more than portraits, there was a revolution no more than a few hours old and a brand new government. Following his mother's advice, Paulo refused to discover whether Pedro was asleep, though he suspected he was not. As a matter of fact, he was not. Pedro saw Paulo's precautions and *he* followed his mother's advice: he pretended not to see anything. So far the advice prevailed, but a touch of jubilation moved Paulo to warble between his teeth, in a low tone, to himself, the first strophe of the *Marseillaise,* which his companions had vetoed on the street:

Allons, enfants de la patrie,
Le jour de gloire est arrivé!

Pedro recognized it more by the tune than the words, and decided that his brother's intention was to hurt him. It was not, but it could have been. He hesitated between a retort and silence, until a fantastic idea crossed his mind —to warble, also in a low tone, the second part of the strophe: "Entendez-vous dans vos campagnes . . ." which alludes to foreign troops, but to turn it from its natural, historical sense and restrict it to the national troops. It was a revenge that was unfulfilled, the idea passed quickly. Pedro contented himself with simulating the supreme indifference of sleep. Paulo did not finish the strophe; he got undressed, still excited, without taking his thoughts off the victory of his political dreams. He did not get into bed right away; first, he went over to his brother, to see if he was asleep. Pedro was breathing so naturally, as if he had not lost anything, that he had an urge to wake him up, to shout at him that he had lost everything, if the institution they had overturned *was* anything. He drew back in time and went and got between the sheets of his own bed.

Neither slept. While they waited for the sleep that would not come, they kept thinking of the happenings of the day, both amazed at how easy and swift they had been. Then they thought about the next day and the ultimate effects. Do not be surprised that they did not arrive at the same conclusion.

"How the devil did they do it without anyone suspecting?" mused Paulo. "It could have been rougher. There was a conspiracy, to be sure, but a barricade would have been nice. Be that as it may, the campaign was victorious. What is needed now is not to let the iron grow cold but to keep striking and keep it hot. Deodoro cuts a fine figure.

They say that his entrance into the barracks, and his sally-ing forth at the head of the battalions, were magnificent. Perhaps too easy: it's just that the Monarchy was rotten and fell of itself . . ."

While Paulo's head was turning out such ideas, Pedro's was thinking the contrary; he called the revolution a crime. "A crime and an absurdity, besides being an act of ingratitude. The Emperor ought to seize the ringleaders and execute them. Unfortunately, the troops were on their side. But it's not over yet. This is a straw fire; it's soon out, and things will be as before. I'll find me two hundred brave lads, ready and willing, and we'll knock over this rickety pile of lath and plaster. It has a look of solidity, but it's nothing. They'll see, the Emperor won't leave, and, even if he doesn't want to, he'll go on ruling or his daughter will, and, lacking her, his grandson. The Em-peror himself ruled when he was still a boy. There'll be time; everything is roses now. But there is still a handful of men . . ."

The final ellipsis of both these speeches means that the ideas were growing frayed, misty, and confused until they disappeared, and the boys slept. During their sleep, the revolution ceased, and the counter-revolution, there was neither Monarchy nor Republic, Dom Pedro II nor Mar-shal Deodoro, nothing with the slightest odor of politics. One and the other dreamed of the lovely inlet of Bota-fogo, of a clear sky, a bright afternoon and a single person—Flora.

LXVIII   *In the Morning*

Flora opened the eyes of both of them and vanished so quickly that they could scarcely see the hem of her dress and hear a sweet word, soft and faraway. They looked at each other without apparent ill will. The fears of one and the hope of the other struck a truce. They ran to see the newspapers. Paulo half out of his mind; he feared there had been some betrayal toward dawn. Pedro had a vague idea of restoration and expected to find in the papers an Imperial decree of amnesty. Neither betrayal nor decree. Hope and fear were gone from this world.

LXIX   *At the Piano*

While they were dreaming of Flora, she did not dream of the Republic. She had one of those nights in which the imagination also sleeps, without eyes or ears, or at most, the retina does not let one see clearly and the ears confuse the sound of a river with the faraway barking of a dog. I cannot give a better definition, though this one is not precise; each of us has surely had such mute, rayless nights.

She did not even dream of music, and yet that evening she had played some of her beloved pages. She played them not only because she loved them, but also to escape from her parents' pain, which was great. Neither of them could believe that the institutions had fallen, that others had sprung into being, and everything changed. Dona Claudia still invoked the morrow for help and asked her husband if he could look into the future, and what did he see? He would bite his lips, slap his thigh, get up, take a few steps, and again tell over what had happened, the reports stuck up at the doors of newspapers, the imprisonment of the ministers, the situation, everything wiped out, gone, gone, gone . . .

Flora was not averse to pity nor to hope, as you know,

but she did not share her parents' agitation and took refuge with her piano and music. She chose some sonata or other. It was enough to free her of the present. For her, music had the advantage of not being present, past, or future: it was a thing outside time and space, pure idea. Whenever she stopped, she would hear some disconnected phrase of her father's or of her mother's: ". . . But how did it happen that? . . ." "Everything on the sly . . ." ". . . any bloodshed?" Sometimes, one of them made a gesture, but she did not see the gesture. Her father, whose soul was unsteady, said a great deal and all of it incoherent. Her mother had a new vigor. She had reached the point where she would fall silent for a few moments as if she were thinking. This was unlike her husband: when he stopped speaking he scratched his head, clasped his hands or sighed, when he was not threatening the ceiling with his fist.

"La, la, do, re, sol, re, re, la," said their daughter's piano, with these or other notes, but they were notes that sounded in order to escape men and their dissensions.

One can also find in Flora's sonata a kind of harmony with the present hour. There was no real government. The young girl's soul was like that first white streak of the dawning day or the last faint glow of twilight—as you prefer—when nothing is so clear, or so dim, that it tempts you to leave your bed, or to light the candles. At most, there would be a provisional government. Flora did not understand forms or names. The sonata gave her the feeling of an absolute lack of government, the anarchy of primitive innocence in that nook of Paradise that man lost through disobedience and will one day win again when perfection brings eternal and unmatched order. Then there will be neither progress nor turning backward, but stability. Abraham's bosom will shelter everything and everybody, and life will be a marvelous spectacle. That is what the keys were saying without words, re, re, la, sol, la, la, do . . .

LXX   *About a False Conclusion*

The events kept happening as fast as the flowers bloomed. And some of the flowers were used for the last ball of the year; others had died the day before. Poets of one and the other regime borrowed an image from the fact to sing the joy and the sadness of the world. The difference was that the second smothered its sighs while the first prolonged its victory dances to great lengths. The metal of trumpets has a different sound from that of harps. But the flowers kept on blooming and dying with the same profusion, the same regularity.

Dona Claudia gathered the roses of the last ball of the year, the first of the Republic, and adorned her daughter with them. Flora submitted and accepted them. Baptista, above everything, a family man, accompanied his wife and daughter to the ball. Paulo went too, because of the young lady and because of the regime. If, in his conversation with the ex-Governor of a province, he told him all the good he thought of the provisional government, he did not hear answering words of accord, nor of opposition. He did not penetrate deeper into the man's confidence, because the young lady attracted him and he was more fond of her than of her father.

Flora saw a similarity between the ball on the Ilha Fiscal and this one, although this was a private ball, and unpretentious. It was given by someone who had been associated with the republican cause from the very beginning, and one of the ministers came though only for a half-hour. This was the reason for Pedro's absence, in spite of his being invited. Flora missed him, as she had missed Paulo on the island: this was the similarity between the two balls. Both meant the absence of one twin.

"Why didn't your brother come?" she asked.

Paulo fell silent. Then after a few moments he said, "Pedro is stubborn. It was his stubbornness that made him refuse the invitation. He probably thinks that the art of dancing perished with the Monarchy. Don't pay any attention; he's a lunatic."

"Don't say that."

"Do you too think that dancing perished with the Empire?"

"No, the proof is that we are dancing. No, I mean that you should not call him bad names."

"Does he seem to you to be a sensible young man?"

"Certainly, like you, Senhor."

"But . . ."

Paulo was going to ask her which of them, if she had to swear devotion to one or the other, would receive her solemn oath; but he reconsidered in time. Then she spoke of the heat, and he thought so too, that it was hot. He would have thought it was cold, if she had complained of the cold. Flora too, if it were only a question of letting her eyes guide her, could have accepted all of Paulo's opinions, just to be in harmony with him. In truth, he now had a bold, radiant air; he held his head high, firm in the belief that it was his writings of the year before that had created the Republic, imperfect though it was without certain ideas that he had put forth and defended, and that were bound to come someday soon. These were the things that he said to her, and she listened with pleasure, without an opinion; it was just the love of listening to him. When the thought of Pedro rose in her mind, sadness dimmed her joy, but joy soon vanquished sadness, and so ended the ball. Then the two of them, sadness and joy, took shelter in Flora's heart like the twin daughters they were.

The ball ended. But the chapter shall not end without allowing a little space for anyone who wishes to speculate about that girl. Neither her father nor mother could understand her, neither could the young men, and probably Santos and Natividade less than anyone. You, milady, mistress of the art of making love, or student of it, you, who listen to various young men, will conclude that she was . . .

I can't bear to write the name of the practice. If it were not for the obligation to tell the story with the right words, I would prefer not to mention it, but you know what it is, so here goes. You have concluded that Flora was a coquette, and your conclusion is wrong.

Milady reader, it is best to deny it right now rather than wait for Time to do it. Flora was not acquainted with the delights of love-making, and still less could she be called a practised coquette. The practised coquette is a plant fed on hopes and sometimes on realities, if the calling demands and the occasion permits. It is also necessary to remember the saying of a great publicist, son of Minas and of the last century, who ended up a senator and used to say against his adversaries the ministers, "Mangoes don't grow on pitanga trees." No, Flora took no notice of her admirers.

The proof of this is that in the state where she lived several months in 1891, with her father and mother, for the reason I will explain later, not one of them obtained a friendly glance from her, or even a kind glance. More than one young man wasted his time in throwing himself in her way and showing his captivation. More than one necktie, more than one cane, more than one pince-nez directed its colors, gestures, and glass at her without any-

thing more than a courteous acknowledgment, and perchance a word of no account.

Flora thought only of the twins. If neither of them
could forget her, they were never out of her mind either.
On the contrary, she wrote to Natividade by every post, so
that she might be remembered by both of them. The letters said little about the land or the people, said nothing
bad or good; they overworked the words "longing" and
"heart's longing," which each of the two brothers took to
himself. They too wrote letters to Dona Claudia and Baptista, with the same double and mysterious intention,
which she understood very well.

This is the way they were when they were apart, she
and they. The ancient discord that divided the brothers in
life continued to divide them in love. They might each
have loved his own young lady, married her, and had each
his own children, but they preferred to love the same woman and not see the world through other eyes, nor hear a
better word, nor different music, before, during, and after
Baptista's mission.

LXXI   *The Mission*

There, the word escaped me. Yes, her father was given a
mission: I do not know anything about it, neither did she.
A hush-hush business. Flora called it a mission to hell.
Her father, without going to such a depth, mentally
agreed with her; orally, he denied the truth of this
definition.

"Don't say that, Flora. It is a confidential mission for
noble political ends."

I think this was true, but to know from this the actual,

specific object of the mission was another matter. Neither is it easy to understand how this governmental gift fell into Baptista's hands. We know that he did not scorn the choice when a close friend ran to summon him to the palace of the Generalissimo. He recognized that it meant that they saw in him great finesse and capacity for work. It is no less certain, however, that he loathed the whole idea of the job from the start, although in the official correspondence he said exactly the contrary. If such letters showed the hearts of people, Baptista, whose instructions were all concerning peace and unity, intended to bring peace and unity by means of fire and sword, but the style is not the man. Baptista's heart was locked when he wrote, and he let his hand go ahead, with the key to his heart tight-clenched in it . . . "It's already time," sighed the muscle, "it's time we got the office of Governor."

As for Dona Claudia, she hated to see the mission end, for it had restored political activity to her husband. There was only one thing lacking in it—an opposition. No newspaper said anything bad about him. The pleasure of reading the vilifications of his adversaries every morning, of reading and rereading them with all their bad names like cat-o'-nine-tails that tore her flesh and at the same time thrilled her—this pleasure was denied her by the secret mission. On the contrary, there seemed to be a kind of bet on to find the emissary just, equitable and concilia-tory, worthy of admiration, a model of citizenship, of spotless character. All this she had experienced in the old days, but to have any flavor it had to be laced with re-bukes and slanders. Without these it was flat and watery. Besides it did not have the ceremonial side that the higher office imposed; still, attentions *were* paid them, and that was something.

181

The Return

When Marshal Deodoro dissolved the National Congress on November 3, Baptista recalled the time of the liberal manifestos and decided to make one. He even began it, in secret, employing the fine phrases that he had by heart, Latin quotations, two or three apostrophes. Dona Claudia pulled him back from the brink of the precipice, with clear, robust reasons. First of all, the measure might prove to be a blessing. Liberty often serves its own purposes by appearing to stifle liberty. In the second place, it was the man who had proclaimed the Constitution that now invited the nation to say what it wanted and to amend this same Constitution, except for the essential parts. The Generalissimo's word, like his sword, was enough to defend and consummate the work he had begun. Dona Claudia did not have the correct style, but she knew how to communicate the warmth of her arguments to a man who was willing. After listening and thinking, Baptista patted her majestically on the shoulder.

"You are right, my child."

He did not tear up the paper he had written. He intended to keep it, just as a souvenir and the proof is that he was going to write a letter to the President. Dona Claudia took this idea out of his head also. There was no need to send him his vote; it was enough to remain on his mission.

"Isn't the government satisfied with you?"

"Yes."

"When it notes that you remain at your post, it will conclude that you approve, and that is enough."

"Yes, Claudia," he agreed after a few moments. "And, on the contrary, anything I wrote against the seditious assembly that the President has just dissolved might seem to be a lack of loyalty. Peace to the dead! You are right, my child."

He remained silent, on the job, faithful to the instructions he had received. Twenty days later, Marshal Deodoro passed the reins of government to Marshal Floriano, Congress was reconvened, and all the decrees of the third annulled.

On learning these facts, Baptista meditated suicide. He remained speechless for several moments, and Dona Claudia could not find the least bit of encouragement to give him. Neither had counted on the rapid march of events, one on top of the other with such a confused trampling that they were like a horde of people in flight. Only twenty days, twenty days of force and tranquillity, of hopes and great future. One day more, and all came tumbling down like an old house.

It was now that Baptista perceived the error of having listened to his wife. If he had finished and published his manifesto on the fourth or on the fifth, he would now have a strong document with which he might rightfully claim some post of honor—or even if it were only esteem. He reread the manifesto; he even considered printing it, incomplete as it was. It had fine turns of expression, like this one: "The day of oppression is the eve of liberty." He quoted *la belle Roland* on her way to the guillotine: "O Liberty, how many crimes are committed in thy name!" Dona Claudia pointed out that it was too late, and he agreed.

"Yes, it was too late. On that earlier day it would not have been too late, it would have come at the proper moment, with sure effect."

Baptista distractedly crumpled the paper; then he

183

smoothed it out and put it away for safekeeping. After that, he conducted an examination of his conscience, profoundly and sincerely. He should not have given in; it would have been better to have held out. If he had held out against his wife's words, his situation would be quite different. He searched himself, and decided it was so, he could have closed his ears and gone ahead. He clung to this idea. If he had been able, he would have turned time backward and shown how the soul by itself chooses the better party. There was no need to know of what had happened before; his own sense told him that in an identical situation with that of the third, he would do something quite different . . . Oh! to be sure!

An official letter or telegram came, removing Baptista from the confidential mission. The trip back to Rio de Janeiro was brief and sad, without the epithets that had regaled him for some months, or the escort of friends. Only one person was happy, his daughter, who had prayed every night for the termination of that exile.

"It seems you are pleased at your father's misfortune," her mother said to her after they were on shipboard.

"No, Mama, I am happy to see the end of that drudgery for him. Papa can do political work just as well in Rio de Janeiro, where he is highly esteemed. You will see, Senhora. If I were Papa, just as soon as I landed, I would go to the Marshal, explain everything, show my instructions, and tell what I had done. Further, I would say that the dismissal was opportune, in order that it might not appear that I was annoyed. Then I would ask to work there, in the city . . ."

Dona Claudia, in spite of the bitterness of the moment, took pleasure in seeing that her daughter thought about and gave advice about politics. She did not notice, as the reader has, that the soul, or heart, of the young lady's discourse was that she should not leave the capital but

184

hold her congress right there, and soon it would be a single legislative assembly as in Rio Grande do Sul; but on which of the houses, Pedro or Paulo, would be conferred this unique political power? That is what she herself did not know.

Both presented themselves to her on board as soon as the steamer entered the harbor of Rio de Janeiro. They did not come in two launches, they came in the same one, and bounded up the side of the ship with such speed that they almost fell into the sea. Perhaps that would be the best ending for the book. As it is, the chapter does not end badly, because the reason for the speed with which they shot up the ship's ladder was an ambition to be the first to greet the young lady—a gage of love that once again made them equal in her soul. Finally they were there, and it is not known which of them really greeted her first: it may have been both.

LXXIII   *An Eldorado*

On the dock Caes Pharoux three carriages were waiting for them—two coupés and a landau, with three handsome pairs of horses. The Baptistas were flattered by this delicate attention of the Santoses, and got into the landau. The twins each rode in his own coupé. The first carriage had a coachman and footman wearing brown uniforms with silver buttons on which could be seen the family coat of arms. The other two carriages had only a coachman, wearing the same livery. And all three set forth, the coupés behind the landau, the horses marching stiffly with sure, measured beat, as if they had trained for this reception for many long days. From time to time they passed other equipages, other liveries, other teams of horses, the same elegance, the same luxury.

The capital still presented a magnificent spectacle to a newcomer's eyes. It was living on the leavings of that dazzling turmoil, that golden epic of the city and of the world, because the general impression was that the whole world itself was thus. Surely, you have not forgotten the word "boom," the great season of enterprises and companies of every sort. He who did not see it, has not seen anything. Cascades of ideas, of inventions, of concessions, rolled out every day, flashing and roaring, to make thousands of milreis, thousands of thousands, thousands of millions, millions of millions of milreis. All the paper, that is stocks and bonds, came fresh and eternal from the printing press: railroads, banks, factories, mines, shipyards, navigation, building, exporting, importing, sacking, loans, all the associations, all the regions, all that these terms imply and more that they leave out. All, bustled in the streets and public squares, with statutes, organizers, and lists. Capital letters filled the public prints, stock issue followed upon stock issue without ever repeating one another; rarely did one die, and only for being fainthearted, but in the beginning none was fainthearted. Each share of stock possessed an intense, republican life, which was increased by that other life, the one with which the soul gathers new religions to its bosom. Shares of stock sprang forth at a high price, more numerous than the old time offspring of slavery, and with infinite dividends.

People from that time who wish to exaggerate the wealth say the money sprang out of the ground, but it is not true. At most, it fell out of the sky. Candide and Cacambo . . . Ai, our poor Cacambo! You know that it was the name of the Indian that Basilio da Gama sang of in O Uruguay. Voltaire took him and put him in his book, and the irony of the philosopher vanquished the sweetness of the poet. Poor José Basilio! You had against you a restricted subject and an out-of-the-way tongue. The great man did not rob you of Lindoya, luckily, but Cacambo belongs to him, is more his than yours, O my soul's countryman.

Candide and Cacambo, I was saying, on entering El Dorado, as Voltaire tells the story, saw children playing in the street with disks of gold, emerald, and ruby. They picked some up and at the first inn they stopped at, they tried to pay for their dinner with two of them. You remember that the innkeeper roared with laughter, first because they tried to pay him with paving stones, second, because in that country no one paid for what he ate: it was the government that paid for everything. It was this hilarity of the innkeeper, together with the liberality attributed to the state, that made people think the same phenomena existed among us, but it is all a lie.

What seems to be true is that our carriages sprang out of the ground. In the afternoon, when twenty or so of them would line up in the Largo de São Francisco de Paula to wait for their owners, it was a pleasure to go up the Rua do Ouvidor, stop and stare at them. The fine matched horses made a person's eyes pop out: they all seemed to have descended from Homeric rhapsodies, even though they were steeds of peace. The carriages too. Juno had surely fitted them with their golden straps, golden bridles, golden reins, all of incorruptible gold. But neither she nor Minerva got into the golden vehicles for purposes of the war against Ilium. Everything here breathed peace. Coachmen and footmen, bearded and stern, waiting rigid and discreet, gave a perfect idea of their office. None of them waited for the boss, lolling back inside the carriages with their legs hanging out. The impression they gave was of an unbending and elegant discipline learned in a high-class school and maintained by the dignity of the individual.

"There are cases," wrote our friend Ayres, "where the impassivity of the coachman on his box, in contrast to the lack of composure of the owner inside, would make one think that *he* is the boss, who for the fun of it has climbed up on the box and is taking the coachman for a ride."

LXXIV   *Textual Reference*

Before going on, it is necessary to say that our friend Ayres was not referring vaguely or in a generic sense to a number of persons but to one particular person. At that time he was known as Nobrega; formerly, he was not known as anything, he was that simple bill collector for souls in purgatory that met Natividade and Perpetua on the Rua de São José at the corner of Misericordia. You have not forgotten that the young mother put a two-milreis note in the collector's bowl. The note was new and fine; it passed from the bowl into his pocket, in the darkness of a hallway, not without a certain amount of struggle.

A few months later, Nobrega left the souls to shift for themselves and went in for other purgatories, for which he discovered other surplices, other alms bowls, and, finally, other banknotes, alms of prosperous piety. I mean he went in for other careers. Suddenly he left the city, and, for all one knows, the country also. When he came back he brought with him several pairs of one-thousand-milreis notes, which fortune doubled, redoubled, and quadrupled. In short, there dawned the famous time of the "boom." This was the grand surplice, the grand alms bowl, the grand alms, the grand purgatory. Who was there now who knew of the collector for souls? The old circle of acquaintances was lost in obscurity and death. He was another man: his features were not the same, except the ones time had repaired and improved upon.

Whether the grand alms bowl, or any of the others, received banknotes that had the same fate as the first one is not known, but it is possible. It was during this time that Ayres saw him in his carriage, leaning over the carriage door, almost falling out, bowing and tipping his hat in all directions, staring at everybody. Since it was the coachman and the footman (I believe they were Scotsmen) that saved the personal dignity of the house, Ayres made the observation that appears at the end of the last chapter, without any general implication.

Although he would no longer find any of his former acquaintances, Nobrega was afraid to return to the neighborhood where he had gone about begging for the first souls. One day, however, his longing to see it was so great that he decided to brave the danger and went there. He had an itch to see the streets and the people, he kept remembering the houses and the shops, a barber, the upper stories of houses with wooden bars before the windows where such and such young ladies would appear . . . When he was about to yield to his desire, he was again seized with fear and went off to another part of the city. He was riding in his carriage. Later he decided to see everything on foot, going slowly, stopping if possible and reliving what was no more.

He went there on foot. He went down the Rua de São José, turned up the Rua da Misericordia, went and stood on the Santa Luzia beach, came back along the Rua de Dom Manuel, threaded his way in and out of alleys. At first, he looked out the corner of his eye, swiftly, from beneath lowered lids. Here he saw the barbershop, and another barber in it. In the barred upper-story windows young ladies leaned on their elbows, and older women, and young girls, and they were all strange. Nobrega gathered courage and stared straight into their faces. Perhaps this *old* lady was a *young* lady twenty years ago; the young lady perhaps a babe in arms, and now with a baby of her own. At the end, Nobrega walked slowly, stopping from time to time.

He went back, again and again. Only the houses, which *were* the same, seemed to recognize him, and some of them almost spoke to him. This is not my fancy. The ex-money-collector felt a need of being recognized by the stones, of hearing their admiration, of telling them his life story, of forcing them to compare the modest fellow of the old days with the grand personage of today, and of hearing their mute words, "Look, sisters, it's he himself, the same man."

He went among them, gazed at them, questioned them, almost laughed, almost put out his hand to shake them hard: "Speak, devils, speak!"

He did not confide that past to any man, but to the mute walls, to the cracked doors, to the old street lamps, if they were still there, to all that was discreet, to all this he would have given eyes, ears, and lips, lips that only he could hear, that would proclaim the prosperity of that old money-collector.

Once, he saw the church São José open and went in. The church was the same: here were the altars, here was the solitude, the silence. He crossed himself, but did not pray, he only looked at one side and the other, as he walked toward the main altar. He had a fear of seeing the sacristan appear, it might be the same one and recognize him. He heard footsteps, drew back quickly, and left.

As he went up the Rua de São José, he flattened himself against the wall to let a cart go by. It came up on the sidewalk; he took refuge in a hallway. It might have been any hallway, but it happened to be the very one in which he had performed the operation on Natividade's two-milreis note. He looked closely; yes, it was the same one. At the rear were the first three or four steps that turned to the left and joined the main staircase. He smiled at the chance happening, relived for a moment that long-ago morning, saw the two-milreis note floating in the air. Others had come into his hands in ways that were just as easy, but he had never forgotten that lovely slip of paper engraved with all those symbols, numbers, dates, and promises, and handed to him by an unknown lady, God knows if she wasn't Santa Rita de Cassia herself. This was his special cult. To be sure, he changed the note and spent it, but the scattered parts only went off to lure other bank-notes into their master's pocket, and they came by the handfuls, obedient and quiet, so that people could not hear them grow.

No matter how deeply he looked into his past life, he did not find any of heaven's favors to equal it, nor any of hell's. After that, if some jewel drew his eyes to it, it did not draw his hands. He had learned to respect other men's property, or he had obtained the wherewithal to buy it. The two-milreis note . . . One day he went further, and called it a gift from Our Lord.

No, reader, you have not caught me in a contradiction. I know very well that in the beginning the collector for souls attributed the banknote to the pleasure a lady had got from some amorous escapade. I still remember his words: "Those two have seen a little green bird!" But if he now attributed the note to the protection of the saint, he did not lie then or now. It was difficult to discover the truth. The only certain truth was the two milreis. Nor can it be said to have been the same then and now. *Then* the two-milreis note was the equivalent, at the least, of twenty (remember the man's worn shoes); *now* it was no more than a cabdriver's tip.

Neither is there any contradiction in putting the saint now, and the lover back then. The contrary would be more natural, when his intimacy with the Church was greater. But, reader of my sins, there was lots of love-making going on in 1871, as there had been in 1861, 1851, and 1841, no less than in 1881, 1891, and 1901. The century will speak for the future. Besides, one must not forget that the opinion of the collector for souls concerning Natividade was formed antecedent to the gesture in the hallway when he put the banknote to rest in his pocket. It is doubtful that, after the gesture, his opinion was the same.

LXXV   *The Proverb Is Wrong*

A person to whom I privately read the last chapter wrote me saying that the cause of the whole thing was the cabocla of the Castello. Without her grandiose predictions, Natividade's gift of alms would have been very small, or nothing, and there would have been no gesture in the hallway, for lack of a banknote. "The occasion makes the thief," concludes my correspondent.

It's not a bad conclusion. Still it contains some injustice or oversight, because the reasons for the gesture in the hallway were all pious. Besides, the proverb may be wrong. One of Ayres' claims—and he too liked to study adages—was that this one was not right.

"It is not the occasion that makes the thief," he said to someone. "The proverb is wrong. The correct form would be this: 'The occasion makes the theft; thieves are born, not made.'"

LXXVI   *Perhaps It Was the*
                              Same One!

Nobrega finally came out of the hallway, but was obliged
to stop, because a woman was holding an outstretched
hand toward him, "My dear sir, a bit of alms for the love
of God!"

Nobrega put his hand in his vest pocket and took one
of the two nickel coins that were there, one a tostão, the
other a two-tostão piece. He took the first, but as he was
about to give it to her, he changed his mind. He did not
give her the coin, he told the old woman to wait, and
went further into the hallway. With his back to the street,
he put his hand in his trousers pocket and pulled out a
roll of bills: he looked through them until he found a two-
milreis note. It was not new, but old, as old as the beggar
woman, who received it in astonishment; but you know
that money loses nothing with age.

"Here you are," he murmured.

When the beggar recovered from her astonishment,
Nobrega had put the roll of money back in his pocket and
was starting to leave. The beggar woman's words were
interspersed with tears, "My dear sir! Thank you, my
dear sir! May God reward you! May the Holy Virgin . . ."

She kissed the banknote, and tried to kiss the hand that
had bestowed the alms, but he hid it, as in the Gospel,
murmuring "no," that she should go away. In truth, the
beggar woman's words had an almost mystical sound, a
kind of celestial melody, an angels' chorus, and it did one

good to look into her wrinkled eyes, at her trembling hand holding the note. Nobrega did not wait for her to go away, he left the doorway, went down the street, with the woman's blessings following him; he turned the corner at a quick pace, and went on, with who knows what thoughts.

He crossed the square, went by the cathedral and the Carmo church, and came to the Carceller restaurant, where he entrusted his shoes to an Italian to shine. Mentally, he looked over him, or below, to the right or to the left—wherever he looked it was far in the distance—and finally he murmured this phrase, which could refer to the banknote, or to the beggar woman, but it probably referred to the banknote: "Perhaps it was the same one!"

No favor, however trifling it may be, is forgotten by the recipient. There are exceptions. There are instances, also, in which the memory of a favor torments, pursues, and bites, like a mosquito; but it is not the rule. As a rule, the favor is kept locked in the memory, like jewels in their jewelcases; the comparison is just, because the favor is often some jewel that the recipient forgot to return.

LXXVII   *Hospitality*

The Baptista family stayed at the home of the Santoses. Natividade could not meet them at the boat, and her husband was busy launching a company: they sent word by their sons that rooms had been readied for them at the house in Botafogo. As soon as the carriage began to move off, Baptista confided he would be ill at ease for a matter of days.

"It would be better in a *pension* until our house on São Clemente is vacated."

"What could we do? There was no other way but to accept," observed his wife.

Flora said nothing, but she felt the opposite of her father and mother. She did not think thoughts. She was so dizzied by the sight of the young men that her ideas did not close ranks in that logical order common to thought. Even sensation was not distinct. It was a mixture of depression and exhilaration, of clouds and bright sky, a happiness that was incomplete, a sorrow that consoled, and all the other things you can find in the chapter of contradictions. I will add nothing more. Nor was she able to tell what she felt. She had strange hallucinations.

Now, however, it must be explained that the hospitality offered to the Baptistas was the idea of the two young graduates. They had their degrees now, although they had not yet entered upon the career either of lawyer or of doctor. They lived off their mother's love and their father's purse—both inexhaustible. Their father shook his head at the idea, but the twins urged this polite attention so insistently that finally their mother, happy to see them in agreement, broke her silence and gave them her support. The thought of having the young girl about her for several days, and noting which brother was the better received, and which one really loved *her,* may have affected her decision, but I do not positively assert anything in this regard. Neither do I make any assertions to the effect that she took great pleasure in receiving Flora's mother and father. Nevertheless, the meeting was cordial on both sides. It was a hug, a kiss, a query, an interminable exchange of compliments. Everyone was more filled out, better color, better looks. Flora was a charming beauty for Natividade and Perpetua: neither of them knew where it would end—this young lady was so elegant, so graceful, so . . .

"Don't say any more," interrupted the young lady with a laugh, "I am of the same opinion."

Santos welcomed them in the afternoon, with the same cordiality—perhaps it was less apparent, but everything is overlooked in a man who is mixed up in great enterprises.

"A sublime idea," he said to Flora's father, "the one I put on the market today, it was one of the best, and the shares of stock gilt edged. It's in sheep's wool and begins with the raising of this mammal on the grasslands of Paraná. In five years we will be able to clothe America and Europe. Did you see the prospectus in the newspapers?"

"No, I haven't read the papers since we docked."

"Well, you shall see it!"

The next day, before breakfast, he showed his guest the prospectus and incorporation papers. There were heaps and heaps of shares, and Santos told him the value of each. Baptista was poor at arithmetic in general, on this occasion worse than ever. But the figures kept increasing before his eyes, they climbed one on top of another, filled the space from floor to windows, and jumped out the windows with a golden roar that deafened him. Baptista left the room spellbound, and went to tell it all to his wife.

LXXVIII   *Visit to the Marshal*

When he finished, Dona Claudia asked him with brutal directness, "Are you going to see the Marshal today?"

Baptista came back to reality, "Of course."

They had arranged that he should go to see the President of the Republic, tell him how he had performed his mission with all secrecy but with impartiality. He would explain the spirit of accord with which he had proceeded and the respect he had won. Then, he would voice approval of a government that, for vigor and liberty, surpassed that of the Generalissimo, and close with a final, erudite phrase.

"As the occasion prompts," said Baptista.

"No, it is better to take one ready made. This one occurs to me: 'Have faith, Your Excellency, that God is on the side of the strong and good.'"

"Yes, that's not bad."

"You can add a gesture indicating heaven."

"Oh, no. You know I don't go in for gestures. I'm not an actor. *I* inspire respect without lifting a finger."

Dona Claudia was willing to dispense with the gesture; it was not essential. She asked him to write the sentence down, but he already had it by heart. Baptista had a good memory.

That same day, Baptista went to see Marshal Floriano. He said nothing about it to the members of the household: he would tell them everything when he got back. Dona Claudia also kept quiet, it was for a short time. She waited anxiously. She waited two mortal hours, and then began to imagine they had thrown her husband into prison, for plotting. She was not devout, but fear inspires devotion, and she prayed inwardly. Finally Baptista arrived. She ran to greet him, excitedly grasped his hand, and led him to their bedroom. Perpetua (see what eyewitnesses to history are worth!) exclaimed tenderly, "They are like two little turtle doves."

Baptista related that the reception was better than he had hoped, although the Marshal had not said anything to him; but he listened to him with interest. The sentence? The sentence came out well, with only a slight change. Not being sure whether he preferred *the good* to *the strong,* or *the strong* to *the good* . . .

"There should have been the two words," interrupted his wife.

"Yes, but I got the idea of using a third: 'Have faith, Your Excellency, that God is on the side of the honorable!' "

Actually, this last word could include the other two, and it had the advantage of giving the sentence his own personal touch.

"But what did the Marshal say?"

"He didn't say anything. He listened to me with courteous attention and then he smiled—a faint smile, a smile of acquiescence . . ."

"Or it might be . . . Who knows . . . You didn't do it right, that's sure. If it had been me, he would have said something. Did you explain everything, just as we arranged?"

"Everything."

"Did you explain the reasons for the mission, and the way you carried it out, and our moderation? . . ."

"Everything, Claudia."

"And the marshal's handclasp?"

"He didn't offer his hand, at first; he made a gesture with his head. It was I who held out my hand, and said, "Always at your service, Your Excellency."

"And he?"

"He took my hand."

"A good, hearty shake?"

"Well, it wasn't like a friend's but it was meant to be cordial."

"And not a word? Not even a *good day to you?*"

"No, there was no call for it. I bowed to him and went out."

Dona Claudia remained deep in thought. The reception did not seem to her to have been bad, but it could have been better. With her, it would have been much better.

LXXIX   *Fusion, Diffusion, Confusion*

I have spoken of Flora's hallucinations before. Truly, they were extraordinary.

On the road, after they left the dock, though the twins were traveling separately and alone, each in his own coupé, she thought she heard them speak—this was the first part of the hallucination. Second part: the two voices fused, so alike were they, and became one. In short, her imagination made of two young men a single person.

I do not believe that this phenomenon is very common. On the contrary, there will no doubt be someone who will not believe me at all and will put down as pure invention what is actually the purest truth. Well, you will be interested to learn that, during her father's mission, Flora heard the two voices fuse into the same voice and the same person, and more than once. And now, in the house in Botafogo, the phenomenon was repeated. When she heard the two brothers without seeing them, her imagination completed the fusion of sound with that of sight, and there appeared to her one single man saying extraordinary words.

All this is no less extraordinary, I admit. If I consulted my own feelings in the matter the two young men would not thus became *one* lad, nor would the young lady remain one damsel. I would rectify nature by doubling Flora. Since this cannot be, I accept the unification of Pedro and Paulo. Because, this effect of vision would be repeated in their presence, as well as in their absence, when she allowed herself to forget the time and the place, and let herself go. At the piano, during a conversation, while out walking in the chácara, at the dinner table, she would have these sudden, brief visions, at which she herself smiled, in the beginning.

If anyone tries to explain this phenomenon by the law of heredity, on the supposition that it was an affective form of the political variation seen in Flora's mother, he will not get any support from me, nor, I believe, from anyone. They are two different things. You are familiar with Dona Claudia's motives. Her daughter must have had different ones, which she herself was not aware of. The single point of resemblance is, that, in the mother, as well as in the daughter, the phenomenon was now more frequent, but, as regards the former, it came from the stampede of external events. No revolution is like simply passing from one room to another; even what are called palace revolutions bring a certain turmoil that remains for a certain length of time until the water sinks to its customary level. Dona Claudia yielded to the unrest of the times.

Her daughter obeyed some other causation, which cannot be readily discovered, nor even understood. It was a vague, dark, mysterious spectacle, in which the visible figures became intangible, double became single, single double, a fusion, confusion, diffusion . . .

Transfusion in Short

A transfusion, or whatever term best defines, through repetition and gradation of forms and states, that particular phenomenon, you may employ in this and the preceding chapter.

Now that the nature of the phenomenon has been stated, it is necessary also to state that Flora thought it droll and charming in the beginning. No, I am wrong: in the very beginning, as she was far away, she did not think much about it. Later, it gave her a kind of start or dizzy feeling, but when she got used to passing two into one and one into two, the alternation came to hold a certain charm for her, and she would evoke it just to have a change of scenery. Finally, not even this was necessary, the alternation took place of itself. Sometimes it was slower than others, on occasion it was instantaneous. The alternations were not so frequent as to border on delirium. In short, she was becoming used to them and taking pleasure in them.

Once in a while, as she lay in bed, before dropping off to sleep, the phenomenon occurred, after much resistance on her part since she did not want to lose her sleep. But sleep would come, and dream complete the waking vision. In the dream, Flora walked, on the arm of the same loved youth, Paulo, if it was not Pedro, and they went along gazing at stars and mountains, or perhaps the sea, as it murmured lovers' sighs, or raged, and at the flowers and the ruins. Not infrequently they were alone, against a piece of sky bright with moonlight, or all studded with stars like a strip of dark blue cloth. It was at the window, for example, from outside came the song of soft winds, a great mirror hanging from the wall reproduced her outline and his, in confirmation of her imagination. As it was a dream, her imagination conjured unheard of sights, so great and so many that one would scarcely believe they could all fit into the space of a single night. But they did, and with room to spare. It sometimes happened that Flora suddenly awoke, lost the picture and the shape, persuaded herself that it was all illusion, and then she rarely went back to sleep. If it was early, she got up, walked about till she was tired, fell asleep again, and dreamed of something else.

Other times, the vision remained after the dream had gone—a single handsome figure, with the same caressing voice, the same beseeching gesture. One night, as she was about to place her arms on its shoulders with the unconscious aim of locking her fingers behind its neck, reality, though absent, demanded its rights, and the single youthful figure became two—the two persons that so resembled each other.

This change gave the two waking visions such a stamp of phantasmagoria that Flora was afraid and thought of the devil.

LXXXI   *Alas, Two Souls*

Come, Flora, help me by quoting some bit of verse or prose that will describe your situation. Quote Goethe, my dear, quote a line of *Faust,* appropriate to the occasion:

Alas, two souls in my bosom dwell!

The twins' mother, the lovely Natividade, could have

quoted it also, before they were born, when she felt them struggling within her:

Alas, two souls in my bosom dwell!

In this the two women were alike—one conceived them, the other took them to her heart. But how does it happen that Flora made this choice, how could she? Not even Mephistopheles himself could explain it clearly and for certain. The verse will have to do:

Alas, two souls in my bosom dwell!

Perhaps that old Placido that we left back there in the first pages, might be able to unravel these later ones. Doctor in obscure and complicated matters, he understood the value of numbers, the meaning of gestures, not only the visible ones but the invisible as well, the statistics of eternity, the divisibility of the infinite. He was dead now, had been dead for several years. You must remember that when he was consulted by the twins' father concerning their original hostility, he explained it handily. Placido died at his post: he was explaining to three pupils the correspondence of the vowels, a, e, i, o, u, to the five senses, when he fell on his face and expired.

Even then, Placido's adversaries—and he had them in his own sect—claimed he had strayed from the true teaching, and, as a natural effect, had gone crazy. Santos never went along with those separatists from the common cause, who ended up forming another little church in another part of town, where they preached that the true correspondence was not between the vowels and the senses, but between the senses and the vowels. This second formula, since it seemed clearer, made many of the early disciples go in with the later ones and proclaim, as their final conclusion, that man is an alphabet of sensations. This group won out, and very few remained faithful to the teaching of old Placido. When his spirit was raised, some time after his death, he once more declared his formula as the only of onlies, and excommunicated all those who preached the contrary. As for that, the dissenters had already excommunicated *him,* pronouncing his memory abominable, with that rigid hatred that strengthens man against the flabbiness of pity.

Perhaps old Placido would have cleared up the problem of Flora in five minutes. But, for this it would have been necessary to summon his spirit, and his disciple Santos was busy right then with some final lucrative liquidations. Man doth not live by faith alone, but also by bread and its composites and counterparts.

LXXXII   *On São Clemente*

After a few weeks, the Baptista family left the Santos home and went back to the Rua de São Clemente. The leave-taking was tender, they began to miss one another before they had separated, but affection, habit, esteem— the necessity, in short, of seeing each other frequently— offset their melancholy, and the Baptistas carried with them a promise that the Santoses would come to see them within a few days.

The twins kept the promise soon. One of them, it seems it was Paulo, went there that same night with a message from his mother, to know if they had arrived all right. They told him yes, and Baptista added, in order to shorten the visit, that they were rather tired. Flora's eyes belied this statement, but in a little while those eyes appeared no less sad than happy. The happiness came from Paulo's promptness, the sadness from Pedro's absence.

Naturally she had hoped for both of them, but, how was it that the two sensations were simultaneous—there's something you won't be able to understand very well, if at all. To be sure, her eyes occasionally strayed to the door, and once it seemed to her that she heard someone on the stairs: all illusion. But these starts, which Paulo did not see, so pleased was he to have stolen the march on his brother, were not such as to make her forget the brother who was present.

Paulo did not leave until quite late, partly so that he could take advantage of Pedro's absence, but also because Flora kept detaining him, in the hope the other might appear. All the while the same duality of feeling filled the girl's eyes, until the moment of leave-taking, when their sadness shone greater than their happiness: for, now there would be two absent instead of one. Draw whatever conclusion you like, my lady. She went off to bed, and discovered that if a person cannot sleep with one sadness in her soul, she is much less able to sleep with two.

LXXXIII   *The Great Night*

There are many remedies for insomnia. The commonest is to count to a thousand, two thousand, three thousand, or more if the insomnia does not give in right away. It is a remedy that has never yet put anyone to sleep, it would appear, but no matter. Up to now, all the efficacious medicines against tuberculosis keep pace with the notion that tuberculosis is incurable. It is meet and proper for men to assert what they do not know, and, if they are professional men, the opposite of what they know: in this way is created that other incurable disease—Hope.

Flora, who was also incurable, if you do not prefer Ayres' definition of her as "mysterious"—the charming Flora had suffered her own brand of insomnia that night. But it was partly her own fault. Instead of lying down quietly and sleeping with the angels, she found it better to stay awake with one or two of them, and spent a part of the night standing at the window or seated, recalling, thinking, comparing, and completing, her linen dressing gown around her, her hair tied back for sleep.

At first she thought about the one who had been there, and called up all his graces, and they were heightened with the special virtue of his coming to see her that night, even though they had seen each other in the morning. She felt grateful and happy. The whole conversation was repeated, there in the solitude of her bedroom, with the various intonations, the various subjects, and the frequent breaks in it, sometimes caused by others, sometimes because of her. She, however, only broke off to think of the one who was absent—and thus did no more than turn a dialogue into a monologue, which, in turn, ended in silent contemplation.

Now, as she thought of Paulo, she asked herself why she did not choose him for her husband. *He* had an extra quality, an adventurous stamp to his character, and this feature was not displeasing to her. Mysterious or not, she let herself be carried away by the impetuosity of a young man who wanted to trade this world and this age for another, purer, happier world and a new age. That head, scarcely yet a man's, was destined to change the course of the sun, which was now going in the wrong direction. The moon too. The moon cried for more frequent contact with men, fewer quarters, with the waning moon decreasing only a half. Visible every night, but without causing the stars to set, it would continue the function of the sun in modest fashion and would bring dreams to sleepless eyes or to eyes wearied with sleep. All this would be achieved by Paulo's soul, in its hunger for perfection. He would be a good husband, in short. Flora shut her eyes tight, the better to see him, and found him kneeling at her feet, with her hands in his; he was smiling and ecstatic.

"Paulo! my darling Paulo!"

She leaned forward to see him closer, and it was not a waste of time, nor did she fail in her intention. Seen thus he was more handsome than when simply talking of ordinary, passing things. She sank her eyes in his and found herself inside the young man's soul. She did not know how to describe what she saw there; it was all so new and radiantly bright that her poor retina could not look steadily at anything, nor for any length of time. Ideas flew up like sparks when a fire is fanned, sensations clashed in single combat, memories rose upward fresh and shining, some sad longings, and ambitions above all else, ambitions with great wings that stirred a wind only with moving. Over all this mixture and confusion fell tenderness, much tenderness, like a gentle rain . . .

Flora withdrew her eyes. Paulo was in the same position, but, near the door, wrapped in penumbra, the figure of Pedro appeared, no less handsome, but somewhat sad. Flora was touched by that sadness. Surely, if she had loved the first exclusively, the second might weep tears of blood without winning the slightest token of sympathy. Love, according to both the ancient and modern nymphs, has no pity. When there is pity for another, these girls say, it means that true love has not yet been born, or is already quite dead, so that the heart does not mind putting on the undershirt of affection. Pardon the figure; it is not noble, nor clear, but the situation, being what it is, does not allow me time to track down another.

Pedro slowly drew near, knelt like his brother, and

took the hands that Paulo had held in his. Paulo got up and disappeared through the other door. The room had two doors. The bed was between them. Perhaps Paulo went away roaring with anger. Flora heard nothing, so gently live was Pedro's gesture, and he was no longer melancholy, his eyes as ecstatic as his brother's. They were not the kind to go forth on adventures. They had the quietness of a man who does not want other suns or moons than the ones that wander there above, a man content with both, and since he thinks them divine does not intend to trade them for new ones. It was the order, if you like, the stability, the accord between himself and other things; all these were no less appealing to the young lady's heart, either because they embodied the idea of perpetual bliss, or because they gave her the feeling of a soul that could stand fast.

Even so, Flora's eyes did not fail to penetrate those of Pedro, until she reached the young man's soul. The secret motive for this second entrance into a pair of eyes may have been a conscientious urge to compare the two entrances in order to judge them, if it was not merely the desire to seem no less curious about one than the other. Both reasons are good, but perhaps neither was the true one. The pleasure of gazing into Pedro's eyes was so natural that it did not require any special intention. And gazing into them was enough to make her slip and fall into the beloved soul. She found it the twin of the other soul: she saw neither more nor less in it.

Only—and here I touch on the difficult point of the chapter—she found here something indefinable that she had not noticed there; in compensation, she had felt there something that she did not come across here. Indefinable, don't forget. And difficult, because there is nothing worse than talking about sensations that do not have a name. Believe me, my dear sir, and you, madam, who are no less dear to me, believe me, I would rather tell over the lace ruffles on the young lady's dressing gown, the hairs that were caught up at the back of her head, the threads in the carpet, the boards in the ceiling, and, when it comes to that, the sputterings of the night lamp, whose flame was dying . . . It would be boring, but readers would understand.

Yes, the lamp's flame was dying but it could still light Paulo's return. When Flora saw him come in and again kneel, beside his brother, and both share her hands, meekly and sensibly, her astonishment was intense and prolonged. Result of a creed, as our forefathers used to say in the days when there was more religion than church steeples. Regaining her composure, she pulled away her hands and placed them on their heads, as if to *feel* the difference, the *quid,* the something, the indefinable. The lamp's flame was dying . . . Pedro and Paulo spoke to her in exclamations, in exhortations, in entreaties, and she answered vaguely and evasively—not because she did not understand them but in order not to provoke them, or, it may be, that she did not know to which of them she should speak with more favor. The last hypothesis would appear the more probable. At least, it is the prologue to what followed when the lamp arrived at its last gasp.

Everything merges together in a half-light. This must have been the reason for the fusion of shapes, so that where there had been two there was now only one. Since Flora had not seen either of the twins leave, she could hardly believe that they now formed a single person, but she came to believe it, especially since this one remaining person seemed to complete her, within herself, better than either of the others separately. It was a great deal of merging and dissolving, of forming and transforming. She thought she had made a mistake, but no, there was a single person made of two and of herself, for she felt the beating of its heart. She was so wearied from emotion that she tried to rise and go outside, but she could not: her legs seemed to be of lead and grown solid with the floor. So she remained while the flame of the lamp in the corner died. Flora gave a start in her easy chair and rose.

"What is this?"

The lamp had gone out. She went to light it. Then she saw that she was without one or the other, without two, without one fused from both. The whole phantasmagoria had dissolved. The lamp, now with a new wick, lighted up her bedroom: imagination had created the whole thing. That is what she supposed, and what the reader knows. Flora decided that it was late, and a cock confirmed this opinion by crowing. Other cocks did the same thing.

"Oh, my God!" exclaimed Baptista's daughter.

She got into bed, and, if she did not go to sleep right away, neither was she slow in doing so. It was not long before she was with the angels. She dreamed of cocks crowing, of a carriage, a lake, a vision of a ship at sea, a speech, and an article. The article was real. Her mother came to wake her at ten o'clock in the morning, calling her a sleepyhead, and while she was still in bed, read her a morning paper that recommended her husband to the government. Flora heard it with satisfaction: the great night had ended.

LXXXIV   *The Old Secret*

Natividade slept tranquilly in Botafogo, but she woke up with her thoughts on her sons and on the young lady of São Clemente. She had been observing the three of them of late. She had thought, at first, that Flora did not favor one over the other, then that she showed favor to both, later still to one and the other alternately. She concluded that the girl had not yet felt anything special and decisive, that she was probably drifting with the times, to see which of them really deserved her. It was her sons who appeared to have a strong inclination and equally strong jealousy. Out of this might come catastrophe. Separation would not put an end to everything, but at least when the families were separated everything would not be present to her eyes, and the visits might be less frequent and even rare. Thus she would have what she wanted.

Besides, it would soon be time to go to Petropolis; strictly speaking it was already time to go. Natividade planned to go up with her sons. Up there, there would be elegant ladies, diversion, gaiety. It might even be that they would find brides, and it would be enough if there was one bride for one son. He who was left without the bride would be free to marry Flora. A mother's schemes; there would be others to modify these, and still others to change them back. Let him who is a mother cast the first stone.

No mother cast the first stone at our friend. I am inclined to believe that the reason for this is to be imputed to Natividade's discretion. Suspicions and schemes filled her heart. She said nothing and waited.

In the end, Flora grew fonder and fonder of Natividade. She loved her as if she were her mother, doubly her mother, in as much as she had not yet chosen either of her sons. The reason may have been that their temperaments were more suited to each other than Flora's and Dona Claudia's. At first, she felt a kind of friendly envy, or aspiration, when she saw that the other woman, though laid waste by time, still preserved something of the lines of ancient sculpture. Little by little she began to discover in herself a burgeoning beauty that promised to be long lasting and delicate and possessed of a life that might be great . . .

Flora learned of the prediction the cabocla of the Castello had made about the twin brothers. The prediction was no longer a secret to anyone. Santos had told it at the time, only concealing Natividade's trip to the Castello: he improved upon the truth by saying that it was the cabocla who had come to Botafogo. The rest was revealed in confidence, as, for example, to the late Placido, and then only after a certain amount of struggle. Three or four times he started to tell it and drew back. One day his tongue made seven turns in his mouth, and out came the secret, in a timid whisper, but it lost its fear in the pleasure of revealing that the lads would be great. Finally the secret fell into oblivion. But Perpetua, for one reason or another, now told it to the Baptista girl, who listened in disbelief. How could the cabocla know the future?

"She did, and the proof is that she divined other things that I am not at liberty to tell, but that were true. You have no idea how that devil of a cabocla could see what was far. And she had eyes that went right through your heart."

"I don't believe it, Dona Perpetua. Come now, the future of people . . . And great in what way?"

"She wouldn't say, no matter how much Natividade begged her to. All she said was they would be great and would rise in the world. Perhaps they will become ministers of state."

It was as if Perpetua had bought the cabocla's eyes. She fixed her friend with them and bored deep into her heart, which, by the way, did not beat hard nor fast, but regularly, as usual. Meanwhile, since it was not impossible that the two lads should attain great heights in this world, Flora left off objecting and accepted the prophecy with no other comment than a gesture—you know what it was, I imagine—she drew down the corners of her mouth, lightly raised her shoulders, and held up the palms of her hands, as if to say, "After all, it could be."

Perpetua added that, in view of the change of government, Paulo would probably be the first to achieve greatness—and she looked piercingly into Flora's eyes. It was a device to discover her sentiments, by leading her on with Paulo's advancement, because it might be that she would fall in love with the destiny sooner than the person. She did not discover anything. Flora went on being inscrutable. Don't ascribe it to calculation; it was not calculated. Actually, she was not thinking of anything beyond herself.

LXXXV   *Three Constitutions*

"Do you really think we'll become great men?" Pedro asked Paulo before the fall of the Empire.

"I don't know. You, at least, might become prime minister."

After the Fifteenth of November, Paulo returned the query, and Pedro answered as his brother had done, making the necessary changes: "I don't know. You might become president of the Republic."

That had been two years before. Now they thought more about Flora than about rising in the world. Morality demands that we place the common good above the individual, but the young men in this respect resembled old men and males of other ages who often give more thought to themselves than to the public. There are exceptions, some of them noble, others *very* noble. History preserves many of them, and the poets, epic and tragic, are full of instances and models of abnegation.

As a matter of fact, it would be asking a good deal of Pedro and Paulo for them to take more interest in the Constitution of February 24 than in the Baptista girl. They thought about both, it is true, and the former had already occasioned an exchange of bitter words. If the Constitution had been a living person, and had been present, it would have heard the most contrary views in this world, because Pedro went so far as to regard it as a sink of iniquity, and Paulo as Minerva herself sprung from the forehead of Jove. I speak in metaphors so as not to degrade my style. Actually they employed words that were less noble and more emphatic, and ended by interchanging them. In the street, where political manifestations were common and the reports put up outside the door of newspaper offices frequent, everything was an excuse for an argument.

When, however, the image of Flora appeared between them, in their imagination, the debate languished, but the insults and abuse continued and even increased, without their admitting a change of motive to one still greater than the first. As a matter of fact, they were reaching a point where they would have traded the two constitutions, the Republican and the Imperial, for the young lady's exclusive love, if such a sacrifice were demanded. Each would form, with her, his own constitution—a better one than any other in this world.

LXXXVI   *Before I Forget*

I must say one thing before I forget it. You know that the twin brothers were handsome and continued to look alike; but they did not consider they had any reason to envy each other on this account. On the contrary, each saw in himself a certain something that accentuated if it did not improve their common graces. It was not true, but it is not truth that triumphs, it is conviction. Convince yourself of an idea, and you will die for it, wrote Ayres, about this time, in his *Memorial,* and he added, "the grandeur of sacrifice is nothing more than this, but if truth joins up with conviction, then is born the sublime, and from it the useful . . ." He did not finish, nor explain, this sentence.

LXXXVII   *Between Ayres and Flora*

That quotation from old Ayres reminds me of a point on which he and young Flora were further apart than in age. I have already told how, before her father's mission, she used to defend Pedro or Paulo, according to whichever happened to be speaking harshly of the other. Naturally she still did the same, but the change of regime brought the need of also defending monarchists and republicans, according to whether she was listening to Paulo's opinions or to Pedro's. A spirit of conciliation or of justice, she placated the wrath or the scorn of the speaker: "Don't say that . . . They too are patriots . . . It is fitting to pardon some excesses . . ." They were only phrases, without the vehemence of passion or the stimulus of principles, and the "speaker" always concluded, "You are kind, Senhora."

Ayres' way was the contrary of this benevolent opposition. You will remember, he made a practice of always agreeing with the speaker, not out of disdain for a person, but in order not to dissent or become embroiled in disputes. He had observed that when convictions are opposed they discompose a person's looks, and he did not want to see other people's faces like that nor give his own an abominable aspect. If there was anything to be gained, fine; but, with nothing to be gained, he preferred to remain at peace with God and men. Hence his scheme of affirmative gestures and phrases that left the parties calm, and himself still more calm.

One day when he was with Flora he spoke of *her* way, told her it seemed studied to him. She denied that it was, said it was a natural inclination to defend those who were absent and could not answer for themselves; besides, in this way, she calmed down the twin with whom she was speaking, and later the other one.

"Yes, I agree with you."

"And why is it that you always agree, Senhor?" she asked with a smile.

"I can agree with you, Senhora, because it is a delightful pleasure to go along with your opinions, and it would be bad taste to combat them, but there is no method in it. As for the others, if I agree with them, it is because they only say what I think."

"I've already caught you in self-contradiction."

"Maybe so. Life and the world are nothing if not contradictory. You probably don't fully appreciate this, Senhora, because you are young and ingenuous, but believe me the advantage is all on your side. Ingenuousness is the best book, and youth the best of schools. You will excuse my tediousness, once in a while it is a necessary evil."

"Don't apologize, Counselor. You know I don't believe anything that goes against your word, nor anything against your person. Even the contradictions I find in you are delightful."

"I agree, they are."

"You agree with everything."

"Look at this, Flora. Excuse me, Counselor."

I forgot to say that this conversation was at the door of a shop on the Rua do Ouvidor. Ayres was going toward the Largo de São Francisco de Paula when he saw the mother and daughter sitting inside choosing a piece of material. He went in, greeted them, and came to the door with the daughter. Dona Claudia's appeal interrupted the conversation for some seconds. Ayres stood looking into the street, where women of all classes, and men of all professions, were going up and down the street, not to mention the individuals standing on either side and in the middle of the street. There was not much stir, nor yet complete quiet, something in between.

Perhaps some of the people were acquaintances of Ayres' and bowed to him, or tipped their hat, but his soul was so wrapped up within itself that if he spoke to one or two of them it was the most he did. From time to time he glanced inside where Flora and her mother were deliberating. He still heard the words he and Flora had exchanged. He felt a curiosity to know whether she had finally chosen one of the twins, and which one. Let it all be told! He was sorry if she hadn't, though it made no difference to him whether it was Pedro or Paulo. He had determined to see her happy—if marriage was happiness, and her husband happy, notwithstanding the exclusion: the excluded would be consoled. Now whether it was for love of the twins, or for love of her, is something one can not really say for certain. Even to raise the corner of the veil, it would be necessary to penetrate his soul even deeper than he himself had gone. There perhaps, among the ruins of a half-celibate, would be found the pale, late-blooming flower of paternity, or, more properly, of a longing for it . . .

Flora returned, bringing back the fresh, red rose of the earth's first hour. They spoke no more of contradictions, but of the street, the people, and the day. Not a word about Pedro and Paulo.

LXXXVIII   *No, No, No*

And *they,* wherever they may have been at that moment, may have spoken or not. The truth is that if neither consented to give her up, on the other hand, neither counted on winning her, no matter how favorably inclined they thought her. They had already arranged that the rejected suitor would accept his fate and leave the field to the victor. When victory did not arrive, they did not know how to decide the battle. To wait would be the easiest way, if passion did not increase, but passion was increasing.

Perhaps it was not exactly passion, if we give the word the sense of violence; but, if we recognize in it merely a strong inclination to love, an adolescent love, or little more, then, it was that. Pedro and Paulo would have given up the lass's hand if it were only a matter of consulting their reason, and more than once they were on the point of doing so—a sudden faint gleam that disappeared on the instant. Absence was already unbearable, her presence a necessity. If it had not been for what happened and will be told in the following pages, there would be material for a book that went on forever. It would only be a question of saying "yes" and "no," and what the young men thought and felt, and what she felt and thought, until the publisher said "Enough!" It would be a book filled with morality and truth, but the story that has been begun would be left without an ending. No, no, no . . . It is my bounden duty to go on with it and finish it. Let us begin by saying that the two brothers had made a pact a few days after that dream or delirium that the gentle Flora had, at night, in their room.

The Dragon

Let us see what the pact was that they made. They had
gone to the theater with Ayres, one night, to kill time.
You are familiar with this dragon. We have all given him
the deepest wounds imaginable, he twitches his legs, ex-
pires, and comes back to life. That is what he did that
night. I do not know what theater it was, nor what play,
nor of what genre it was. Be that as it may, the question
was to kill time, and the three of them left him stretched
out on the ground.

They went from there to a restaurant. Ayres told them
that, in the old days, when he was young, he would end
the night with friends of the same age. It was in the time
of Offenbach and the operetta. He related anecdotes, told
of plays, described the actresses and the factions that cham-
pioned them, he almost caught himself repeating a scene,
words and music. Pedro and Paulo listened attentively but
they felt nothing of what awakened echoes in the old diplomat's soul. On the contrary, they felt a desire to laugh.
What did they care about an old café on the Rua Uru-
guayana which was later turned into a theater, and now
into nothing, about people who lived and shone, and
passed away before they came into the world? The world
began twenty years before that night, and would never
end, like the vivarium of eternal youths it was.

Ayres smiled, because he too had felt the same at
twenty-two years of age, and he till remembered his father's smile, his father was old of course, when he had
said something of the sort. Later, when he acquired the
ideal notion of time that he now held, he knew that this
dragon was at once alive and dead, and there was no

more use in killing him than in keeping him alive. Nevertheless, his recollections were sweet, and many of them as alive and fresh as if they had come from the day before.

The difference in age was great, he could not enter into details with them. He remained alone in his memories, and spoke of other things. Pedro and Paulo, however, fearing he had guessed their feelings and understood the derision that his longings for strange, remote times had inspired in them, begged him to tell them about various things, and he told them all he could, of an impersonal nature.

After all, the conversation was worth more than this summary, and they were not eager to part. Paulo asked him for more Offenbach, Pedro for a description of the Seventh of September and the Second of December parades; but the diplomat found a way of leaping back to the present, and particularly to Flora, whom he praised as a handsome woman. The eyes of both agreed that she was *beautiful*. He also praised her spiritual qualities, the sensitivity of her fine intellect, gifts that Pedro and Paulo had also noticed. Out of this grew the conversation, and finally the pact I mentioned at the beginning of this chapter; but it demands another chapter.

XC   *The Pact*

"So far as I can see, one of you is in love with her, if not both of you."

Pedro bit his lips, Paulo consulted his watch: they were now going along the street. Ayres decided he was right, it was both of them, and he did not hesitate to say so, adding that the young lady was not like the Republic, which one could defend and the other attack: it was necessary to win her or lose her once and for all. What would they do when she made her choice? Or was the choice already made, and the one passed over still trying to win her for himself?

Neither spoke right away, although both felt the necessity of making some explanation. Their belief was that no clear, decisive choice had been made. Also that they both had the right to hope for the preference and would do their damnedest to win it. These and other ideas floated around silently inside them without coming out in the open. The reason is not hard to see, and must have been more than one: first, the subject of the conversation; second, the importance and dignity of their interlocutor. No matter how wide Ayres threw open the doors to the young men's confidence, they were still young men, and he old. But the subject itself was so seductive, the heart, in spite of everything, so indiscreet, that they needs must speak, though they spoke in denial.

"Don't tell me it isn't so," interrupted Ayres, "we old fellows know the ways of the young and can easily surmise what they are about. It's not even necessary to surmise; it's enough to see and listen. You are in love with her."

They smiled, but this time with such bitterness and constraint as to show the unpleasantness of the rivalry. The rivalry was recognized by others, it must also be known to Flora, and the situation now seemed to them more complicated and hopeless than before.

They had reached the Largo da Carioca, it was one o'clock at night. Santos' victoria was there waiting for the young men: it was their mother's idea, and by her order: she kept searching for occasions and means of making them live together, like brothers. She tried hard to correct nature. She often took them with her, out driving, to the theater, to make calls. That night, as she knew they were going to the theater, she ordered the victoria to take them to the city and wait for them.

"Get in, Counselor," said Pedro, "the carriage is big enough for three. I'll ride on the little seat in front."

They got in and went off.

"Well," continued Ayres, "it's certain that you are in love with her, and equally certain that she has not yet chosen between you. She probably doesn't know what to do. A third man would break the deadlock, and you would soon console yourselves; I too consoled myself when I was a young man. Since there is no third man, and the situation can no longer be endured, why don't you agree upon some plan?"

"What plan?" asked Pedro with a smile.

"Any plan, some way of cutting this Gordian knot. Let each follow his own inclination. You, Pedro, will first try to untie it. If he can't, Paulo, you will take Alexander's sword and slash it. It will be all over and finished. Then destiny, which is waiting for you with two beautiful women, will come leading them by the hand for one and the other, and everything will be harmony on earth as in heaven."

Ayres said other things before he got out at his front door. From the street, he still asked, "Are we agreed?"

They both nodded their heads, and when they were alone they said nothing. It is probable that they were thinking, and no doubt the time between Cattete and Botafogo seemed short to them. They arrived home, went up the garden stairs, spoke of the temperature, which Pedro thought delightful, Paulo abominable, but they did not say so, in order not to irritate each other. It was the hope of a pact that brought about this sort of temporary moderation. May the fruit still hang on tomorrow's tree!

Here was their room waiting for them—a model of

neatness and charm, of comfort and restfulness. It was their mother who gave it its finishing touches each day; it was she who saw that flowers were placed in the little porcelain vases; and she herself always went to take them away at night and place them outside the windows, where her sons would not breathe them as they slept. Here were the candles at the foot of the two beds, set in their silver candlesticks, one engraved with the name of Pedro, the other with the name of Paulo. Table covers made by her own hands, and bows she had tied on the drapes, and finally her portrait, and her husband's, hanging on the wall between the two beds, in that space where there used to be the portraits of Louis XVI and Robespierre bought on the Rua da Carioca.

At the base of each of the candlesticks the twins found a little note from Natividade. Here is what it said: "Would one of you like to go to Mass with me tomorrow? It is the anniversary of your grandfather's death, and Perpetua doesn't feel well." Natividade had forgotten to speak to them before, and, as for that, she could go very well without them, especially by carriage; but she liked to have them with her.

Pedro and Paulo laughed at the invitation and the form of it, and one of them suggested that, to please their mother, they both go. The acceptance of the suggestion was prompt: *this* was not accord, it was a kind of dialogue within the same person. Heaven seemed to be writing the peace treaty that both were to sign, or, if you prefer, Nature was correcting their dispositions, and the two brawlers had begun to reconcile being and seeming. I do not swear to this, I only say what seems credible from the looks of things.

"We'll go to Mass," they repeated.

A long silence ensued. Each was thinking about the pact and how to propose it. Finally, from bed to bed, they said what seemed best to them, made proposals, discussed, changed, and concluded the agreement without benefit of the notary's seal, with only the given word. The terms were simple. Since they could not be sure that Flora *would* choose, they agreed to wait a short space of time —three months. After she made her choice, the one who was rejected, bound himself not to make any further attempt. As they were to have the final certainty of Flora's choice, agreement was easy: each would do no more than exclude the other. Since, however, at the end of the stipulated time, no choice might have been made, it would be best to add a final proviso. The first that occurred to them was for both to abandon the field, but this did not attract them. Then they thought of having recourse to chance: the one designated by Lady Luck would leave the field to his rival. So passed an hour in discussion, after which they closed their eyes.

XCI

A Boy Owes It to His Mother

At nine o'clock the next morning, Natividade was ready to go to the Mass she had ordered said at the Gloria church. Neither of her sons appeared.

"They must be asleep."

And two, three, four, five times she went to the door of their room to see if she could hear a noise in answer to her note. Nothing. She decided they had come in late. Only, she did not know they were sleeping on the pact, nor that there was a pact. As long as they had made it in soft beds, it was all right. Finally, she finished putting on her gloves, went downstairs, got into the carriage, and went off to church.

It was an anniversary Mass, as she had said in the note. An old custom: her father had his Mass, her mother hers, her brothers and other relatives theirs. She was not one to forget obituary dates, as she did not forget birthdays, whosesoever they were, friends' or relatives'. She knew them all by heart. O sweet memory! there are people you do not help, and they even get into rows with you and with others, because of your neglect. Happy are they whom you protect; *they* know what the 24th of March is, the 10th of August, the 2nd of April, the 7th and the 31st of October, the 10th of November, the whole year with its special sorrows and joys.

When she got home Natividade saw her two sons waiting for her in the garden. They ran to open the carriage door, and after they had helped her out and had kissed her hand, they explained what happened. They had both decided to go, but sleep . . .

"Sleep and laziness," concluded their mother with a laugh.

"It was only sleep," said Pedro.

"We just woke up," added Paulo.

They argued over which should give her his arm. Natividade settled the matter by giving them each an arm. In the house, as she was changing her clothes, she reflected that if Flora had made some request of them, they would have awakened in time, no matter how late they had gone to bed: memory would have served as an alarm clock. A momentary shadow passed over her, but she was soon reconciled with the difference. And it was not out of jealousy, but to lead them to other temptations, and so separate them from war rather than from the lovely Flora, that their mother tried to take them to Petropolis with her. They would go up the first week of January. The season was going to be excellent: she told of the balls, mentioned names, reminded them that Petropolis was the city of peace. The government might change here below and in the provinces . . .

"Provinces, Mama?" put in Paulo.

Natividade smiled and corrected herself, "In the states. You must forgive your mother's mistakes. I know very well that they are states; they are not like the old provinces, they don't wait for a governor to come to them from here in the Court . . ."

"Court, Baroness?"

Now they both laughed, mother and son. Then, Natividade continued, "Petropolis is the city of peace. It is, as Counselor Ayres said the other day, a neutral city, an international city. If the capital of the nation were there, there would be no overthrowing of the government. Petropolis—you see, the name in spite of its origin, remained, and will remain—belongs to all. They say the season is going to be delightful . . ."

"I . . . I don't know if I can go right now," said Paulo.

"Nor I," put in Pedro.

Once more they were in agreement, but this time the agreement would probably cause division, their mother reflected, and the pleasure these last two words gave her was short-lived. She asked them what reason they had for staying behind and for how long. If they had already been established in their own offices, as doctor and lawyer, it would be different; but, if neither of them had yet begun his career, what would they be doing down here, while she and her husband . . .

"That's just the point, I have to make some clinical studies at the Municipal Hospital," answered Pedro.

Paulo explained his situation. He would not be practicing law, but he needed to consult certain eighteenth-century documents in the National Library: he was writing a history of landholdings.

None of it was true, but a boy owes it to his mother to tell her something besides the truth. Natividade expressed the opinion that they could do it all between the arrival and departure of the Petropolis boat each day: they would go down to the city, have a late breakfast, work, and at four o'clock come back up, as many others did. Up there they would enjoy visits, music, balls, a thousand fine things, not to mention the mornings, the temperature, and the Sundays. They defended their study as being the better for long continuous hours.

Natividade did not insist. She would sooner wait for her sons to finish the library documents and the clinical work at the hospital. This idea made her consider the necessity of seeing the young doctor and the young lawyer established. They would work with other professional men of reputation and would go forward and upward. Perhaps it was their learned careers that would give them the greatness promised by the cabocla of the Castello, and not a political, or some other, future. One can shine and rise to eminence in anything. And she criticized herself for imagining that Baptista could open up a political career for one of them, without noticing that Flora's father could hardly go on with his own career, even though it was an obscure one. But the idea of power returned again and again to occupy a mother's thoughts, and her eyes were filled with it as she fixed them now upon Pedro, now upon Paulo.

They reached an agreement. The boys would come up on Saturdays and go down on Mondays—the same on holy days and national holidays. Natividade was counting on habit and the diversions.

A subject of conversation on the boat and in Petropolis

was the difference between the sons, who went there only once a week, and the father, who with all his many business affairs went up every afternoon. What could they be doing down here when there were eyes willing to attract and hold them, up there? Natividade defended her sons, explaining that one was busy at the hospital and the other at the National Library, and that they studied hard at night. The explanation was acceptable, but, besides snatching a choice morsel from the pearly teeth of the summer season, it could have been a fabrication of the young men's: they were probably chasing around with women.

As a matter of fact, they made a stir in Petropolis, during the few hours they passed there. In addition to everything else, they looked like each other and had charm. Mothers said nice things about them to their mother, and inquired into the real reason that kept them at the capital, not as I put it in this raw, unvarnished manner, but with fine, subtle art—wasted art, because their mother stuck to the story of the library and the Municipal Hospital. By means of this ritual, falsehood, already served at firsthand, was served at secondhand, but for all that was no better received.

XCII   *Awakened Secret*

After all, what secret is there that is not found out? Cunning, determination, curiosity, call it what you like, there is a force that brings out in the open everything people try to hide. The secrets themselves get tired of keeping quiet —of keeping quiet or of sleeping. Let us stick with this second verb, which better serves our imagery. They get tired and, in their way, help that which we impute to another's indiscretion.

When they open their eyes, the darkness hurts. One ray of sunlight is enough. Then they beg the gods (because secrets are pagans) for a teeny bit of twilight, dawn or evening, although dawn promises day, while evening slips back into night, but even though it be evening light . . . the whole thing is to breathe the light of day. For, secrets, my dear lady, are also people: they are born, live, and die. Now, what happens when a glance of sunlight penetrates their solitude is that it scarcely ever comes out again, it generally increases, tears among them, overpowers them, and drags them by the ear out into the open. Dismayed by the great light, they first go from ear to ear in whispers, or sometimes written down in notes, but so vaguely and without names that it is hard to tell who they are and where they're from. This is the period of childhood: it soon passes, youth vaults over adolescence, and they stand forth strong, and scatter abroad, wise as gazettes. Finally, if old age comes and they are not dismayed by their white hairs, they take charge of the world, and perhaps succeed, I don't say in being forgotten but in being a bore; they enter into the family of the sun himself, who, when he rises, belongs to all, according to the motto on a signborad of my childhood.

O signboards of my childhood! I would like to end this chapter with you, but the subject would not have dignity, nor hold interest, and would be one more interruption of our story. Let us stick with the divulged secret: it is all we need. An elegant summer visitor did not conceal her astonishment at learning that the two brothers had made a pact on a point that would break up the greatest friendship in this world. A legation secretary insinuated that it might be a joke on the part of the two young men.

"Or of the three men," added a second lady vacationer.

They were taking a ride on horseback to Quitandinha. Ayres was along and he said nothing. When they asked him if Flora was pretty, he said "yes," and spoke of the temperature. The first lady asked him if *he* could enter into such a bargain. Ayres took a deep breath, like one who has come from far off, and asserted that in the presence of a priest he would be obliged to lie, so great were his sins, but there, in the road, in the open air, among ladies, he confessed he had killed more than one rival. So far as he could remember he had seven deaths on his conscience by various weapons. The ladies laughed; he spoke in a somber tone. Only once did he let one go before killing him, and he invented a Neapolitan tale. He eulogized the dagger. One he had many years ago, the best steel in the world, and he felt obliged to give it as a present to a bandit, a friend of his when the fellow proved that he had completed his twenty-ninth assassination the day before.

"Here, this is for your thirtieth," I said handing him the weapon.

A few days later he learned that the bandit had used the dagger to kill a lady's husband, and then the lady herself, whom he had been courting without success.

"I left him with thirty-one crimes of the first order to his credit."

The ladies went on laughing. In this way Ayres succeeded in diverting the conversation from Flora and her suitors.

While they were trying to find out about her in Petropolis, Flora's spiritual situation remained the same—the same conflict of affinities, the same equilibrium of preferences. Once the conflict was ended, the equilibrium shattered, the solution would come promptly, and however much it hurt one of her suitors, the other would win, unless the dagger of Ayres' anecdote intervened.

So passed several weeks after Natividade went to the mountains. Whenever Ayres came to Rio de Janeiro he did not fail to go to visit Flora in São Clemente, where he found her just as she was before, except once he found her immersed in silence. The next day he received a letter from her asking him to forgive her inattention, if there had been any, and sending him her love. "Mama asks to be remembered to you and to the Baroness' family." This remembrance represented the permission she obtained from her mother to write the letter. When he returned to Rio, he hurried to São Clemente, and Flora repaid him with her gaiety for the silence of that other morning. Still it was not spontaneous nor constant: she would lapse into melancholy. Ayres even came back several times in the same week. Flora greeted him with her usual gaiety, and then later showed the same changeableness as the times before.

Perhaps the reason for those lapses in conversation was the voyage that her mind kept making to the Santos house. On one occasion, her mind returned to say to her heart: "Who are you that you neither bind or unbind? It is best to let them go once for all. It will not be hard, because the remembrance of one will eventually destroy that of the other, and both will be lost in the wind that tears off old leaves and new, and particles of things that are so light and small that they escape the human eye. Go on, forget them. If you cannot forget them, don't see them any more: time and distance will do the rest."

It was all over. It was only a matter of writing these words on her heart as a reminder. Flora wrote them, with trembling hand and blurred vision. As soon as she finished, she saw that the words were jumbled, the letters ran together and then began to fade away, not all of them, but here and there until the muscle cast them off. In its courage and strength, her heart could be compared to the twin, Paulo; her mind, because of its art and subtlety, to the twin, Pedro. That is what she decided after a certain length of time, and in this way she explained what cannot be explained.

In spite of all this, she did not really understand the situation, and she resolved to put an end to it, or to herself. The whole day was disturbed and puzzling. She got the idea of going to the theater so that the twins would not find her in that evening. She would go early, before the usual hour of their visit. Her mother sent for tickets, and her father approved of the diversion when he came home to dinner, but his daughter ended with a headache, and the tickets were wasted.

"I'll send them to the young Santoses," suggested Baptista.

Dona Claudia objected and kept the tickets. Her reason was a mother's reason: though choice of a bridegroom, and marriage, might be slow in coming, she liked to see the twin brothers there before her, talking, laughing, even arguing, with their eyes on her daughter. Baptista did not immediately understand, nor afterward, but not wishing to displease his wife he passed up the opportunity of offer-

232

ing the lads a gift. Such a good opportunity! It was not much for them—they had means to squander, and did so. The gift was in the thought, and also in the note he would write them enclosing the tickets. He went so far as to compose it mentally, although it was no longer of any use. His wife, seeing him silent and serious, thought it was anger, and tried to make amends. Her husband pushed her gently away with his hand. He went on composing the note, gave the contents a judicious playfulness, and in a bold hand wrote on the outside, "To the young apostles Pedro and Paulo." His intellectual efforts made Dona Claudia's opposition all the more unendurable. Such a beautiful note!

XCIV   *Contradictory Gestures*

How can a single roof cover such diverse thoughts? It is the same with the sky, whether it is clear or clouded—a vast roof that covers a multitude of them with the same zeal as the hen her chicks . . . And do not forget the human skull either, which also houses thoughts, not only diverse ones, but even contradictory ones.

Flora, up in her room, no longer thought of tickets and theater stalls. Neither did she pay any attention to the headache that she did not have. If she mentioned it, it was because of its being a handy and acceptable excuse, short or long as occasion demanded. Do not imagine she was praying, although she had an oratory in her room, and a crucifix. She would not have come to ask Jesus to deliver her soul from that diverging inclination. Seated on the edge of the bed, her eyes on the ground, she was probably thinking of something serious, unless of course she was thinking of *nothing,* which also lays hold of a person's eyes and thoughts. She bit her lips, but not in annoyance. She placed her head between her hands, as if to smooth her hair, but her hair remained as it had been before.

When she rose to her feet, it was dark night, and she lighted a candle. She did not want the gas. She wanted a soft light that would give only a little life to the room and its furniture, that would leave some parts in half-darkness. If she had looked in the mirror, it would not have given back her usual beauty, in the light of the candle now placed on an antique desk at some distance. It would have shown the note of pallor and melancholy, it is true, but she did not know she was pale, nor did she feel melancholy. Yet, in her bewildered sadness there was a trace of despair.

How this all fitted together I do not know, nor did she. On the contrary, at times she seemed struck with amazement, at others with a vague restlessness, and if she sought the repose of a rocking chair it was to leave it at once. She heard eight o'clock strike. Soon, Pedro and Paulo would probably call. She thought of telling her mother not to send for her, that she was in bed. This idea did not last as long as it took me to write it, and there it is already in the line above. She recalled it in time.

"It would be an impertinence," she said to herself, "it's enough not to go down. Mama will say I'm ill, enough for us to miss the theater, and if she comes to my room, I'll tell her I can't go down . . ."

She uttered the last words aloud, to strengthen her resolution. She started to lie down on the bed, then she decided it would be better to do it when she heard her mother's footstep in the hall. All these alternatives may have come of themselves; it is not impossible, however, that they were also a way of shaking off troubling thoughts—thoughts she was afraid to follow for fear of where they might lead.

XCV   *The Third Party*

Fearing to follow where they led, what would Flora do?
Open one of the bedroom windows that gave on the
street. She leaned against the grating and peered below
and above. She saw the starless night, few people passing,
silent or in conversation, living-room windows thrown
open, lights inside, in one a piano. She did not see a certain man's shape on the sidewalk across the street, standing still, looking at Baptista's house. She did not see it,
and she would not have been interested in knowing who
it was. The figure, however, as soon as it saw her, trembled and never took its eyes off her, nor lifted its feet from
the ground.

Do you remember the lady vacationer at Petropolis who
attributed a third suitor to our young lady? "Or of the
three men," she said. Well, here is the third lover, and it
may be that still another will appear. This world belongs
to lovers. Everything else in it can be dispensed with—a
day will come when they will even dispense with governments, anarchy will organize itself, as in the first days of
Paradise. As for food, Boston or New York will originate
a process by which people can sustain themselves simply
by breathing air. Lovers will be everlasting.

This one was an officer in the Secretariat. Usually Sec-
retarial employees marry early. Gouvêa was a bachelor, he
ran around with women. One Sunday, at Mass, he
noticed the ex-Governor's daughter and went out of the
church so madly in love that he asked for no further
promotion. He had been in love with many, had gone
with several, this was the first that had really smitten him.
He thought of her day and night. The Rua de São Cle-

235

mente became the path that took him to and from the government office. If he saw her, he looked long at her, stopped at a distance, in a doorway, or he pretended to be looking at a passing carriage then turned his eyes from the carriage to the young lady.

When he was a clerk, he used to write verse. After he was made an officer, he gave up the habit, but one of the effects of his passion was to restore it to him. Alone, in his mother's house, he wasted paper and ink versifying his hopes. The verses ran off the end of his pen, the rhyme with them, and the stanzas followed in neat lines, like companies of a battalion; the title was like the colonel, the epigraph the music, once he got command of the march of his thoughts. Would these forces be strong enough to conquer? Gouvêa got some of them published in newspapers, with this dedication, *To someone*. Even with this, the fortress did not fall.

Once, he got the idea of sending a declaration of love. Passion engenders foolish acts. He wrote two letters, but not in the same style, rather in opposite styles. The first letter was poetic: it addressed the lady as *thou,* as in his verses, it adjectivized all over the place, called her goddess in allusion to the name Flora, and quoted Musset and Casimiro de Abreu. The second letter was the officer's retaliation upon the clerk. It came out in the style of government reports and official letters, heavy, respectful, full of Excellencies. When he compared the two letters, he could not choose either. It was not only the diverse, contrary nature of the text, it was mainly the lack of authorization that led him to tear up the letters. Flora did not know him: what is more, she shrank from becoming acquainted with him. If her eyes met his, she withdrew them immediately with an indifferent air. Only once did he think her eyes bore a look of forgiveness. And it is possible, even certain, that this brief ray of light unfolded the flowers of hope (I am beginning to talk like the first letter)—for it made him late to work at the government office. Luckily he was an excellent employee: the director extended the quarter of an hour of grace, and listened to the headache, cause of a wretched insomnia.

"I didn't go to sleep until dawn," ended the officer.

"Sign in."

And then Gouvêa's godfather up and died, and, in his will, left his godson three thousand milreis. Anyone would consider this a blessing; Gouvêa considered it two: the legacy and the opportunity of establishing relations with Flora's father. He hastened to ask him to represent him in the collecting of the legacy, and they quickly arranged the matter of the fees and expense. Shortly thereafter he sought him out at home, and, that the lawyer might inform his family about his client, he employed many subtle, witty speeches, told anecdotes of his godfather, expounded philosophic concepts and his program for a husband. He also described the administrative situation, his imminent promotion, the words of praise he had received, the responsibilities entrusted to him, the bonuses, everything that set him apart from his fellows. In addition, no one in his department was against him. Even those who felt he stood in their way admitted the preference given him was just. It was not all exactly true. He believed it was so, at any rate, and if he did not believe all of it, neither did he disbelieve any of it. He wasted time and effort. Flora never knew of the conversation.

She did not know of the conversation nor notice the figure in the street, as I mentioned above. I have already said the night was dark. I now add that a fine rain began to fall, and a cold wind came up. Gouvêa had his umbrella and was about to open it, but he hesitated. What was taking place in his soul was a struggle comparable to the two texts of his letter. The officer wanted to shelter himelf from the rain, the clerk wanted to get wet, that is, the poet was reborn in the face of the intemperate weather, without fear of harm, ready to die for his lady, as in the days of knighthood. An umbrella was ridiculous; to spare oneself a cold in the head would give the lie to one's adoration. This was the struggle, this the upshot: the clerk triumphed, while the rain began to pour and other people rushed by under umbrellas. Flora went in and closed her window. The clerk still waited awhile, until the officer opened his umbrella and did the same as the others. At home, he enjoyed his mother's sad consolation.

XCVI   *Withdrawal*

That night ended without incident. The twins came, Flora did not appear, and on the following day two notes inquired of Dona Claudia how her daughter was. The mother answered "well." Even so, Flora did not receive them that evening with her customary gaiety. There was something that made her speak little. They begged her for music; she played: it was good, because it was a means of withdrawing within herself. She did not return their handclasp as they imagined she had until just recently. So passed that evening, so passed other evenings. Now one twin, now the other arrived first; and imagined that it was the presence of his rival that cast a restraint on the girl, but arriving first did not help any.

All this was so painful to her that she finally begged her Christ for a governorship for her father—or any sort of government office away from here. Jesus Christ does not distribute the public offices of this world. It is the people that bestows them on whoever deserves them, by means of closed ballots placed inside a wooden ballot box that are counted, opened, totaled, and multiplied. The election to office might come, yes indeed; the question was whether Jesus Christ would answer all those who asked for the same thing. The number of those seeking office would be infinitely greater than the number of offices. This objection was immediately expelled from Flora's mind because she prayed to *her* Christ, one of yellowed ivory, left to her by her grandmother, a Christ that never refused her anything, whom other people did not importune with their humble petitions. Even her mother had her own personal Christ, confidant of her ambitions, solace of her bitter disappointments; she would never appeal to her daughter's. This was the kind of ingenuous faith the young lady had.

To be sure, she had already asked him to deliver her from this snarl of feelings that would not yield one to the other, from this wearying indecision, from this pull in both directions. She was not heard. The reason may have been that she did not give her request the clear form that I have given it, to the scandal of the reader. As a matter of fact, it was not easy to make a request in this way, in connected discourse, whether spoken or only thought: Flora did not formulate her prayer. She turned her eyes toward the image and forgot herself, in order that the image might read the wish that was in her heart. It was too much—to expect a favor from Heaven and oblige the celestial power to guess what it was . . . That is what Flora concluded, and she resolved to change her procedure. She did not succeed in doing it; she did not dare say to Jesus what she would not say to herself. She thought about it, but she did not confess to either one. She felt the contradiction without daring to actually face it.

XCVIII   *Doctor Ayres*

One day it seemed to the mother that her daughter was nervous. She questioned her and with difficulty learned no more than that Flora suffered fits of dizziness and of forgetfulness. It happened to be a day when Ayres came to call, with messages from Natividade. The mother spoke to him first and confided her alarm. She asked him to question her also. Ayres assumed the role of physician, and when the girl appeared and her mother left them alone, he made ready to cautiously question her.

A useless design, because she herself began the conversation by complaining of a headache. Ayres observed that a headache was a pretty girl's malady, and having admitted that this was a trite remark, he explained his motive in making it. He did not want to miss an opportunity of saying to her what everyone knew and was saying, not only here, but also in Petropolis.

"Why don't you go to Petropolis?" he concluded.

"I hope to make another, longer voyage, a very long one . . ."

"To the other world, I'll bet?"

"You guessed it."

"Do you already have your ticket?"

"I'll buy it on the day I leave."

"Perhaps you won't be able to. There's been a great rush to those parts. It's better to buy it beforehand, and, if you like, I'll take charge of this; I'll buy another for me, and we'll go together. The crossing, when you don't know anyone, must be tiresome; sometimes, even people you know are boring, as happens in this world. It's the memories of life that are agreeable. The people on board are ordinary, but the captain inspires confidence. He doesn't open his mouth, he gives his orders by gestures, and there has never been any report of his ship being wrecked."

"You are making fun of me. I even believe I have a fever."

"Let's see."

Flora held out her wrist. He, with a profound air, said, "You have, a fever of forty-seven degrees, your hand is hot, but this in itself proves that it's nothing, because that voyage is always made with cold hands. It must be a cold in the head, speak to your mother."

"Mama can't cure it."

"Yes, she can, there are household remedies. Anyway, ask her, and she can send for a doctor."

"The doctor will prescribe barley water, and I don't like barley water."

"Nor I, but I endure it. Why don't you experiment with homeopathy: it doesn't have a taste, like allopathy?"

"Which seems best to you?"

"The best? Only God is great."

Flora smiled, a pale smile, and the Counselor saw something that was not a passing sadness, nor a childish whim. He again spoke to her of Petropolis, but he did not insist. Petropolis would be an aggravation of the present moment.

"Petropolis has the disadvantage of rainstorms," he went on. "If I were you, I would leave this house and this street, go to another neighborhood, to some friend's house, with your mother, or without her . . ."

"Where?" Flora asked anxiously.

And she kept looking at him, waiting. She did not have a friend's house to go to, or did not remember of one, and she wanted him to choose one for her, wherever it might be, and the farther away the better. That is what he read in her spiritless eyes. It is a great deal to read in a pair of eyes, but good diplomats retain their talent for understanding everything a silent face says to them, and even the contrary. Ayres had been an excellent diplomat, in spite of the Caracas adventure, if it wasn't that this too sharpened his gift for uncovering and for covering up. All diplomacy is in these two related verbs.

XCIX *On the Pretext of a Change of Air*

"I am going to arrange a fine house for you," he said as he left.

Since he had been in Petropolis, Ayres had not gone to Andarahy to have dinner with his sister on Thursdays, as they had arranged and was reported in Chapter XXXII. Now he went there, and five days later, Flora moved to her house, on the pretext of a change of air. Dona Rita would not let Dona Claudia bring her daughter to her, she herself went to fetch her from São Clemente, and Ayres accompanied the three of them.

Flora's youth in Dona Rita's house was like a rose sprung up beside an old wall. The wall grew young. The single flower, though pale, gladdened the cracked mortar and the bare stones. Dona Rita was enchanted. Flora repaid her hostess' warmth with such artless grace that the latter ended by telling her she would steal her from her mother and father, and it was another occasion for laughter between them.

"You gave me a beautiful present in this girl," Dona Rita wrote to her brother, "it is a new soul for me, and it came in the nick of time, because my old one was all worn out. She is very docile, she converses, plays, and draws delightfully, she has made sketches of various things around here, and I go out with her to show her views worthy of her attention. Sometimes her face takes on a sad expression, her gaze wanders far off, and she sighs; but when I ask her if it is longing for São Clemente, she smiles and makes a gesture of indifference. I don't speak to her of her nerves so as not to pain her, but I believe she is feeling better . . ."

Flora also wrote to Counselor Ayres, and the two letters arrived at Petropolis in the same post. Flora's was a long, cordial expression of gratitude, only occasionally interlarded with a note of longing. Thus it confirmed the other woman's letter, even though she had not read it. Ayres compared the letters, reading the young woman's twice to see if it held more than appeared on the paper. In short, he had confidence in the remedy.

"Not seeing them, she is forgetting them," he thought. "And if there should happen to be someone in the neighborhood who has the sense to fall in love with her, it is possible she may get married after all."

He answered both of them, the same night, telling

them he would come have breakfast with them on Thursday. He wrote to Dona Claudia, enclosing his sister's letter, and went to spend the evening at the home of Natividade, to whom he showed the five letters. Natividade approved of everything. She only remarked that her sons did not write to her, and that they must be despondent.

"The Municipal Hospital cures, and the National Library also," retorted Ayres.

On Thursday Ayres went to the city and had breakfast in Andarahy. He found the two women as he had read in their letters. He questioned them separately in order to hear from their own mouths the confessions put down on paper: they were the same. Dona Rita seemed even more enchanted. Perhaps the fresh reason was something the young girl had said the day before. As they were speaking of hair, Dona Rita related what was reported in Chapter XXXII, that is, that she had cut off hers to place it in her husband's coffin when it was carried off for burial. Flora did not let her finish; she grasped her hands and squeezed them hard.

"No other widow would do that," she said.

Whereupon Dona Rita took the girl's hands and placed them on her own shoulders, and concluded the gesture with an embrace. Everyone had praised her for the unselfishness of the act; this was the first person to find it unique. And so another long embrace, much longer . . .

C   *Two Heads*

The embrace was so long that it took the rest of the chapter. This one begins without it or a third one. Even Ayres' and Flora's handclasp, though lingering, finally ended.

Breakfast took a longer time than usual because Ayres, besides being a conversationalist emeritus, could not get enough of listening to the two ladies, especially the younger one. He found a touch of listlessness in her, or dejection or something of the sort that I do not find in my vocabulary.

Flora showed him the sketches she had made, landscapes, figures, a stretch of the road to Tijuca, an antique fountain, a *Beginnings of a house*. It was one of those houses that someone began many years before and no one finished, with only two or three walls standing, a ruin without a history. There were other sketches, a flight of birds, a vase in the window. Ayres, filled with curiosity and patience, kept on turning through them: idea took the place of perfection; and fidelity, of necessity, was approximate. Finally, she tied the strings of the portfolio. Ayres thought he caught sight of one sketch remaining, which was covered; he asked her to show it to him.

"It's a rough sketch, it's not worth the trouble."

"Everything is worth the trouble. I want to accompany the artist's attempts. Let me see."

"It's not worth your while . . ."

Ayres insisted. She could no longer refuse, she opened the portfolio and took out a sheaf of heavy paper on which were sketched two heads close together and exactly alike. They may not have had the perfection she wished; nevertheless there was no need of names. Ayres studied the work for several minutes, and two or three times he raised his eyes to look at its author. Flora waited for his glance, questioningly; she hoped to hear praise or criticism, but she heard nothing. Ayres finished his examination of the two heads and laid the sketch among the others.

"Didn't I tell you it was a rough sketch?" asked Flora, to see if she could wrest a word from him.

But the ex-Minister preferred to say nothing. Instead of finding the influence of the twins almost extinguished, he found it turned into a solace of their absence, so vigorous and full of life that memory sufficed without the presence of the models. The two heads were linked by an invisible bond. When Flora saw that Ayres' silence continued, she perhaps understood part of what was passing in his mind. With a quick gesture she took the sketch and gave it to him. She did not say a word, still less did she write one. Either would have been indiscreet. What is more, it was the only sketch to which she had not put a signature. She gave it to him as if in token of repentance. Afterward she once more tied the ribbons of the portfolio, while Ayres silently tore up the sketch and put the pieces in his pocket. For a moment, Flora stood motionless, her mouth half open, then she grasped his hand as if to thank him. She could not help but let fall two tiny tears, like two more ribbons that would forever tie up the portfolio of the past.

The image is not good, nor true. It occurred to the Counselor as he walked along, on his way back from Andarahy. He went so far as to write it in his *Memorial;* later he crossed it out and wrote a reflection that was less final: "Perhaps it was a tear for each twin."

"It may end with time," he thought on his way to the boat for Petropolis. "In any case, it's a tangled web."

CI   *The Tangled Web*

The twins also found it a tangled web. Whenever they went to São Clemente, they received news of the young lady but no definite information as to her return. Time was passing; it would not be long before they consulted the oracle like two men of ancient Greece.

Adhering to the letter of the agreement, they did not count these interrupted weeks, since no choice was forthcoming, and they might get from the consultation the opposite of the young lady's eventual inclination. A just reflection, though not a disinterested one. Each of them asked for nothing more than to prolong the battle, hoping to win it. Meanwhile, they did not confide this twinly thought to each other. Both thought the feelings they enjoyed were exclusively their own; and love brought a feeling of shyness and made them mute. They no longer spoke of Flora.

Not only not of Flora. As their antagonism grew, they took refuge in silence. They avoided each other. Whenever possible they did not eat together; if they did, they spoke little or not at all. At times they spoke to keep the servants from suspecting; they were not aware of it, but they spoke awkwardly and in a forced manner, and the servants discussed what they said and their manner of speaking in the pantry. The satisfaction with which these communicated their findings and conjectures is one of the few things that sweeten domestic service, in general so rude. They did not succeed, however, in conjecturing everything that was making the brothers more and more cross-grained, the barb of hatred that increased in their mother's absence. It was more than Flora, as you know: it was their own irreconcilable natures. One day there was great news in the pantry and in the kitchen. Pedro, on the pretext of suffering from the heat more than Paulo, moved out of their bedroom and went to sleep just as badly in another room that was no less hot than the first.

A Vision Calls for Half-Shadow

Meanwhile the beautiful young gentlewoman could not remove them from her own bedroom, no matter how hard she tried to be rid of them. Memory would lead them back by the hand, they entered and stayed. Later they would go away, either of themselves or thrust out by her. When they returned, it was by surprise. One day Flora availed herself of their presence to make a sketch like the one she had given the Counselor, but more perfect, more finished.

She also would grow weary. Then she would leave her room and go to her piano. They went with her and sat one on each side of her, or stood facing her, and listened with religious attention, whether it was a nocturne or a tarantella. Flora played to please the taste of each, without deliberation: her fingers obeyed her soul's mechanics. She bent her head over the keyboard in order not to see them, but her field of vision kept them still, if it was not their breathing that made itself felt in front of her, or at her side. So great was her sensitivity.

If she closed the piano and went down to the garden, it often happened she found them there, walking about, and they would greet her with such a kindly look that she forgot her impatience, for the time. Then, without her telling them to go, they would leave. The first few times, Flora was afraid they had abandoned her completely, and would call them up within herself. They both returned at once, so obediently that she became convinced that their flight was not flight, that they did not scorn her, and she never evoked them again. In the garden, their disappearance was more instantaneous, perhaps because of the extreme brightness there. Vision calls for half-shadow.

The Fourth

I know, I know, three times I know there are a lot of visions in the last few pages. Ulysses admitted to Alcinous that it was a bore for him to tell the same things more than once. For me too. I have a duty toward them, however, because without them our Flora would be less Flora, she would be another person that I never knew. I knew this one, with all her obsessions, or whatever you may call them.

Not for this reason, nor even because she may have acquired some dejection of spirits and nervousness, did Flora cease to take on charm, to grow more beautiful, and to have more than one unknown suitor sighing for her. There was no lack of admirers who turned to look, and came to stare at her as she sat with Ayres' sister on the green bench by the garden gate. It may be she recognized one now and then, Gouvêa, for example: actually, it was as if she did not see them.

One of them was worth more than all the others together for his carriage alone—drawn by a handsome pair of horses: the neighborhood capitalist. His house was like a palace, the furniture made in Europe, Empire style, his table set with Sèvres and solid silver, rugs from Smyrna, and a vast bedroom with two beds, a single bed and a double bed. The second awaited his bride.

"She shall be my bride," he said to himself one day when he saw Flora.

He was a mature man; his face was battered by life's winds, in spite of many applications of unguents and toilet waters; his person lacked hauteur, and his manners had neither grace nor naturalness. He was Nobrega, that fellow of the two milreis, the teeming note that bore so many others, more than two thousand contos de reis. For the recent notes, that grandmother of theirs was lost in the night of time. Now it was a time of fair weather, of sweet, pure morning.

When he saw the young lady and made the reflection that is recorded above, he was surprised at himself. He had seen other ladies, and more than one with messages written in their eyes, telling him that their hearts were vacant. But she was the first to really catch his fancy and hold his thoughts. He came back to look at her again; the people of the district perchance noted the capitalist's frequent presence in the neighborhood. He finally succeeded in gaining admittance to Dona Rita's house, to the great annoyance of his habitual guests, who imagined they would be forgotten by their Lucullan host. Nobrega, however, had given lavish orders that they all be served and taken care of as if he were present.

His absence did not cause him to go without their hymns of praise. On the contrary, the servants could testify to what they all thought of the "great man." This was the name his private secretary had given him, and it stuck. Nobrega knew little spelling, no syntax—useful subjects to be sure but nothing compared to spirituality, and spirituality was his strong point. The faithful scribe added that if it were necessary to take his shirt off and give it to a beggar, Nobrega would do it, even if the shirt were embroidered.

Even now, in the present instance, this love was, after

all, a charitable impulse. In a short time, this chance attraction turned into a *grande passion,* so grand that he could not repress it, and he resolved to avow it. He was uncertain whether he should speak to the young lady herself or to the mistress of the house. He did not have the courage for either. A letter would take care of everything, but even a letter called for words, ardor, respectfulness. If only Flora's looks or gestures had told him something, even a little something—fine, the letter would then be an answer. But they told him nothing. They were only courteous and graceful: they did not go beyond these two terms.

Dona Rita noticed Nobrega's interest and thought he would be the best possible life solution for her young guest. All her uncertainties, distress, and melancholy would end in the arms of this estimable, highly respected old moneybags, in a house like a palace, with a carriage at her command . . . She herself would enhance the splendor of this grand prize of the Spanish sweepstakes.

Finally, Nobrega's secretary composed in his best style, a letter in which the capitalist requested Dona Rita to consult the wishes of the young lady he loved.

"Don't write sentimental stuff," he told his secretary. "I love this young lady with a protective feeling rather than anything else. It is not a lover's letter. Dignified style . . ."

"A cool letter," concluded the secretary.

Nobrega corrected him. "No, not completely cool. The letter should be flattering, without forgetting that I am not a child."

That was the way it was done. It would have been more so but Nobrega thought the style could be somewhat bland, it would do no harm to put in two or three words appropriate to the purpose, *beauty, heart, sentiment* . . . That is the way it was finally done, and the letter was

251

carried to its destination. Dona Rita was delighted. It was exactly what she wanted. She had her plan already laid: she would write finis to a melancholy story, giving it, as a final page, a spectacular conclusion. She did not intend to tell her brother beforehand, because she wanted him to receive the complete news, all done and finished. She re-read the letter, made ready to go at once, but there are persons for whom the saying "The best of the feast is the anticipation" sums up all life's pleasure. Dona Rita held this opinion. Still, she knew that letters of this sort are not to be kept secret for an indefinite period of time, nor is their message to be communicated without caution. She waited twenty-four hours. The following morning, after breakfast, she read the letter to the young lady. The natural thing would be for Flora to be astonished. She was, but soon she broke into a laugh, a frank, ringing laugh such as she had not laughed at Andarahy. Dona Rita was *most* astonished. She supposed that not his person but his advantages and circumstances would have pleaded in favor of her candidate. She was forgetting the locks of hair she had once placed in her husband's tomb. She gave her counsels to the young lady, described in glowing terms her suitor's position, the present and the future, the splendid situation this marriage would give her, and, as a final touch, Nobrega's spiritual qualities. The girl listened without saying anything, then once more broke into laughter.

"You're sure I'll be happy, Senhora?" she asked.

"I believe so. The future will decide whether I am right or not."

"Let us wait for the future, although it seems to me very slow in coming. I do not deny his virtues, he seems to be good, he has treated me kindly, but I do not want to marry, Dona Rita."

"Of course, his age . . . But don't you, at least, want to think it over for a few days?"

"I've thought it over."

Dona Rita still waited one more day. The refusal, if Flora should change her mind afterward, would be a disaster for her. I use Dona Rita's own words to herself, *great disaster, splendid position, deep feeling.* Dona Rita went to extremes, before that noble grandee of the last years of the century.

CIV   *The Reply*

Not wishing to reply with the bald, unvarnished truth, Dona Rita consulted the young lady, who answered simply, "Say I do not intend to marry."

When Nobrega received the few lines Dona Rita sent him, he was thunderstruck. He had not counted on a refusal. On the contrary, he was so certain of being accepted that he already had a wedding program worked out. He imagined the young lady, her timid eyes, silent lips, the veil that covered her beautiful little face, his delicate courtesy, the words he would say to her as they entered his house. He had already composed a prayer to the Holy Mother that she might make them happy. "I will give her a carriage," he said to himself, "jewels, many jewels, the best in the world . . ." Nobrega did not have an exact idea of the world; it was a manner of speaking. "I will give her everything, silk slippers, silk stockings that I myself will put on her . . ." His heart trembled as he put on her stockings. He kissed her feet and her knees.

He had imagined that when she read his letter she would be so amazed and thankful that in the first moments she could not speak in reply to Dona Rita; but soon words would pour from her heart in a rush. "Yes, Senhora, I would be willing, I would accept; I had not thought of anything else." She would write at once to her father and mother to ask their permission. They would come running; though incredulous, when they saw the letter, and heard their daughter and Dona Rita, they would no longer doubt the truth, and would give their consent. Perhaps the father would come to give it in person. And nothing, nothing, nothing, absolutely nothing, a simple refusal, a bold-faced, insolent refusal, for, after all, who was she, in spite of her beauty? A young woman without a penny, modestly dressed, without earrings, he had never seen her with jewels in her ears—not even two little insignificant pearls. And why did they pierce her ears if they did not have earrings to give her? He reflected that the poorest girls in the world had their ears pierced for the rings that might fall from heaven. And along comes this one and refuses the rich earrings that heaven was going to shower upon her . . .

At dinner, the habitual guests noticed that he was pre-occupied. In the evening, he and the secretary went out for a walk. Nobrega summoned the coldest, most in-different gesture he was capable of, an almost gay gesture, and announced to the secretary that Flora did not wish to marry. One could not put in words the secretary's amaze-ment, then his consternation, finally his indignation. Nobrega answered magnanimously, "She meant no harm, it was perhaps because she thought herself beneath, far beneath, the fortune offered her. You may be sure she is a good girl. It may be, too, who knows, that the prompting of her heart was wrong. That girl is ill."

"Ill?"

"I don't state it positively. I say it may be."

The secretary was positive. "Only sickness," he said, "can explain her ingratitude. Because, her act is pure ingratitude."

254

Hereupon, the note of indignation returned, a sincere note, like the others. Nobrega enjoyed hearing it: it was a consolation. Finally, he put into execution the idea he had when he came out of the house: he increased the secretary's salary. It may have been in payment for sympathy. The recipient of the benefit went further, he regarded it as the price of silence, and no one found out about anything.

CV   *Reality*

The illness, given as an explanation for the refusal of marriage turned into a reality in a matter of days. Flora became slightly ill. Dona Rita, in order not to alarm her parents, undertook to treat her with home remedies. Then she sent for the doctor, her doctor, and the expression of his face was not good, but bad. Dona Rita, who was accustomed to read the gravity of her own illnesses in his countenance, and he always found them *very* grave, thought best to send for the girl's mother and father. They came at once. Natividade also came down from Petropolis, though not to stay: up there they feared some disturbance here below. She came to visit the young girl, and at her request remained some days. "Only you can make me well," Flora told her, "I don't believe in the remedies they give me. It's your words that are good for me, and your care . . . Mama too, and Dona Rita, but, I don't know, there is a difference, a . . . Look, I think that presently I'm going to laugh."

"Go on, go on. Laugh."

Flora smiled, even though with that pale smile that appears on the lips of a sick man when the illness permits or when he himself overpowers the sadness that accompanies pain. Natividade spoke words of encouragement to her, made her promise to come convalesce in Petropolis. The illness began to lessen. Dona Claudia accepted Dona Rita's offer and stayed in the house. Natividade went to Botafogo at night and returned each morning. Ayres came down from Petropolis every other day.

The twins also went there to learn how the sick girl did. Now more than before, they felt the strength of the chain that bound them to her. Pedro, already a doctor, though without a practice, injected more authority into his questions and drew better conclusions from the symptoms, but both had the same hopes and fears. Sometimes they spoke louder than was customary and proper. The reason, egotistical as it may have been, was pardonable. Suppose that visiting cards spoke: some, more forward than others, would shout their names that one might know at once of their presence, their courtesy, and their anxiety. This eagerness on the part of the twins was needless, because she knew about them and received the messages they left.

So Flora's days passed. She wanted Natividade always beside her, for the reason that she had given, and for another that she did not mention nor perhaps know of, but we can suspect it and write it down. This was the blessed womb that had born the twin brothers. Instinctively she found something special about her. As for Natividade, she knew nothing of the influence she exercised on Flora for this or any other reason. She was glad to see that even now, in this crisis, Flora had not lost her fondness for her. They spent the hours together, talking if it did not make her worse to talk, or then with one holding the hands of the other in her own. When Flora slept, Natividade sat looking at her, at her pale countenance, the sunken eyes, the feverish hands, but still without loss of the charm of healthier days. The other women came into the room on tiptoe, craning their necks to see whether she was asleep, speaking in gestures or so low that only the heart could hear.

When she seemed to be improving, Flora asked for a little more light and sky. One of the two windows was thrown wide, and the sick girl filled herself with life and laughter. It was not that Fever had completely gone away. The ugly witch was still in the corner of the room, with her eyes fastened on her. But, either from weariness or because she was bound by a spell, she frequently drowsed, and for long periods. Then the sick girl felt only the warmth of Disease, which the doctor gauged at thirty-nine or thirty-nine-and-a-half degrees, after consulting his thermometer. Fever, seeing his gesture, laughed noiselessly, laughed to herself.

CVI   *Both? What Do You Mean Both?*

We were at the point where one of the windows of the room had increased its dose of light and sky at the request of Flora, in spite of her fever, which, however, was not great. What happened thereafter deserves a book. It did not take place right away; it took long hours, and some days. There was time enough for a reconciliation, or a farewell, between life and Flora. Either could be long drawn out; or they could be brief. I knew a man who fell sick when he was old, if it was not of old age, and he spent an almost infinite time in making the final break. He would pray for death, but when he saw the gaunt visage of this his last mistress peeking through the half-open door, he turned his face the other way and warbled a nursery song to fool her and go on living.

Flora did not resort to any such songs, though they were closer to *her*. When she saw the sky, and a patch of sun on the wall, she was naturally overjoyed, and once she wanted to sketch, but they would not let her. When death peeked through the door, she would shiver, it is true, and close her eyes. On opening them she would look at the gloomy figure, without either avoiding her, or calling to her.

"Tomorrow you will be able to sketch, and a week from today, or before, we will go to Petropolis," said Natividade, holding back her tears, but her voice did the office of her eyes.

"Petropolis?" sighed the sick girl.

"There you will have lots of things to sketch."

It was seven o'clock in the morning. The day before, when the twins left, quite late, their fears of her death were growing; but fears are not enough, reality must overtake them—this is how hopes spring up. But hopes are not enough, either, reality is still essential. Dawn brought some relief: at seven o'clock after these words of Natividade's, Flora was able to fall asleep.

When Pedro and Paulo came back to Andarahy, the patient was awake, and the doctor, though he did not hold out much hope, ordered applications that he asserted should be effective. Everyone showed traces of tears. In the evening, Ayres appeared, bringing news of disturbances in the city.

"What is it?"

"I don't know: some talk of demonstrations for Marshal Deodoro, others of a plot against Marshal Floriano. There is something."

Natividade begged her sons not to get mixed up in any

trouble; they both promised and kept their promise. When they saw the situation in some of the streets, groups of men, patrols, weapons, two machine guns, Itamaraty Palace lighted up, they had a curiosity to find out what had happened, and what was going on—a vague urge that did not last two minutes. They went and shut themselves up at home, and slept badly the whole night. The next morning the servants brought them the morning papers with news of the day before.

"Is there any message from Andarahy?" one of them asked.

"No, Senhor."

They still tried to read, superficially, here and there. They could not; they were anxious to leave the house and obtain news of the night. Although they took the newspapers with them, they did not read clearly nor connectedly. They saw names of persons arrested, a decree, movement of men and of troops, all so confused that they found themselves in Dona Rita's house before they found out what had taken place. Flora was still alive.

"Mama, you are more sad today than you've been these last few days."

"Don't talk so much, my dear child," replied Dona Claudia. "I am always sad when you get sick. Get well and you'll see."

"Do, do get well," put in Natividade. "When I was young, I had an illness like this that prostrated me for two weeks, and then I got up, when no one any longer expected it."

"Then no one expects me to get up again?"

Natividade tried to laugh at this prompt conclusion, in order to cheer her. The sick girl closed her eyes, opened them a little while later, and asked them to see if she had a fever, they checked: she had, she was very feverish.

"Open the window wide for me."

"I don't know if it will be good for you," reflected Dona Rita.

"It will do no harm," said Natividade. And she went to open it; she did not throw it wide open, but halfway. Flora, though now very weak, made an effort and turned toward the light. She remained in this position, with her thoughts far away: at first her eyes roamed restlessly, then they became motionless, and finally fixed. The others came into the room slowly, muffling their steps, bringing messages and taking ones back; outside they were waiting for the doctor.

"He's late, he should be here by now," said Baptista.

Pedro was a doctor, he suggested going in to see the patient. Paulo, since he could not go in also, reflected that it would offend the attending physician, and besides he lacked experience. Both of them wanted to be present at Flora's passing, if it had to be. Their mother, who heard them, went out into the drawing room, and, learning what it was, said "no." They could not go in; it was better for them to go for the doctor.

"Who was it?" asked Flora when she saw her come back into the room.

"It was my boys: they both wanted to come in to see you."

"Both?" Flora asked. "What do you mean both?"

This remark made them think that it was the beginning of the delirium, if it was not the end of it, because, you see, Flora did not say another word. Natividade insisted it was delirium. When they repeated the dialogue to Ayres, he rejected the delirium.

Death was not long in coming. It came more quickly than they had feared. All the women, and her father, hovered about the bed, where signs of the final agony were rapidly appearing. Flora died like a brief afternoon, an afternoon that dies suddenly, but not so suddenly that

260

the pain of longing for the day is not felt. Her end was so serene that the expression of her face, when they closed her eyes, was more that of sculpture than of the dead. The windows, thrown wide, let in the sun and sky.

CVII   *State of Siege*

There is no novelty in funerals. That one happened to pass through streets that were in a state of siege. Come to think of it, death is nothing more than the suspension of the liberty to live, perpetual suspension, whereas the decree of that day lasted only seventy-two hours. At the end of seventy-two hours, all the liberties were restored, except that of returning to life. Whoever died, was dead. That was the case with Flora. But what crime could that girl have committed, except the crime of living, and perchance of loving, it is not known whom, but of loving? Forgive these obscure questions, which are not appropriate, but rather strike a discordant note. The reason for them is that I do not record this death without pain, and I still see the funeral . . .

CVIII   *Old Ceremonies*

Now the coffin is coming out. Everyone takes off his hat as soon as it appears in the doorway. People going by, stop. The neighborhood leans out its windows, some of them are jammed because the families are bigger than the space. Servants stand in the doorways. All eyes examine the persons who grasp the handles of the coffin: Baptista, Santos, Ayres, Pedro, Paulo, Nobrega.

The last, although he no longer paid visits to the house, had sent to inquire about the sick girl and was invited to help carry out her lovely body. In his carriage, in which his secretary rode with him, and which was drawn by the most handsome pair of horses in the procession, they were so to speak unique, Nobrega reminded the secretary, "Didn't I say she was ill? She was very ill."

"Very."

I will not go so far as to assert that he took pleasure in Flora's death only because it confirmed his remark about her illness while she was perfectly sound. But it was a sort of consolation to him that no one was her husband. There was a further one: supposing she had accepted him and they had married, he thought now of the magnificent funeral he would have given her. He sketched in imagination the hearse, the most expensive possible, the horses and their black plumes, the coffin, an infinity of things that by dint of inventing he made real. Then there was the tomb, marble, gold letters . . . The secretary tried to draw him from his sad mood by speaking of objects along the way.

"Do you remember, Your Excellency, the fountain that used to be here years ago?"

"No," growled Nobrega.

Once again there is no novelty in funerals. Hence the evident boredom of grave diggers, opening and closing graves every day. They do not sing, like the ones in *Hamlet,* who tempered the sadness of their calling with songs about the same calling. They bring the coffin, lime, and trowel for the guests, and for themselves the spades with which they shovel the earth into the grave. Her father and some friends remained beside Flora's grave to see the earth fall, at first with that mournful thud, then with a tedious slowness, no matter how the poor men hurried. Finally all the earth had been shoveled in, and they placed above it the wreaths from parents and friends: *"To our beloved daughter," "To our sainted, darling Flora her loving friend Natividade," "To Flora, an old friend,"* etc. When it had all been done, they began to leave, her father between Ayres and Santos, who were holding him up, for he was stumbling. At the gate of the cemetery they went to their carriages, and drove off. They did not notice the absence of Pedro and Paulo, who had remained behind, near the grave.

CIX   *Near the Grave*

Neither of them counted the time spent there. They only knew it was a time of silence, contemplation, and of longing. I do not say it, in order not to embarrass them, but it is possible that they wept also. They had a handkerchief in their hand, they frequently wiped their eyes, then, with their arms hanging limp, hat in hand, they stared, apparently at the flowers that covered the grave, but in reality at the being that was there below.

Finally they tried to tear themselves away from that place, and take their leave of the dead; it is not known with what words, or if they were the same ones: the feeling was identical. As they stood facing each other, the idea of clasping hands above the grave occurred to them. It was a promise, an oath. They went away together, silently descending the hill. Before they reached the entrance gate they put into words the gesture their hands had made above the grave. They swore everlasting concord.

"She separated us," said Pedro. "Now that she is gone, let her unite us."

Paulo nodded agreement. "Perhaps she died for that very purpose," he added.

Then they embraced. There was nothing emphatic, or affected, in either the gesture or the words: they were simple and sincere. Flora's shade surely saw them, surely heard that promise of reconciliation and inscribed it on the signboards of eternity. Both, with a single impulse turned their eyes to see Flora's grave once more, but it was far off and hidden by great sepulchers, crosses, columns, a whole world of bygone folk, folk almost forgotten. The cemetery had an air almost of gaiety, with its wreaths of flowers, bas reliefs, busts, and the whiteness of the marble and lime. Compared with the fresh grave, it seemed a rebirth of life that had been forgotten here in a corner of the city.

It was hard for them to leave the cemetery. They would not have supposed they were so shackled to the dead girl. Each of them heard the same voice, with the same sweetness and special words. They had reached the entrance gate, and their carriage came forward. The driver's face was radiant.

This expression on the driver's face cannot be explained, unless it was that, worried by their delay—for he could not imagine his two fares had remained at the grave-side so long—he had begun to fear they had accepted some friend's invitation and ridden home with him. He had already resolved to wait a few minutes more and then leave—but the tip? The tip was doubled, like their grief and their love: it was, let us say, twins.

Flying Along

Just as the carriage flew along from the cemetery, so this chapter will fly along. First of all it will tell how the twins' mother succeeded in carrying them off to Petropolis. They no longer gave as excuses the clinic at the Municipal Hospital or the documents in the National Library. Clinic and documents now lay buried in Grave No. . . . I will not set down the number lest some curiositymonger, finding this book in the above-mentioned library, take the trouble to investigate and complete the text. The name of the dead lady is enough; it has been stated again and again.

This chapter will fly along like the train from Mauá, over the mountain, to the city of peace, luxury, and gallantry. There goes Natividade with her sons, and Ayres with them. Up there, that night, when he called at the Baron's house, he could see the effects of the sworn peace, the final conciliation. He knew nothing of the young men's pact. Neither father nor mother knew anything about it. It was a secret guarded with silence and the sincere desire to commemorate a woman who had bound them together by dying.

Natividade's whole heart, and life, was in her sons. She took them everywhere with her, or kept them to herself, in order the better to enjoy them, to test them in action, to push forward time's corrective work. News and rumors from Rio de Janeiro were objects of conversation in the houses they visited, but did not persuade them to abandon their voluntary abstention. Little by little, various pastimes caught them up: a drive in a carriage, or a ride on horseback, and other pleasures, took them out together.

So, they came to the time when the Santos family went down to the city, to the dismay of Natividade. She was afraid that when they were closer to the government, political discord would put an end to her sons' recent harmony, but she could not stay there. The rest were going down. Santos longed for his old habits, and gave some good reasons, which Natividade heard afterward from Ayres also. It may have been a coincidence, but if the ideas were good they had to be accepted.

Natividade entrusted the completion of her work to time. She believed in time. In my childhood, I used to see him painted as an old man with a white beard and a scythe in his hand, which frightened me. As for you, my dear sir or madam, depending on the sex of the person who is reading me, if there are not two of you and of both sexes—a pair of lovers, for example—curious to know how it is that Pedro and Paulo came to have the same Creed . . . Let us not speak of this mystery . . . Content thyself with knowing that they had every intention of keeping their oath. Time brought the end of the season, as in other years, and Petropolis abandoned Petropolis.

CXI   *A Summary of Hopes*

"It takes two to make a fight," so goes the old proverb that I heard as a boy, which is the best age to hear proverbs. In maturity they should already be part of life's baggage, fruits of ancient, common experience. I believed in this one, but it was not what made me resolve never to fight. It was because I already found it inside me that I gave it credence. Even if it had not existed, it would have been the same. As to my habit of refusing to fight, I can't answer, I don't know. No one forced me. All temperaments were agreeable to me; I had few differences, and lost only one or two friendships, so peacefully, what is more, that the friends I lost never left off tipping their hats to me. One of them asked my pardon in his will.

In the case of the twins it was two that refused to fight: it seemed to them they heard a voice from outside or from on high that constantly begged them for peace. Theirs was a greater force, and a change of formula: "If two refuse, no one fights."

Naturally the acts of the government were approved and disapproved, but the certainty that this might again kindle their hate, caused the opinions of each to remain within a small circle of his personal friends. They ceased to have thoughts at the sight of each other. Differences at the theater or in the street were suppressed at once, however much it hurt to hold their tongue. It did not hurt Pedro as much as it did Paulo, but he too suffered a little. Shifting their thoughts, they would forget the whole thing, and both were rewarded with their mother's laugh.

Different careers would soon separate them, while the same residence kept them united. Everything might work out: professional interests would serve this end, their personal relationships also, and finally, habit, which is worth a great deal. I have been summing up, as I could, Natividade's hopes. She had other hopes, which I will call conjugal; the young men however, did not show any inclinations that way, and their mother (if you sounded her heart) already felt an anticipated jealousy of her daughters-in-law.

The day before a month from Flora's death had been completed, Pedro had an idea, which he did not share with his brother. He would have lost nothing by doing so because Paulo had the same idea, and he too said nothing. Out of it came this chapter.

On the pretext of going to visit a sick man, Pedro left the house before seven o'clock. Paulo left a short time later, without any pretext. My devout lady reader, you have guessed that they both went to the cemetery; you have not guessed, nor is it easy to guess, that they each took a wreath. I do not say they were of the same flowers, not only out of respect for the truth, but also to remove any idea of intentional symmetry in the act and in the chance. One was of forget-me-nots, the other, I believe, of immortelles. Which was the wreath of the one and of the other is not known, nor is it of interest to this narrative. Neither bore an inscription.

When Paulo arrived at the cemetery and saw his brother from a distance, he felt like someone who has been robbed. He thought he would be the only one, and he was second. The assumption, however, that Pedro had not brought anything, not even a leaf, consoled him for being anticipated in his visit. He waited a few moments, then, noting that he might be seen, he left the road and hid among some graves until he could go and take his place by Flora's. Here he waited about a quarter of an hour. Pedro was in no hurry to tear himself away from there: he appeared to be talking and listening. Finally he took his leave and went down the hill.

Paulo walked slowly toward the grave. As he was about to lay his wreath on it, he saw another there, of fresh flowers, and, comprehending that it was his brother's, he had an impulse to go after him and call him to account for the memento and for the visit. Don't concern yourself about the impulse: it passed immediately. What he did was to place the wreath Pedro brought at the feet of the dead woman so that it would not fraternize with his, which was laid at her head.

He did not notice, he did not even guess that Pedro would probably stop a moment to turn his head and send a last glance toward the girl's grave. But he did, and when he caught sight of his brother in the place where he had been, his eyes on the ground, he too had his impulse to go and drag him away from that hallowed ground. He thought it preferable to hide and wait. Whatever his brother's rites of mourning might be, *he* had given the first rites to their common beloved. He had been the first to call upon Flora's shade, speak to it, bemoan with it their eternal separation. He had come before the other; he had remembered her sooner.

Thus consoled, he could go on his way: if Paulo came out after him, and saw him, he would know that he was second in visiting her, and it would be a blow to him. He took a few steps in the direction of the cemetery gate, stopped, went back and once more hid himself. He wanted to see the fellow's gestures, see him pray, see if he crossed himself, so that he could give him the lie when he heard him make fun of the ecclesiastical ceremonies. But he knew it was false, he would not admit to anyone that he had seen him praying at Flora's grave. On the contrary, he would be quite likely to deny it, or at least make a gesture of incredulity . . .

While these thoughts were passing through his head, fading one into the next, and while he discoursed without

words, accepting, rejecting, hoping, he did not take his
eyes off his brother, nor the latter his off the grave. Paulo
did not make a gesture, he did not move his lips, he kept
his arms crossed, his hat in his hand. Nevertheless, he
might have been praying. He may have been speaking
silently, to the shade or to the memory of the departed
gentlewoman. The fact is, he did not go away. Then
Pedro saw that his conversation, evocation, adoration,
whatever it was that kept Paulo at the grave, was much
more prolonged than *his* had been. He had not noted the
time he spent, but it was evident that Paulo had already
been there a much longer time. Discounting his impatience, which always makes the minutes longer, even so, it
would seem certain that Paulo was more prodigal with
regrets than he, and, thus, gained through the lengthen-
ing of his visit what he had lost in his late arrival. It was
Pedro's turn to feel robbed.

He decided to leave, but a force that he could not explain would not permit him to raise a foot, nor take his
eyes from his twin. With difficulty he finally succeeded in
withdrawing his eyes and letting them roam around over
other graves where he read some of the epitaphs. One, of
1865, he could not make out well enough to tell whether
it was a tribute of filial love, or of conjugal, maternal, or
paternal love, because the adjective was worn away. It was
a tribute all right, it was in the formula adopted by
marble-cutters to economize their client's style. Noticing
that the adjective had already been eaten away by time,
Pedro told himself *his* love was an eternal substantive that
needed nothing else to define it.

And he thought other thoughts, with which he covered
his humiliation. He had done everything in a hurry. If he
had waited a little, it would be the other who would now
be watching. Time was passing, the sun beat on his
brother's face, yet he made no move to go. Finally, he

looked as though he were going to leave the grave, but he only walked around it, as if searching for the best place in which to see or evoke the person buried in its depths.

At last, Paulo turned away, walked down the hill and out the gate, carrying with him Pedro's curses. The latter got an idea, which he rejected at once, and you would do the same, my dear reader: it was to return to the grave and add to the time he had spent there before—another, longer period. He rejected the idea, wandered about a few minutes, and left without seeing any sign of Paulo.

CXIII   *A Beatrice for Two*

If Flora had seen their gestures, she probably would have come down from heaven, and tried to find a way of listening to them forever, a Beatrice for two. But she did not see them, or it did not seem best for her to come. Perhaps she saw no need of coming back here to be godmother to a duel she left in the middle.

As for the duel, if it was going to continue it would not be over the same grievance. Don't forget that it was at the foot of that same grave that the two brothers had sworn eternal peace, and though it was not the grave that unmade the peace, it is certain that it rekindled some of the old anger. You will tell me, and with apparent logic, that if the body buried in the tomb still separated them, she would separate them still more if her spirit came down from heaven. A complete fallacy, my friend. At first at least, they would swear whatever she told them to.

Some months later, Pedro opened his doctor's office, where sick folk came; Paulo his law office, sought by those in need of justice. One brother promised health, the other to win your case, and they often succeeded, because they lacked neither talent nor luck. Besides, they did not work alone, but each with a colleague who already had a name and some experience.

In the midst of the happenings of the time, among which loomed the revolt of the fleet and the fighting in the South, the continuous bombardment of the city, the fiery speeches, imprisonments, bands, and other hubbub, they did not lack ground for disagreement. Politics was not even necessary. Opportunities and subjects were now greatly increased in number. Even when they chanced to agree apparently, it was only to disagree soon after for all time, not deliberately, but because it could not be otherwise.

They had destroyed the accord brought about by reason and sworn to in the name of love, love for the dead maiden and for their mother who lived. They could hardly endure the sight of each other, listening to each other was worse. They tried to avoid everything that time and place might combine to put them more at odds. So it was that they let their professions lead them down separate paths into separate worlds of men. Natividade could scarcely detect the ill will between them, since they appeared resolute in their love for her, but she did detect it, and kept trying to bind them close, in every way. Santos rejoiced in prolonging himself by means of the medicine and the legal advice of his sons. The only thing he was afraid of was that Paulo, out of party loyalty, might bring home a Jacobin bride. Not daring to say anything to him on this matter, he took refuge in religion, and never heard Mass but what he inserted a special, secret prayer to obtain the protection of Heaven.

CXV   *Exchange of Opinions*

On a sudden, Natividade noticed the first signs of a change of feeling, but it seemed to be intentional rather than a natural effect. And yet it was most natural. Paulo began to be opposed to the government, while Pedro began to moderate his tone and feeling and ended by accepting the Republican regime, which had been the object of so many quarrels between them.

His acceptance was not sudden nor complete: it was enough, however, for one to see that there was not an unbridgeable chasm between him and the new government. Naturally time and reflection had brought about this effect in Pedro's spirit; not to mention that his ambition for a great destiny, his mother's hope, was also growing. Indeed, Natividade was overjoyed. She too had changed, if there was anything to change in her simple maternal soul, for whom all regimes were evaluated in terms of her son's glory. Besides, Pedro had not completely surrendered, he had some reservations, in respect to the individuals and to the system, but he accepted the principle, and that was enough: the rest would come with age, she said.

Paulo's opposition was not against the principle, but against its execution. "This is not the republic of my dreams," he would say. He proposed reforming it in three stages with the fine flower of human institutions, not of the present nor of the past, but of the future. When he spoke of them one would see his conviction in his lips, and in his eyes that looked afar, like a prophet's soul . . . It was another chance for them to speak at cross purposes. Dona Claudia held that it was part of their intention to never be in agreement—an opinion that Natividade would have finally accepted if it had not been for Ayres.

He too had noted the change and was inclined to accept this explanation because of the cosy comfort he found in going along with other people's opinions: it kept him from getting worn out and disgusted. It was the more agreeable if acquiescence could be conveyed with a simple gesture. This time, however, he was concerned for the person.

"No, Baroness," he said, "don't ever believe it is intentional."

"But what can it be then?"

Ayres spent some time in choosing his words that they might not be either affected nor insignificant: he wanted to say what he thought. Sometimes speaking is no less difficult than thinking. At the end of three minutes, he said privately to Natividade, "I think the reason is that the spirit of change resides in Paulo, and that of conservation, in Pedro. One is content with what is, the other finds it too little, and would like to advance to a point to which men have never gone. In short, forms of government do not matter to them, as long as society remains firm, or pushes ahead. If you do not agree with me, you may agree with Dona Claudia.

Ayres did not have that wretched fault of the opinionated: it made no difference to him whether you accepted his ideas or not. It is not the first time I have said it, but it is probably the last. Actually, the twins' mother asked for no better explanation. Even so, the discord between them would not end; they had only exchanged weapons to go on with the same duel. Hearing this conclusion, Ayres made a gesture of assent, and called Natividade's attention to the color of the sky, which was the same before and after rain. As she supposed there was something symbolic in this, she began to search for it, and you would have done the same, reader, if you had been there; but there was not anything symbolic about it.

"Have confidence, Baroness," he continued after a little. "Count on circumstances; they too are enchantresses. Count still more on the unforeseen. The unforeseen is a kind of free-lance god, for whom it is best to celebrate a certain number of thanksgivings: he may have a deciding vote in the assembly of events. Imagine a despot, a court, a message. The court discusses the message, the message praises the despot to the skies. Each courtier takes it upon himself to define one of the despot's virtues: his kindness, his piety, his justice, his modesty . . . finally they arrive at his greatness of soul. There also arrives the news that the despot has died of apoplexy, a citizen has assumed power, and liberty has been proclaimed from the throne. The message is approved and copied. An amanuensis serves to change the course of history: the whole thing is that the name of the new chief be known, and the contrary is impossible: no one ascends the throne without this, and not even you, Senhora, know what an amanuensis' memory is. As in funeral Masses, all that is changed is the name of the person commended—Petrus, Paulus . . ."

"Oh! Don't mention my sons with bad omen!" exclaimed Natividade.

"Then, they were elected to the Chamber of Deputies?"

"They were: they take their seats on Thursday. If they were not my sons, I'd say that you will find them more handsome than you left them a year ago."

"Say it, say it, Baroness. Pretend they are my sons."

Ayres had just returned from Europe, where he had gone with a promise to remain only six months. He miscalculated, he spent eleven. Natividade called it a year to make a round number of his absence, which she had felt deeply, as had Dona Rita. Blood in the one woman, habit in the other—it was hard for them to endure the separation. He had gone on the pretext of mineral baths, and, however much they recommended Brazil's, he refused to try them. He was not accustomed to the local brands, and was persuaded that the waters of Carlsbad or Vichy would not have cured much without their names. Dona Rita insinuated he was going in order to see how the girls were that he had left over there, and she concluded, "They must be old, as old as you."

"Perhaps older. It is their business to get old," replied the Counselor.

He tried to laugh but could not go beyond the threat of it. It was not the reminder of his own old age, nor of the decrepitude of others, it was the injustice of a fate that took away one's inner vision. Girls, he knew, surrendered to time, like cities and institutions, and even more quickly than these. Not all of them would go straight off, to prove the saying that attributes early death to the gods' love, but he had seen some of this sort, and he was reminded of the gentle Flora, who was gone, with all her delicate graces . . . He did not go beyond the threat of laughter.

The two women had tried to keep him from going, Santos also for he would lose in him a fixture of his evenings. But our man resisted, took ship and left. As he wrote often to his sister and to his friends, he gave the exact reason for his staying longer, and it was not love affairs, unless he was lying, but he was past the age of lying. He asserted, yes, that he had regained some of his strength, and he looked it when he disembarked, eleven months later, on the Pharoux docks. He had the same air of an elegant, lively, well-groomed old fellow.

"So they were elected?"

"Elected, and they take their seats on Thursday."

CXVII   *Taking Office*

On Thursday, when the twins took their seats in the Chamber, Natividade and Perpetua went to see the ceremony. Pedro or Paulo arranged a box in the gallery for them. The mother invited Ayres to go also. When he arrived he found the ladies already seated, Natividade looking at the president and the deputies through her binoculars. One of these was reading the minutes and no one paying any attention to him.

Ayres sat down a little farther back, and after a few minutes said to Natividade, "You wrote me they were candidates of two different parties."

Natividade confirmed the report. They had been elected by opposing parties. Both supported the Republic, but Paulo wanted something more than it was, and Pedro thought it was enough and to spare. They proved themselves sincere, ardent, ambitious; they were well liked by their friends, were studious, well informed . . .

"They love each other at last?"

"They love each other in me," she replied, after formulating this phrase in her head.

"Is it big enough—this friendly terrain?"

"Friendly, but worn and broken. Any day I may fail them."

"You won't. You have many, many years of life before you. Take a trip to Europe with them and you'll see, you'll come back even more robust. I feel I'm twice the man I was, however much it offends my modesty to say it—but my modesty forgives all. And then when you have set their feet on the right path, and seen them great men . . ."

"Why does politics have to divide them?"

"Yes, they could become great in their scientific fields, a great physician, a great jurist . . ."

Natividade was unwilling to admit that science was not enough. Scientific glory seemed to her comparatively obscure: it was mute, cloistered, understood by few. Politics, no. She would have liked only politics, but so that they did not fight, but loved each other, climbing together, hand in hand . . . This is what she was thinking to herself while Ayres, dropping the subject of science, finally agreed that nothing could be done without love.

"Passion," he said, "is half the battle."

"Politics is their passion, their passion and their ambition. Perhaps they are already aiming at the presidency."

"Already?"

"No . . . that is, yes. Can you keep a secret? I questioned them separately: they admitted that this was their ultimate dream. It remains to be seen what one will do if the other gets the office first."

"He'll throw him out, probably."

"Don't joke, Counselor."

"It's not a joke, Baroness. You imagine it is politics that sets them at odds, frankly, no. Politics is an incident, like the gentle Flora . . ."

"They still remember her."

"Still?"

"They went to the anniversary Mass for her, and I suspect they also went to the cemetery, but not at the same time. If they did, it means they truly loved her; then, it was not an incident."

No matter what he could have said in reply, he did not insist on his opinion; rather, he gave substance to hers by making a fact out of the visit to the cemetery.

"I don't *know* if they went," she added, "I suspect it."

"They must have gone; they really loved the girl. And she loved them. The difference was that, since she could not make them one, as she saw them within herself, she preferred to close her eyes. Don't let the mystery bother you. There are other mysteries that are more obscure."

"It looks as if the ceremony is about to begin," said Perpetua who had been looking toward the floor of the Chamber.

"Move over here, Counselor."

The ceremony was the usual one. Natividade thought only of seeing them come in together and together take the oath of allegiance—come as she had kept them, in her womb and in life. She was content to admire them separately—Paulo first, then Pedro, both serious—and from here above, she heard them repeat the formula in a clear, sure voice. The ceremony was interesting to the galleries because of the similarity of the two men; to their mother, it was moving.

"They are legislators," said Ayres at the end.

Natividade's eyes were filled with pride. She rose and asked her old friend to accompany them to their carriage.

In the entrance hall, they found the two new deputies, who rushed up to their mother. It is not known which of them kissed her first; since there were no house rules in this *chamber,* perhaps it was both at the same time when she placed her face between theirs, one cheek for each pair of lips. What is certain is they kissed her with equal tenderness. Then they went back to the floor of the Chamber.

CXVIII   *Things Past, Things to Be*

As she was about to get into the carriage, Natividade caught sight of the São José church to one side, with a piece of the Morro do Castello in the distance. She stopped.

"What is it?" asked Ayres.

"Nothing," she answered getting in and holding out her hand to him, "till this evening?"

"Till this evening."

The sight of the church and the morro awakened in her all the scenes and words that are set down in the first two or three chapters. Do not forget that it was near the church, between it and the Chamber of Deputies, that the coupé waited that day for her and her sister.

"Do you remember, Perpetua?" said Natividade when the carriage began to move off.

"Remember what?"

Perpetua remembered. Natividade observed that there should be, somewhere nearby, that steep road they climbed, with difficulty and curiosity, all the way to the cabocla's house, with people all around them going up and coming down. The house was on the right, it had a stone stairway . . .

Don't worry, my friend, I'm not going to repeat those pages. But *she* could not help recalling them, nor keep them from coming back of themselves. The whole thing reappeared with its old-time freshness. She had not forgotten the dainty figure of the cabocla when her father led her into the room: Enter, Barbara. The idea of her being old, and far away, returned to the state she had left a province, rich where she was born poor, did not occur to Natividade. No, all of her went back to that morning of 1871. The pretty cabocla was the same light little thing, with her hair caught up on top of her head, looking, speaking, dancing . . . Things past.

When the carriage was about to go around the Santa Luzia beach, as they passed the length of the hospital, Natividade had an idea, but it was no more than an idea, of returning to the Castello road, of going up it to see if she would find the seeress in the same place. She would tell her that the two nursing babies that she had predicted would be great were already deputies and had just taken their seats in the Chamber. When would they fulfill their destiny? Would she live to see them great men, even though she lived to be very old?

The presidency of the Republic could not be filled by two men, but one would hold the vice-presidency, and if he thought this too little, they would exchange offices later. Greatness would not be wanting. She still remembered the words she had heard from the cabocla when she asked what type of greatness was in store for her sons. "Things fated to be!" answered the Pythia of the North, in a voice she could never forget. Even now she seemed to hear it, but it was an illusion. At most, it was the carriage wheels and horses' hooves that beat out, "Things to be! things fated to be!"

CXIX *Announcing Succeeding Chapters*

All stories, if you cut them in slices, end with a last chapter and a next-to-the-last chapter, but no author will call them that. They all prefer to give them special titles of their own. I have adopted a quite different method. I will write at the head of each of the two remaining chapters their climactical designations, without indicating the particular subject matter of either. I show the kilometer we are at on the line, supposing the story is a railroad train. Mine is not properly that. It could have been a canoe, if I had put water under it and given it some wind, but you have seen that we travel only over land, on foot, not in a carriage, and are more concerned with the people than the ground covered. It is not a train, nor a boat: it is a simple story that has happened and is still to happen, as you will see in the two chapters not yet told, and they are short.

CXX *Next-to-the-Last*

This is another death notice. Some chapters back the youthful Flora died; in this one, we have the death of Natividade, who was old. I call her old because I have seen her baptismal certificate, but, as a matter of fact, neither her deputy-sons nor her white hair gave her an appearance corresponding to her age. Her elegance, which was a kind of sixth sense with her, fooled time so that she kept, I won't say the freshness, but the charm of former days.

She did not die without having a private talk with her two boys—so private that not even her husband was present. And he did not ask to be included. The truth is, Santos went about weeping in corners, he would not have been able to hold back his tears if he had heard his wife make her final requests of their sons. Because, the doctors had already given her up. If I had not recognized in those guardians of health the examiners of life and death, I might have twisted aside my pen, and, contrary to science's prediction, let Natividade escape. I would have committed a vulgar and contemptible act, besides it being a lie. No, sir, she died on schedule, a few months after that session of the Chamber of Deputies. She died of typhus.

So secret was her talk with her sons that they refused to tell it to anyone, except to Counselor Ayres, who had guessed part of it. Paulo and Pedro confided the rest to him, asking him to say nothing.

"Didn't you swear not to tell?"

"No, not really," said one of them.

"We swore only to what she asked us to," explained the other.

"Then you may tell it to me. I will be as secret as the grave."

Ayres knew that graves are not secret. If they don't say anything it is because they would always tell the same story: hence the reputation for secrecy. It is not a virtue, it is a lack of news.

Well, what their mother did when they came in and closed the door of the room was to ask them to stand one on each side of her bed and to each give her their right hand. She gently joined the two hands and held them in her own, which were on fire. Then, in a faint voice, and with her eyes lighted only by the fever, she asked a single, great favor of them. They were weeping and silent; perhaps they guessed what the favor was.

"A last favor," she insisted.

"Tell us, Mama."

"You must be friends. Your mother will suffer in the other world if you are not friends in this one. It's a little thing I ask. Bringing you into the world was hard for *me,* and raising you, and my hope was to see you great men. God will not have it so. Well . . . But I want to be sure I am not leaving behind two ungrateful sons. Come, Pedro, come, Paulo, swear that you will be friends."

The young men wept. If they did not speak it was because their voice would not pass from their throat. When it could, it came forth tremulous, but clear and loud.

"I swear, Mama!"

"I swear, Mama!"

"Friends for ever?"

"Yes."

"Yes."

"I don't want any other remembrance. Only this, true friendship, never to be broken."

Natividade still held their hands in hers, she felt them trembling with emotion, and she was silent a few moments.

"I can die in peace."

"No, Mama," they both interrupted, "you are not going to die."

It seems their mother tried to smile at this confident speech, but her lips did not respond to her intention, and made a grimace that frightened her sons. Paulo ran for help. Santos entered wildly, in time to hear his wife breathe a few last words. The final agony soon began, and lasted several hours. If you counted all the hours of death agony there have been in the world, how many centuries would it make? Some of them probably terrible, others sad, many desperate, occasional ones boring. Finally death arrives, for all its delay, and plucks the person away from the weeping, or from the silence.

CXXI   *Last*

Castor and Pollux were the names another deputy gave the twins when they returned to the Chamber of Deputies after the Mass of the seventh day. So great was their unity, as if they were trying to outdo each other. They entered together, stayed together, left together. Two or three times they voted together to the great dismay of their respective political friends. They had been elected to fight each other, and they were betraying the voters. They heard hard names, sharp criticism. They had about decided to resign from office. Pedro, however, thought of a compromise.

"Our political duty is to vote with our friends," he said to his brother. "Let us vote with them. All Mama asked of us was personal concord. On the rostrum, yes, no one will get us to attack each other; in the discussion and in the voting we can, and must, differ."

"Agreed. But if you someday find you belong in my camp, why come on over. Neither you nor I pledged our judgment."

"Agreed."

Personally, there was not always this kind of agreement between them. Clashes of temperament were not unusual, and furious impulses, but the memory of their mother was so fresh, her death so close to them, that they suppressed every urge, however much it cost them, and lived in unison. In the Chamber, political disagreement and personal fusion made them more and more objects of wonder.

The Chamber ended its session in December. When it reconvened the following May, only Pedro appeared. Paulo had gone to Minas—some said to see his betrothed, others to hunt for diamonds, but it seems it was only a pleasure trip. Soon after, he returned, and came to the Chamber alone, unlike the year before when the two brothers used to climb the stairs together, almost arm in arm. Friendly eyes were not long in discovering that the brothers were not getting on well, and, soon after, that they detested each other. There was no lack of indiscreet persons to ask one and the other what had happened in the interval between the two sessions. Neither made any reply. The president of the Chamber, on the advice of the leader, named them to the same committee. Pedro and Paulo, in turn, went and asked to be excused.

"They are changed," said the president in the coffee room.

"Completely changed," agreed the deputies that were present.

Ayres learned of this conclusion on the next day, from a deputy that was a friend of his, who lived in one of the *pensions* in Cattete.

He had gone to have breakfast with him, and, in the course of the conversation, as the Deputy knew of Ayres' friendship with his two colleagues, he told him about the year before and the present year, and the radical and inexplicable change. He also told him the opinion of the Chamber.

It was no news to the Counselor, who had already been a witness to the uniting and the disuniting of the twins. While the other man spoke, he was going back through the years, through their lives, reviewing their battles, the clashes of temperament, the reciprocal aversion that was barely concealed and, though occasionally displaced by some stronger motive, persisted in the blood as a virtual necessity. He did not forget about their mother's request, nor about her ambition to see them great men.

"You, sir, are their old friend, tell me what it was that made them change," concluded the Deputy.

"Change? They haven't changed. They are the same."

"The same?"

"Yes, they are the same."

"It's not possible."

They had finished breakfast. The Deputy went up to his room to get his hat and gloves. Ayres went and waited for him at the street door. When the Deputy came down, he had a bright look in his eye.

"Now mightn't it be . . . Who knows if it might not be the inheritance, from their mother, that changed them? It might just be this inheritance, matters of the inventory . . ."

Ayres knew it was not the inheritance, but he did not care to repeat once more that they were the same, and had been from the womb. He preferred to accept the hypothesis, to avoid argument, and went out fingering his lapel where there bloomed the same eternal flower.